White Tigers

Men of Tokyo: Forbidden Cravings
Men of Phuket: Tongue-Thai'd

For more excerpts, information and fund stuff on
Sedonia Guillone's White Tigers series, please
visit:

www.the-white-tigers.com

Men of Tokyo: Sudden Bliss
ISBN 978-1-937796-58-7
ALL RIGHTS RESERVED.
Title Copyright © 2014 Sedonia Guillone

Edited by Claire Semaskiewicz
Cover art by Les Byerley
Interior design by Allison Jacobson

Trade paperback Publication April 2014

Men of Tokyo: Sudden Bliss

Sedonia Guillone

Dedication

For Mitch, the love of my heart and guide of my spirit

Author Note

A note about Japanese names – sometimes the suffix – *san* is used, sometimes *-chan*. San denotes a formal respect while –chan is often used between lovers, close friends and family members, denoting the closer level of relationship. Technically, the use of suffixes is even more complex than this, but does not apply in this story. Also, I use the word *soji* for the screens that are used as doors. Technically, the word is *shoji* but the word and concept are familiar to Western readers in the former spelling.

For those unfamiliar with the few Japanese words I use, they are as follows:

Domo arigato – thank you very much; *Nande* – literally, 'what?' Also used to say, What's going on? *Kuso* and *shimatta* – basically like saying 'shit' or damn'. My apologies to those completely familiar with Japan and Japanese culture, if anything is inaccurate. I had more than one beta reader, (one of whom lived in Tokyo for twelve years) and have gotten as correct as I can see. <wink>.

Pocky – biscuit sticks from Japan. They can be covered with chocolate, strawberry, green tea or any other kind of flavour candy makers find appealing.

Ryokan - a traditional Japanese establishment providing food and lodging for travellers.

Hattenba – bath houses that serve as cruising joints for gay men.

I hope you enjoy the story! Sedonia

Love is a silent thread strung across the universe. I would know you in my own heart anywhere. — Mitchell Halper

One who has a man's wings and a woman's also is in himself a womb of the world, and being a womb of the world, continuously, endlessly, gives birth... — Lao Tzu

Chapter One

Koji-san…Koji-san?

Koji heard his name repeat in the air close by. Like a mosquito, it buzzed in his ear, annoying and insistent. He'd answer…in a minute. This was too important. He kept typing, eyes glued to the monitor. The Meiji Memorial Hospital account was his baby. Nothing else mattered.

The mosquito buzz stopped a moment, followed by the sound of a throat clearing. Once. Twice. Then a third time.

The sound was soft and feminine. He caught a whiff of perfume, and then long, pink lacquered nails drummed softly on the desk beside his keyboard.

His hands stilled over the keys and he looked up, following the scent of perfume. The symbols and letters he'd been focusing on hovered in his vision. Behind them was Tomoko. His boss's secretary. He blinked and her face came into focus. Worry lines marred her usually smooth forehead.

Worry lines? Tomoko standing at his desk, working so hard to get his attention? A strange feeling tickled in his gut, penetrating the fog of words and numbers imprinted like ticker tape across his vision.

"Koji-san, Mr. Miosuke wants to see you." Tomoko's voice was soft and courteous as usual, though it sounded as if she were speaking from the end of a tunnel.

Her words took a few extra seconds to process. When they did, his stomach tightened. "Do you know what he wants?" Miosuke usually only summoned people to his office when they'd done something wrong.

The young woman shook her head, though her frown remained. "No, Koji-san. He just said *now*."

Shimatta. When Miosuke said *now*, it was never good. He was in trouble, no doubt, though he couldn't imagine what he'd done wrong. Maybe he should have been working eighty-hour weeks instead of seventy-five.

Slowly he rose from his desk, heart pounding, and followed Tomoko past the rows of cubicles where his fellow engineers tapped away at their keyboards. The clacking sound that he'd stopped noticing long ago, now echoed through his brain and matched the rhythm of his heart. Then there was that ache in his neck, the one he never noticed while typing, and now rubbed it with one hand as he walked.

Too bad he wasn't into women. He couldn't even distract himself by watching Tomoko's stockinged legs as she walked in front of him. Tomoko was pretty and her round bottom pressed against her tight skirt with each step she took. But he might as well have been watching his sister, Gina, for all the sight aroused him. The only thing that drew him was Tomoko's long sleek hair. But it stopped there. He tried to imagine that long sleek hair brushing across the back of a broad-shouldered guy full of hard, rounded muscles and a thick cock. It worked...for a second. Miosuke's door loomed ahead. Besides, a fantasy didn't work as well as the real thing.

Not that there was anyone in the office to distract him either. None of the guys around him fit the visual either. The only guy who'd ever come a bit close had left for another job a long time ago. Koji remembered him briefly as he followed Tomoko. A few stolen blowjobs in the broom closet before stealing back out into the hallway, making their way back to the office separately, as if nothing had happened. It had been hell. A hell he hadn't wanted to repeat. Other than that, eighteen hours a day at his desk didn't allow time for more than jacking off in the shower.

"Go on in, Koji-san." Tomoko smiled though the worry still showed in her eyes. She held the door to Miosuke's office open for him.

Koji pulled in a deep breath and walked in.

The older man looked up from his desk, gave a brief nod and gestured to a chair. Like Tomoko, the man had worry lines, but unlike Tomoko, the hard look in his dark eyes made Koji feel pierced through the middle.

The door shut behind him. Koji bowed, his breath caught somewhere in his windpipe. "You wanted to see me, sir?"

Miosuke nodded. "Yes. Have a seat."

Koji bowed again quickly and lowered himself into the chair indicated. His palms already sweated and he folded his hands in his lap, prepared to take whatever verbal lashing was coming.

Miosuke leaned forward on his elbows. "Watanabe-san, you're a valued member of this firm."

Koji lowered his head, a gesture of modesty when accepting praise. "Thank you, sir."

"You're welcome. But," Miosuke continued slowly, "the talk flitting about the office is that you're here every night until at least eleven and then in again early, well before eight most mornings."

Koji's heart did a strange little flip. Others around him worked nearly as many hours. At least he thought they did. "I am only trying to do my best. The Meiji Memor —"

"When was your last vacation?" Miosuke fixed him with pointed look.

Nande? Koji caught himself staring a moment at the older man. What was he getting at? He tried to recollect, then the memory of last summer came to him. He'd taken one day for Gina's wedding and then come back to work. Two months later, after his stepmother had died of cancer, he'd taken two days for the funeral, one for the service and then the next for Shizuko's cremation ceremony.

He cleared his throat. "Um, last summer. I...took...a few days."

"For a funeral. That's no vacation." Miosuke's voice softened appropriately.

Koji fought down the memory of Shizuko in her coffin. "The Sanyohama account had to be looked after," he went on, "and I was afraid to leave it to someone else. A health clinic, you know...I couldn't take any chances of their system running down."

"Yes, I remember that." Miosuke cleared his throat again. "Watanabe-san, have you looked at yourself in the mirror lately?"

Koji furrowed his brow. Funny, Gina had asked him if he had the flu or something when he went to her house for dinner last night. He'd gone into her bathroom and looked at himself to see if he appeared as ill as she thought. All he saw were the usual dark circles under his eyes. But he'd never exactly been a vibrant picture of health, even when he'd played sports and practiced karate. "When I brush my teeth I look in the mirror."

Miosuke scratched at his head, a strange look on his lined face. "You are not only a good employee, Watanabe-san," he said, "you're an investment."

"Sir? An investment?"

"Yes." Miosuke gestured towards him. "You are a producer, bringing income to Toshio Systems. It is my job to protect this firm's investments."

Koji's heartbeat sped up, the way it always did when he used to play soccer. It hadn't pounded quite this way in a long time. "I don't understand. I'm sorry." It didn't sound like he was about to be reprimanded or terminated. Yet, Miosuke was getting at something.

"What I'm trying to tell you is as of this moment, you're officially on vacation. For at least one week."

Icy heat prickled down Koji's arms. "Miosuke-san, no, I mean, I'm in the middle of corrections to the Meiji account." Knowing he was being disrespectful, he fell silent and bowed. He squeezed his eyes shut, praying his plea would move Miosuke. He *had* to finish this account. Had to. And he was the only one who could make sure it was done and done right.

"Watanabe-san," Miosuke's voice had taken on an edge. "You failed to mention to me that twice this week the office manager has come in at six in the morning and found you asleep at your desk. I am all for your being a productive employee, but if you burn out and your health fails, you will not be able to produce at all." Miosuke held up a folder and set it back down. "According to my file on you, all your projects are up and running perfectly. Not a glitch. All they now require is minimal maintenance. That can be done by me or one of your colleagues. His face softened a bit. "I promise, we will take good care of them for you while you're gone."

Gone. The word rang through Koji's mind like a death knell.

Miosuke picked up the receiver of his desk phone. "I have booked you a room in the Crown Hotel for a week, starting this morning."

Koji shot up from his seat. "No, sir, I...beg you." He was behaving in the most unseemly manner but couldn't help himself. Not only was he being forced away from the most important account of his career, but also Miosuke was forcing him to go to the Crown! Toshio Systems reserved several rest-cure rooms there for employees at all times. He'd die, absolutely die, if they stuck him in one of those small rooms with nothing in it but a bed, no space for his laptop, no cell phone allowed and no other clothing than T-shirts and shorts. And then to be put through a daily regimen of exercise, being sat down to meals. *Kuso!*

Miosuke's face settled into a neutral tone, as if he'd steeled himself against all of Koji's objections. The older man pushed a button on the phone and waited. "Security? Yes, I need you to escort an employee out of the building and down to the Crown." He hung up the receiver. "I'm sorry, Watanabe-san. I anticipated this response. You are fast on the road to complete burnout. Toshio Systems cannot allow this. Your failed health will cost us more in insurance payments in the long run. The Crown is a luxury hotel. One of the finest in Tokyo. They have a spa, massages, fine cuisine. You'll enjoy it."

Desperation fanned through Koji's chest. Images of that little room, being locked in, insane because he couldn't work, cut off from...the world. No! He had to think fast, had to find a middle way solution. Then the idea hit him.

And none too soon. The door to Miosuke's office opened and two uniformed security guards entered.

Koji's heart jumped. He sank bank into his chair, not knowing whether to be terrified or humiliated. "Miosuke-san, you are right. I'll take my vacation. Just, please, I beg you, let me choose the place. I'll go right now." His heart pumped and his hands trembled in his lap.

Miosuke held up a hand to the guards. "Just a moment." His hard look fell on Koji. "What place is this?"

Koji bowed his head. No doubt, some of the guys in his office went to the place he had in mind, but none of them needed to broadcast it to their boss the way he did now. And Miosuke would understand immediately once Koji named the neighbourhood it was in. However, faced with even two minutes at the Crown, he'd strip down naked and play a Mozart sonata on his violin in the middle of the office if it would keep him from being forced there. "The White Tiger. It's a...hotel...a *ryokan*...in Ni Chome."

A men's hotel in Tokyo's premier gay neighbourhood.

He'd actually thought about going there on his last vacation, at least for a couple of days. The last time he'd been at a gay bar, he'd heard some guys talking about the White Tiger. Koji had never been a big one for eavesdropping, but more than his ears had pricked up when he'd heard them say that the men at the White Tiger were gorgeous and gave incredible blowjobs, whenever you wanted one. He couldn't believe what he was hearing— baths and massages, pampering and...those same gorgeous men walking around in skimpy clothes all the time. Sounded like paradise. But he'd never made it there.

How ironic. Now he was basically being forced to go.

Then he thought of something else. He didn't have a reservation. Shit! What if they didn't have an opening? He'd be fucked, and not in the good way.

The older man's expression remained even, giving away no particular response to Koji's admission. "All right, Watanabe-san. Do you have the number for this place?"

He nodded. Thankfully, he'd jotted it down in his address book a long time ago, where it had remained tucked in his briefcase. "I'll call right this minute."

Miosuke nodded. "I'll wait to hear that you've gotten a reservation."

Koji launched from his chair and bowed deeply, holding back the overpowering urge to fall to his knees, partly from relief and partly from gratitude to Miosuke for not forcing him to go to the Crown. "I'll be right back."

Immediately he turned and left the office, not looking to either side of him as he walked briskly to his desk. He could just imagine all the eyes on him, all the thoughts in people's heads as to why he had been called into the boss's office with security guards there.

At his desk, he sank down into his chair. Hands shaking, he yanked open his briefcase and fished out his address book. There it was, the phone number, right in the front, because he never bothered to alphabetise the names and numbers he jotted in.

With a quick glance towards Miosuke's office, he dialled.

Someone picked up on the second ring. "*Moshi moshi*, White Tiger." The voice was smooth, deep and male and caused a distinct tickle in Koji's middle despite the scene he'd just caused in Miosuke's office. "Yes, I'm calling to see if you have a room available?"

"When would you arrive?"

Koji sighed. Under normal circumstances, he would have wanted to go to his apartment and throw a few things into a bag before heading to the hotel. That didn't seem to be an option at all under the circumstances. "Within the hour. For…a week."

A few seconds' pause followed. "It just so happens we do have a room available. Name, please?"

Koji's heart pumped. He looked up, catching a few curious glances his way, then hunched closer to the phone. "Watanabe Koji. Do you need a credit card or anything?"

"No, Watanabe-san. We'll take care of that while you're here. Do you need directions?"

"No. I…know where you are."

"Very good." That smooth male voice made the tickle in Koji deepen. He wondered what the man on the other end looked like. He'd find out soon enough, no doubt. "See you soon."

"Yes, soon. *Arigato.*" Koji hung up the phone and slowly rose from his chair. Back in Miosuke's office, he was vividly aware that the security guards were still there. Damn, Miosuke wasn't playing around. He bowed to his boss. "Miosuke-san, my reservation is made. I will take a cab from here straight to the hotel." He'd have to make do without his things and find a way to steal home during the week and get them. Maybe even sign onto the company's network from his laptop.

Miosuke had come out from behind his desk and nodded. His expression had softened and his eyes appeared almost…pained. "Enjoy your vacation. Your accounts will be well cared for."

Koji bowed again. Relief couldn't begin to describe not having to go the Crown. When he straightened, he saw Miosuke nod to the security guard. He breathed a sigh of relief over getting away from the uniformed men, and with another brief bow to his boss, left.

And found himself suddenly flanked by the security guards who matched each step to his. Shit! His face burned and he kept his head turned down, just knowing his co-workers were staring at him and would soon be discussing his departure over the coffee machine in the break room.

Stopping at his desk only long enough to collect his briefcase, he didn't dare even glance at his monitor, for fear one of the security guards breathing down his neck might hold him at gunpoint. So it was no surprise when the two uniformed men remained with him the whole way down the elevator, through the lobby to the curb where one of them hailed a cab and then both climbed into the backseat with him.

The taxi pulled away from the curb and onto the busy street. Clutching his briefcase on his lap, Koji watched the streets of Tokyo pass by the window, all under the clear spring light. Tremors shook in his limbs, and his heart clawed around in his chest. With each passing moment, he imagined the hospital, seeing every computer monitor in every nurse's station go dead. Patient after patient would die, not receiving the proper monitoring. And it would be his entire fault. All these dead people because he was in a hotel somewhere getting a blowjob. His right eyelid began to twitch and he heaved several short breaths.

"Are you all right?"

Koji's gaze whipped to the security guard on his left. The uniformed man looked concerned for the first time.

His throat tightened suddenly and his hands tingled. "You don't understand what's happening. They'll die. They'll all die. You must let me out." The cab stopped at a light and Koji leaned over the guard to grab at the door handle.

Firm hands pushed him back against the seat. "You're not going anywhere. Except to your hotel. No one's going to die."

Hunkered over his briefcase, Koji stared down at his hands, vision blurred now. Several deep breaths and the panic passed a tiny bit. Miosuke would never let anyone die, right? He'd said he'd make sure another engineer covered the hospital's mainframe system. Didn't he?

Koji heaved another breath. He should have been glad for this trip to the White Tiger. He'd avoided going to the Crown, to the horrid isolation of a forced rest cure. He knew he should be grateful that within the hour, he'd probably be in the care of some gorgeous muscular male at his beck and call. And well, he was *kind* of glad about that. It had been forever since he'd gotten a blowjob and even longer since he'd had actual *sex*. He couldn't even count how long.

Koji looked down, took deep breaths against another rising wave of panic. The only thing that calmed him was a promise to himself that somehow, during his vacation, he'd find a way to check up on work.

~~~~~

Mondays always made Naoto feel blue. After the rush of guests that flooded the White Tiger on the weekends, Monday morning was quiet and left him too much time to think To remember.

Lee Cheung had died on a Monday.

Or rather, he'd been *shot* on a Monday by *yakuza* coming around for the money Lee owed him. Those bastards couldn't have cared what the money had been borrowed for—doctors' bills for his dying father. They just wanted their money. They'd taken it from the till after filling Lee full of holes.

Naoto straightened his posture and took a deep breath, trying to put his attention back on meditation, but all he could see was Lee, the crimson staining his shirt, his eyes rolling back in his head. There'd barely been time to say good-bye...

At least he'd been the last person Lee saw. Lee had even said as much one night when they were lying in bed together, bodies still sweating and musky from great sex. Lee had run his fingers down the smooth fall of Naoto's hair, which to this day, he kept long enough to reach the middle of his back. "Naoto, I hope you're the last person I see before I die." As if he'd known.

The words had sent a chill through Naoto's body at the time. "'That had better be a damn long way off, Lee,'" was all he'd been able to say.

It hadn't been. Only a few weeks later, Lee had bled to death in his arms.

Three years later, the pain was still there. Worse on Mondays.

Kiku-sensei would tell him not to fight it or suppress it but to let the pain wash through him. But that wasn't easy to do, especially when it involved the loss of the one person you'd wanted to spend your whole life with, but then you were only twenty-nine and facing the rest of your life without him—

"Naoto-kun."

He looked up. "Kiku-sensei." Immediately he unfolded himself from the lotus posture and bowed to his mentor.

Kiku-sensei was watching him from the doorway of the small meditation room with that soft set to his dark eyes and full lips that conveyed compassion. Kiku had once been a *yakuza*, had run his own illegal gambling parlour right here in this building. But Kiku had gone legit years ago, devoting himself to improving other's lives rather than living in the underbelly of society.

It was because of Kiku that Naoto hadn't gone over the edge after Lee's death when all he could do was fantasise about finding and murdering the yak who'd killed his lover. He'd gone so far as to begin searching for the bastard and planning his revenge. Kiku hadn't even known him then. He'd only brushed against Naoto accidentally on a crowded street corner. But Kiku was a man of eerie psychic intuition, and that brief contact had given him visions of Naoto's plans.

Naoto remembered that moment. "Don't do it," Kiku had said. A complete stranger on the street. Naoto's blood had run cold. He'd stopped and stared. Kiku had held up his left hand, showing the pinkie he'd mutilated as his price for leaving his crime family. "It can only end badly for you," he'd said. "Whatever has happened...don't throw your life away." Then he'd reached into his pocket and given Naoto a card. "If you need help..." he'd said, and handed Naoto the card. "Please."

Naoto had accepted the card. The White Tiger, it had said, with a phone number and website address.

What had possessed Naoto to go to the White Tiger and let Kiku divert him from his plan, Naoto didn't understand. But he was grateful. Maybe it had been the way Kiku begged him, seemed to care so much about what happened to him, more than his own parents cared...

"There's a guest coming today," Kiku said. "He'll be here in a few minutes." He paused. "I had the sense from speaking to him on the phone that you were the best one to attend him."

Naoto's stomach did a small flip. The same psychic intuition that had led Kiku to urge Naoto into his fold, away from the mob was probably the same force operating today. Nodding, he bowed. Doing service for a guest would probably go a lot longer way toward dispelling his ghosts than chewing over painful memories when he should have been hearing his mantra. "I will be there to meet him, *sensei*."

Kiku stepped his broad form aside and let Naoto precede him through the doorway. "The gentleman gave me no details, but considering he called for a reservation less than an hour before arriving and that he sounded—" Kiku paused as if searching for a word—"there was an edge of something in his tone. I would almost hazard the word 'desperation.'" He smiled gently. "Something told me you'd be the best person here for him."

A ripple of warmth passed through Naoto. It was no small thing to have his mentor's approval this way. He stopped and bowed. "Thank you for your confidence in me, Kiku-sensei."

Kiku smiled and Naoto could see why Ryu, one of the other White Tigers, always said that Kiku looked like a golden Buddha. Naoto had to agree, even though he wasn't in love with Kiku as Ryu was. "My confidence in you is well earned, Naoto-chan. You work hard. You've developed the most compassion of your brothers. And this guest needs a lot of that, from what I could hear." He gestured for Naoto to precede him out the door. "Now, I've put down Room Three on the roster for our guest." He accompanied Naoto to the front entrance. "His name is Koji Watanabe. He sounded young, perhaps around your age and quite stressed."

They'd reached the front entrance and Kiku led him into the vestibule, where the sidewalk and curb were visible through the glass doors. Kiku's gaze grew serious. "Now, Naoto-chan, listen, it's very important that you remember – your role is simply to help this man relax."

Naoto glanced at his mentor, whose tone, though, deceptively soft, was serious. "Of course, Kiku-sensei."

The other man continued as if he hadn't spoken. "You are not to try and save him, no matter what feelings he might bring up in you." Only then did Kiku turn and look directly into Naoto's eyes. "Do you understand, my friend?"

He knew that Kiku didn't warn all the White Tigers in this way, but did so now because of his tendency to get too deeply attached to a certain type...guys like Lee who needed saving. Naoto bowed his head. "Yes, *sensei*. I understand. I'm sorry it's taking me so long to learn."

Kiku's hand came out and squeezed his shoulder. The gesture was warm and conveyed the friendship that had evolved over the last three years since Naoto had come to the White Tiger. They'd begun with a brief period as lovers, while Kiku had shown him the White Tiger path he'd learned on business trips to Shanghai. It had been a revelation to Kiku, how to harvest a man's yang and how to pleasure him so that he was uplifted, body, mind and soul. The love making, gentle and caring, had helped to comfort his grief over Lee's death.

Directed towards healing, the sex had mysteriously raised energy to his heart, giving him the strength he needed to face his grief. It wasn't the searing passion he'd had for Lee, but it was quiet and sweet. What he'd needed to get through. After that initial time, when the physical part between him and Kiku had spent itself, their friendship had continued and deepened.

"The deepest lessons take the longest. I know. And of course, you know you may always come to me if things become too difficult. There is nothing you cannot discuss with me." He patted Naoto's shoulder. "You're an exceptionally passionate man, but I don't want to see that fire consume you until there's nothing left."

Naoto bowed his head a final time. "Thank you, Kiku-sensei."

Kiku shook his head then. "I'm sorry it's has been so difficult to find a proper partner for you to work with. The White Tiger path is meant to be worked with a partner. But, I keep hoping. For all of us."

Not that the other White Tigers weren't decent guys. The twins, Tatou and his brother, Mod from London were terrific. Half Thai like Ryu, they were beautiful and devoted to Kiku and to this place. So was Basho who did most of the cooking. They were all his good friends now, but after what he'd had with Lee, he just wasn't drawn to any of them in the way necessary to practice something so intimate.

Through the glass doors, Naoto saw a taxi pull up to the curb. His eyes widened at the sight of a uniformed guard stepping out of the backseat…then another from the other side. Last of all a slender young man emerged, his ashen face almost as white as the white, long-sleeved dress shirt he wore. His slightly rumpled suit jacket and the battered briefcase in one hand only emphasised his state. The words Kiku had used earlier came back to him: *He sounded young, perhaps around your age and quite stressed*.

Once again, Kiku's intuition had not failed him. Judging from the man's pallid complexion and the dark circles under his eyes…

"Koji Watanabe, if I'm not mistaken," Kiku said softly. "And it appears our guest is not here of his own free will. Forced rest cure, probably."

Naoto nodded. Another workaholic. They came to the White Tiger regularly to relax, but not usually by force. *Ay.*

Kiku studied the scene with him a moment longer and then Naoto felt another pat on his shoulder. "I know you'll do your best to help him." And then he was gone.

Naoto watched the men approach the glass doors. The guards led Watanabe as if he were a criminal. He sure didn't appear to be one. He seemed to need about a month's worth of sleep, massages and blowjobs to erase that unhealthy pallor and sad, haunted look.

Well, Naoto thought as he took a deep breath and prepared to greet Koji Watanabe, that's what he was here for. Massages, blowjobs and everything in between.

Chapter Two

Up close, Koji Watanabe looked like shit hit with a hammer. Naoto held open the glass door for him, thinking of the phrase a guest from New York City had used to described how he felt when he'd come to the White Tiger. Naoto had laughed as he'd rubbed the American's shoulders and had always remembered those words.

They certainly fit Koji Watanabe. In spite of his beautiful bone structure, his face was gaunt, cheekbones a bit too sharp, skin pale. The man's large almond-shaped eyes probably could have been luminous but instead appeared work-deadened, exhausted with dark circles. *Haunted.*

The guy hadn't even brought an overnight bag, only a briefcase. Kiku was probably right about the hasty nature of his reservation.

"Koji Watanabe?"

The man stared at him a moment then nodded. "Yes."

Watanabe looked so lost that Naoto couldn't help the squeeze of compassion in his heart. Naoto bowed. "Welcome to the White Tiger, Watanabe-san. I'm Naoto, I'll be your attendant during your stay."

Koji Watanabe's eyes widened briefly and then he returned the bow. "Thank you."

Naoto's gaze flickered to the security guards. "Do you two need a room?"

"No, they don't," Watanabe-san said quickly. He turned to them. "Please tell Miosuke-san that I arrived safely."

Both uniformed men nodded silently, then turned and went back down the walk to the waiting taxi.

As the glass doors floated shut in their wake, the new guest uttered a deep sigh.

Naoto touched the man's elbow briefly, over his suit jacket. "Come, slip off your shoes and I'll show you to your room."

Wordlessly, he obeyed and Naoto picked up his leather shoes, in need of polishing, put them on the nearby rack and set down for him a pair of slippers with the hotel's emblem printed on the top. When Watanabe had stepped into them, Naoto slid back the inner door for him. Gently, he retrieved the briefcase from Watanabe's hand then gestured to the hallway. "I hope you'll be comfortable here," he said, giving Watanabe the customary line while leading him past the inner courtyard with its potted bamboos and Zen garden. Kiku had worked very hard to transform his illegal gambling parlour into a place of peace and repose for work-ridden businessmen and tourists.

"*Arigato*."

"You're welcome." Apparently, Koji Watanabe was going to need serious decompression. He seemed unable to respond in other than one-word sentences, the tone tight, like a guitar string pulled nearly past its breaking point. Even during the short elevator ride to the third floor, Naoto sensed that the slimmer man was in another world. His body was here at the White Tiger but his mind seemed elsewhere. From the suit and tie look of him, most probably back in his office.

At the door, Naoto stopped and slid back the *soji* screen, revealing a small but comfortable space. Just as Kiku had done with the main parts of the hotel, he'd made the rooms peaceful and alluring with neutral colours and potted plants. Black lacquer furnishings and raised futons in simple black fabric covers made a pleasing contrast, along with wall hangings depicting beautiful men in erotic poses, bodies entwined, lips pressed together.

Bowing, Naoto gestured around the room's interior. "Please, Watanabe-san, make yourself at home."

Wordlessly the other man stepped in. Naoto followed him and slid the *soji* closed. Watanabe was glancing around at his accommodations with that absent, preoccupied look in his eyes. Quickly, Naoto showed him the closet where he set the briefcase down and then pointed out the small washroom off to the side and the buzzer by the bed where he could ring for service at any time of the night or day.

Watanabe thanked him again in that tight, distracted way of his and then sank down onto the bed, hands hanging between his knees, elbows on his thighs. Naoto noticed the guy wasn't even bothering to remove his jacket or loosen his tie.

Well then, it was up to *him* to do it.

Stepping forward, Naoto knelt on the *tatami* that covered the dark polished wood floor. "Please, Watanabe-san, let me help you. First, your jacket."

Wordlessly, Watanabe slipped off his jacket and surrendered it. Naoto took it and hung it in the closet, then knelt down again. "Now, your tie." He reached out, fingers landing on the knot and fall of the other man's tie.

Watanabe started as if he'd been given a mild electric current and his eyes widened briefly again, but he didn't try to stop his tie from being gently worked open and slipped off.

"This is your time to relax, Watanabe-san." Naoto kept his voice a soft murmur as he let his protective desire to nurture another man in distress come out. That was one of the things he was good at. Otherwise, Kiku wouldn't have given him what was appearing to be a hard case. "Everything you could want or need is here while you're our guest. *Everything*." With the last word, Naoto let his hand rest briefly on the other man's chest.

Koji Watanabe didn't answer but Naoto could see that his eyes, for the first time seemed to focus for more than a couple of seconds.

It was then that Naoto had a glimpse of what Watanabe might look like if he hadn't been so haggard. Large dark eyes with thick lashes drew his gaze. He followed the straight bridge of his nose to the nostrils, which widened slightly at the end. The high cheekbones that looked a bit too sharp now would probably give him a kind of star quality when he'd put on a few pounds, as would the light gold of his complexion when less sallow.

The one thing that stood out, untarnished by stress, was his lips. Firm yet full, a dusky pink and beautifully shaped, like a slightly pulled back bow, there was one word for Koji Watanabe's lips — kissable. Well, maybe lickable and suckable too. Naoto caught himself staring a moment longer than was appropriate.

Oh, and Watanabe's hair, cut in a typically conventional office-guy style, short around the sides and barely longer on top, was also really beautiful. Just long enough to sift one's fingers through, if given a chance.

Naoto's heartbeat had kicked up a notch. He had always been a close observer and admirer of the male face and form, and it was clear this man was better looking than most of the men he serviced. Of course, there *were* good-looking guys that came in, but only once in a while did one have a certain something that gave him that…*feeling*…

Firmly putting his attention back on the task at hand, he dared to work open the top button at Watanabe's collar. A small expanse of pale gold skin peeked through, making Naoto suddenly itch to see more. To see what the rest of Koji Watanabe looked like. "Is that better, Watanabe-san?"

Now he caught the other man looking directly into his eyes. Watanabe's lips had parted slightly and his breathing sounded shallow. "You have long hair," he said, then shook himself as if starting from a trance. "I—I'm sorry, I meant please, call me Koji." Then he covered his face with both hands and slumped over. "I don't know what I meant."

Naoto stared at the top of Koji-san's head, at the beautifully-shaped fingers peeking out from where they were buried in his hair. How he yearned to pull the man to him. But he held back, sensing Koji-san might not be ready. "You have no need to apologise. If you prefer a man with short hair we can—"

Koji-san's head shot up, eyes wide. "No! I'm sorry. It wasn't a complaint." His breath started to come in short bursts and his pale face grew even paler.

Anxiety. Naoto recognised the signs. If Koji-san was as work-ridden as he appeared, he was probably in withdrawal. It wasn't uncommon among the guests who came here, especially the Japanese men. "Koji-san," he said, keeping his tone soothing. His hands came up and he rubbed the other man's shoulders. Through the thin white shirt, Koji-san's muscles were wiry, though also a bit too thin. "There is nothing to apologise for."

"This was so wrong. So wrong. I should be there." The words tumbled from Koji-san's lips and his eyes were wide with that haunted look.

"It's all right, Koji-san." Without thinking, Naoto rose higher on his knees and embraced the slimmer man. Koji-san was trembling as if he'd been outside in snow without any clothing on and his breathing had that choked sound Naoto had heard men make in terrible circumstances...like when they actually *were* dying...from gunshot wounds.

He rubbed the man's back in gentle circles and tilted his head aside so Koji-san's forehead could rest on his shoulder, all the while trying to erase the image of his lover's gunshot wound. "It'll be all right. You'll see, Koji-san. I know it will." He kept rubbing, feeling the wiry muscles of the other man's back flex as his body trembled and shook. The poor guy was a basket case. It was going to take much more than a massage with a happy ending to help him unwind.

Naoto held the other man for what seemed a long time, rubbing his back and just simply letting his anxiety attack run its course. Venturing one hand upward, he massaged the nape of Koji-san's neck. The man had a gracefully curved neck. Naoto had noticed it when unbuttoning his collar, and the skin there was warm and smooth. Not only that, but he smelled good, like clean laundry and soap with just a hint of male musk.

What a waste. A guy like this with such beauty, holed up in some office somewhere, driving himself insane over what was probably nonsense. Since his own father was a garbage collector, Naoto had always felt that Take Shimura provided a necessary service for society, something people just couldn't go without. So had Lee when he'd stopped teaching at the university to run his parents' grocery store in Little Asia. People always needed food. But some of the men who came here in suits, it seemed they'd be so much happier digging in the earth and growing things or building cabinets and *soji* screens. The man in his arms probably tapped on a computer the whole damn day. And night, from the looks of him.

Koji-san's trembling began to lessen. He seemed to like Naoto's fingertips on the tendons of his neck and on the smooth sides of his throat. Naoto resisted the urge to turn his face and press a kiss to the side of his head, but he did dare to let his massaging fingers venture upward, into Koji-san's hair. Naoto's breath caught. How sleek Koji-san's hair was. He raked gently upwards and nearly closed his eyes in pleasure as if tasting a luscious pastry. Naturally luxurious this hair was, like Lee's had been, sifting so easily between his fingers, teasing the pads of his fingertips with its soft beauty.

With each slide of his hand into Koji-san's hair, the other man grew calmer. His trembling ebbed to a slight shiver and his breathing, thankfully, began to lose that choked panicky sound of a man in his death throes. It was only then that Naoto felt Koji-san's arms around him, his hands gripping the back of his vest with the force of a man hanging on for his life.

Suddenly, Koji-san released him and sat up. His eyes were wide and still haunted, though he looked more sheepish than anything else. He took a deep breath. "Forgive my outburst." His gaze darted back and forth and then he looked down, shoulders slouching again. "This has been nothing but a shameful day." One hand came up and raked a second time through his hair.

Naoto sat back on his heels and watched him a moment. "What happened, Koji-san? Perhaps it would help if you tell me about it. That is, if you want to." Some men just needed to unload at first, and he was used to playing the role of simple listener, too.

Koji-san heaved a deep sigh. "I've been forced to go on vacation." Slowly, he looked up, eyes sheepish. "I begged my boss to let me choose a place to go, and he finally agreed.

But I had to do it right then and there. He even had those security guards escort me all the way here without letting me stop to get a change of clothes. He knew I'd refuse to take the time otherwise."

"What do you do?"

Koji-san pushed his hands into his hair. "Software engineer."

"Computers?"

He nodded.

Just as I thought. Not unlike his older brother, Shin, who'd turned out to be a math genius by age five and now did some kind of work for the government he couldn't talk about. Shin was two years older than he was and since Naoto could remember, he'd watched Shin get all kinds of special schooling while his parents let Naoto run wild. Of course, being left alone had its good points. He might never have met Lee if his parents had roped him in the way most parents did. But still...

Naoto gently took hold of Koji-san's wrists. "Well, as long as you're here, I can try to help you." He expected the other man to resist him, but to his surprise, Koji remained passive, letting Naoto draw his hands down to his sides so that he could move in closer and undo more buttons on his shirt. He worked open the second and then the third, trying to ignore the invasion of intense heat in his groin as the opening shirt revealed more smooth golden skin. No undershirt. "You'll see, Koji-san, if you relax and give yourself time to unwind, you'll begin to feel better. That's what I'm here for."

Koji-san made a sound that was somewhere between a huff and a wry chuckle. "I don't know how to relax."

Naoto smiled up at him. "Don't worry. I'll show you how." He undid the last couple of buttons and pulled in another breath. Though Koji-san was a bit too thin, Naoto could see that at the proper weight, the man was shaped like a swimmer or diver. Slim yet finely muscled, v-shaped torso. And those large dark nipples. Naoto's mouth watered to taste them, to feel them pebble against his tongue...

Wordlessly, he lifted one of Koji-san's wrists and undid the cuff, repeating the same with the other one. The tightening in his groin intensified as he slipped the shirt off Koji-san's arms and set it aside. "I would recommend a massage to start with."

Koji-san was staring at him like before, as if just noticing him. "Yes," he said softly. "A massage." He continued to stare at Naoto, letting Naoto undo his belt and the fastening of his slacks.

Naoto swallowed, his throat suddenly dry. He perused Koji-san's toned abdomen down to the waistband of his thoroughly conventional yet still alluring white briefs. It was actually the bulge pushing out the white fabric that inspired the lump in his throat and the itch in his palm to pull down the elastic and let the guy's cock out so he could stroke it. But that would have been pushing, so he distracted himself with removing Koji-san's slippers and socks so he could pull the man's slacks off.

Smiling, he rose up on his knees again and took hold of the open waist of the slacks. "Let's just get these off and then we can begin your massage."

Obediently, Koji-san lifted his ass off the bed enough for Naoto to pull down the slacks and slide them down. It was difficult not to stare at the other man's thighs and calves, which, like the rest of him were toned in spite of their needing some weight.

"Should I leave these on?" Koji-san looked up at him and tugged the elastic of his underwear.

Naoto swallowed. It had been awhile since someone had turned him on quite like this. He busied himself with hanging the other man's clothing neatly in the closet. "Only if you wish to, Koji-san. You can leave them on now and remove them later if you want to." He smoothed down the slacks on the hanger and turned around.

And froze.

Koji-san was naked. Wearing nothing but a distraught look on his beautiful face.

Naoto forced himself not to stare, not to peek down at the guy's dragon. Too late. The flicker of an eye caught the man's partially erect stalk resting against one smooth thigh.

"I wasn't sure what to do."

Koji-san's voice pulled him from his inappropriate stare. The man's eyes were clouded, not as badly as a few minutes earlier, but still uneasy.

Naoto cleared his throat, realising his error. He shouldn't have left any kind of decision up to his guest. Koji-san was in no shape to make even the smallest choice. "You're fine, Koji-san." He paused a moment and refocused his attention. He was here to pleasure this man and ease the stress from him as best he could, not to ogle him.

Just then, someone called out his name from the hallway. Ryu. His heart leaped and he saw Koji's eyes go wide. The other man hunched over, obviously to cover himself. *Shit.* "Yes?"

"Saké." Ryu's voice came through behind the rice paper screen.

Relief prickled down Naoto's arms. *Damn.* Koji-san had him so...worked up, he'd forgotten about the customary offering of saké Kiku had delivered to a guest to welcome him. "Thank you," he called.

"You're welcome. Let me know if you need anything else."

He heard Ryu set the tray down outside the door and leave.

Koji-san was still slumped over, elbows on his bare knees.

"I'm sorry, Koji-san," he said gently. "I forgot about your welcoming gift."

Koji-san sat up, eyes wide. "It's okay." His voice was still tight and he spoke as if he'd expected Naoto to scold him for something. *Poor guy.*

"I'll be right back." At Koji's nod, Naoto spent a few moments preparing a towel and bowl of warm water for after the massage, set the items to the side and then went to the screen. Sliding it back, he retrieved the small tray with the cup and decanter and closed the screen behind him. He knelt by Koji-san, who hadn't moved from his seat on the edge of the bed, and poured some saké into a small cup, which he held up to his guest. "Here, have some. It will help you relax."

Koji now sat up, shoulders hunched. He nodded once and accepted the cup, his fingertips brushing Naoto's. "*Kampai*," he toasted softly, lifting the cup to his lips.

"Yes." Naoto smiled. "To an empty glass."

Naoto watched the other man take a sip, his eyes closing as he swallowed. Koji-san's Adam's apple bobbed with the movement of his throat and Naoto ached to press a kiss to the spot.

Koji-san drained the cup in one swallow. When he opened his eyes again, Naoto could see the light glaze over his dark irises. Apparently, Koji-san wasn't much of a drinker and already felt the effects.

Naoto refilled the cup and offered it to him again. With the same toast, Koji-san accepted it and downed it as he had the first.

Koji-san's eyelids dropped slightly over his large eyes and his breathing grew calmer. "That was very good." His words had grown slower. "Please, one more."

Naoto felt an objection rise to his lips. But Koji-san was the guest and as long as he wasn't doing something life-threatening, he would be indulged. Naoto poured him a third cup and watched him gulp it down, no toast. This time, when Naoto took the cup back, he set it aside.

"Naoto-san." Koji-san's voice was soft and less shaky than before.

Naoto looked at him, surprised he'd called him by name. Showed how uptight he was, needing three cups of saké before addressing Naoto directly like that. "Yes?"

A strange look flooded Koji-san's eyes. "May I touch your hair?"

Naoto's gut tightened, both at the request itself and at the hushed wonder in it. He remembered how Koji-san had remarked about his hair earlier. "Of course." He pulled out the tie that kept the length hanging neatly down his back and lifted it to fall over his shoulder, down one side of his chest.

Koji-san's lips parted in what appeared almost a smile, the first since he'd gotten here. His hand came out slowly, fingers extended and he touched the dark fall gingerly, as if handling his mother's forbidden porcelain tea set. "Oh, so beautiful."

Naoto's heart sped up slightly. The touch on his hair tugged in a pleasant way against his scalp and the sensual wonder in Koji-san's eyes made a strange ache in his chest. What kind of life did this man have? He seemed so…deprived.

On the first down stroke, his guest's seeking fingertips pressed inadvertently on his nipple. Pleasure darted through it and Naoto let out a small breath. "Thank you, Koji-san," he murmured, aware he wasn't only thanking the other man for liking his hair.

"I love long hair," Koji-san said. In spite of the saké-induced slur in his voice, he spoke with a reverent hush. "Yours is especially nice. So shiny." He caressed it again, as if petting a cat or dog and with each stroke, his fingertips grazed Naoto's nipple. Naoto felt it harden, as did his dragon.

Thankfully, Koji-san was too buzzed to notice anything beyond the hair he caressed. His gaze rested on Naoto as if he were watching an engrossing film. "You're amazing," he breathed.

Naoto stared at him, remembering at the last second to smile. "You're very kind, Koji-san," he answered. No one had ever called him amazing, not even Lee. Too bad his guest was on liquid courage. He probably wouldn't even remember this, after sleeping it off.

"I mean it, Naoto. Amazing. All of you." Koji continued to stroke his hair. His fingertips sent another tingle of heat through Naoto's nipple. If he kept doing this, Koji-san was going to end up getting more than a massage.

Gently, Naoto stilled the other man's hand by covering it with his. "Whenever you're ready, Koji-san," he said softly, "we can begin your massage."

Releasing Koji-san's hand, he pulled back the bedcover and arranged the pillows. "Koji-san, if you lie on your stomach, I can give you a relaxing massage. Would you like that?"

Koji continued to stare at him like a love-starved puppy. "You're going to massage me?" The question sounded hopeful.

"If you'd like that."

Koji-san nodded. "Yes, thank you."

Now that the man was past his initial crisis, he could begin his guest's serious relaxation.

Chapter Three

Heart pounding now, Naoto guided Koji to a lying position on his stomach, arms folded under his chin.

"Naoto-san, you may think I don't know what I'm saying because I'm drunk now, but I do." Koji-san turned to look up at him. His gaze was almost worshipful now. "You're beautiful, like a samurai. A strong, handsome samurai, who's gentle too." He fell silent, sculpted lips slightly parted, as if he were waiting for Naoto to kiss him.

A shiver of want passed down Naoto's back. He'd never thought of his wide flat face, rugged cheeks and strong jaw as beautiful. But if Koji-san felt that way, so be it, even though the man's opinion was definitely alcohol-inspired. "Thank you, Koji-san," he murmured. He stared another moment at Koji-san's lips. He'd have loved nothing more than to kiss the man, to slip his tongue inside his mouth and taste him. But he generally didn't kiss guests and they generally didn't request it.

"You're welcome."

Naoto brushed a soft caress over Koji's hair, gently bidding him to rest his chin again on his hands. His own dragon was hard now, pushing against the snug white shorts that comprised the bottom half of the hotel's uniform. The smallest movement, such as reaching for the massage oil in the bedside table, made the material of his shorts rub him, increasing his longing to free his cock and release the pressure. To hide his reaction, he asked, "Are you comfortable?"

"Yes. Very comfortable, thank you."

Naoto perused his form again. The man was all sleek lines and smooth expanses of golden skin, just inviting

Naoto to cover him, press the length of his front down that body and push his dragon between a pair of perfectly round ass cheeks…

Nande? He froze. Had he seen correctly? Looking more closely, he examined what appeared vicious-looking white streaks across the other man's buttocks. Scars. His heart squeezed in his chest, but he had to pretend nothing was wrong.

"Just ignore them, Naoto-san."

Naoto whipped his gaze up. "I beg your pardon?"

Koji-san twisted his head around again to look at him. "The scars. I sensed your hesitation. That must have been what it was."

Naoto's heart lurched. The man was more perceptive than he appeared, drunk or not. "I…I didn't mean to—"

"Forget it. They're from a long time ago. They don't hurt anymore." There was a strange catch in his voice, something that made Naoto not believe that last bit.

But truly, it wasn't any of his damn business. No doubt, Kiku would tell him the same. He could practically hear his *sensei's* voice in his mind, urging him to put his attention back onto his guest's pleasure.

Breathing a small sigh, he reached to the wall and turned a knob to the sound system. Kiku always had a recording playing of gentle *shamisen* and bamboo flute music to make the atmosphere as calming as possible. It worked, the *shamisen's* quietly plucked string sounds filtered into the air with the flute. That done, he lit a stick of sandalwood incense and picked up the massage oil. Usually massages were given downstairs in one of the massage rooms, but Koji-san's need was too immediate.

Warming the oil in his hands, Naoto knelt by the futon. He closed his eyes a moment and got still, not wanting his arousal to come through in his touch. He was supposed to *relax* Koji-san, not make him into a sudden sex partner. Usually, this was not such a difficult task. Today was different. Perhaps because it *was* Monday and Mondays were so goddamn difficult.

Naoto opened his eyes and put his hands on the other man's back. He pulled in a quick breath. That golden skin was as warm and as smooth to the touch as he'd thought it would be. He began a circular motion with his oiled palms.

"Ohhhhh." Koji-san murmured.

The sound shivered through Naoto and he could swear the man's skin was so creamy it could melt under his touch. His dragon pushed against his shorts, more insistent now, but Naoto pulled his attention back to his rubbing. He slid his palms back down, pressing gently, especially with his thumbs.

"Mmm." Koji-san's body sagged the tiniest bit into the futon and he heaved a deep sigh. "You're so good at this. So beautiful."

A tingle cascaded through Naoto's chest. "I'm glad you're enjoying it."

"I meant that *you're* beautiful, Naoto-san."

Naoto felt his cheeks heat up. Strange, a guy nearly six feet tall, built like a heavyweight fighter, blushing the way he knew he was right now. He only wished Koji-san meant what he was saying. Get enough saké into a guy and the hairy ass of a goat could be beautiful. "That's very nice of you."

"I'm not saying it to be nice. I'm not *nice*. I'm saying what's true."

Naoto frowned but continued his massage. "I'm sure you have nice qualities."

"Ask Hiru. He'll tell you what I am."

"Who's Hiru?" *A lover, perhaps*? Naoto didn't want to know, but he sensed Koji-san's need to ramble.

"He's a friend of mine who sits near me at work. If you ask him, he'll tell you. I'm not nice, I'm not mean. I'm not anything. I'm nothing."

Naoto pulled in a breath, not so much at the words, but at the matter-of-fact way they were spoken. Only the smoothness of Koji-san's skin and his sorry condition could bring his attention back to the massage. The muscles under his touch couldn't be tighter, as if Koji-san had hundreds of pounds of pressure coiled in every inch of him. The pads of Naoto's thumbs found knot after knot, in the man's upper back, along his spine and into his shoulders. *Deltoids, trapezoids, latissimus dorsi*, the poor man's body was a roadmap of tension. "You're not nothing, Koji-san," he said as he made another circle of the other man's tight back with his hands. "If you were nothing, you wouldn't have been forced to go on vacation."

"Don't be fooled. I'm an investment to them. Nothing more."

"An investment?" Naoto shifted around so that he faced the foot of the bed. Why he asked the question, he wasn't sure. He already understood what Koji-san meant, and it was disgusting. The very reason he was grateful to be slipping through the cracks of this rat's maze called society.

"Yeah, an investment. A delivery truck in the shop for a tune-up. So I won't break down and make them lose business. And then cost them more money in repairs."

Naoto stared down at the back of the other man's head as he continued his slow, easy massage. "People aren't machines, Koji-san. You're a man." *A really beautiful man who feels incredible under my hands.*

Koji-san made a strange sound, something like a chuckle but strangled. Not a happy sound. "If I'm a man then how come I don't want Tomoko? She has long beautiful hair like yours. But I don't want her. I want *you*."

Naoto's heart lurched. He lifted his hands as if Koji-san's back had caught fire. Okay, he could deal with this. Koji-san wasn't the first man who'd ever come to the White Tiger because it was the only place he could really let go and be himself. Naoto didn't know who this woman was that Koji-san spoke of, but it didn't matter. Lowering his hands, he resumed rubbing. "There's nothing wrong with wanting a man, Koji-san. Nothing at all. Ever."

As if to emphasise his words, he let his hands dip towards Koji-san's slim waist. His heartbeat rose slightly. That curl of heat he'd felt earlier in his dragon now resurged. The flow clicked and Naoto let his mind and body pour into the stream of the moment.

Koji-san's breathing deepened. "It feels wrong," he breathed. "But I…"

"What, Koji-san?" Naoto dipped his fingers lower. His touch grazed the tops of Koji-san's buttocks. Mmm. Skin smooth and soft over the hard muscle. He made another round upward and then further down towards the tops of his thighs.

"That's very good." Koji-san's voice was husky now. "I can't help it that it feels so good."

"You shouldn't have to help it, Koji-san." Naoto pushed the heel of one hand into Koji-san's left ass cheek, pushed down and rubbed in tight circles.

"Oh, oh, oh," Koji-san murmured with each round of Naoto's hand.

Naoto looked down. The other man's thighs had parted, revealing the firm plumpness of his balls between them. The sight made Naoto forget about the scars.

Shimatta! His mouth watered to lick that delicious, ripe-looking sac, to venture his tongue in the crease of Koji-san's ass and explore every hidden part. To tease his tiny hole until Koji-san groaned.

Naoto dipped his fingers between Koji-san's ass cheeks and brushed one fingertip over the tight opening.

"Ohhh." Koji spread his legs apart some more.

Naoto smiled, caught up in the flow of the moment now. "You see, Koji-san? If it were wrong, it wouldn't feel so good. If men weren't made to love other men, we wouldn't have been given these…" He caressed Koji's entrance again, loving the rougher feel in contrast to his smooth ass.

Koji-san's hips lifted off the futon, widening the gap between his cheeks even more. "Yessss…maybe you're right." He sounded breathless now.

"Don't worry, Koji-san, I'm right." Naoto rested his fingertip there with more pressure. With his other hand, he squeezed one firm ass cheek, manipulated the taut round muscle in a rhythm against his caressing finger. "How is that, Koji-san?"

The slimmer man was panting, lifting his ass with each brush of Naoto's fingertip over his hole, and his back heaved with each harsh breath, the sound of a man releasing years of built-up pressure. "So…good."

Naoto took a deep breath. Even though every inch of his own body throbbed now, his hands had a life of their own, seeming to know just naturally what Koji-san needed.

He wiggled the tip of his index finger, slick with oil, over the tight hole and then pushed, just enough to penetrate Koji-san to his first knuckle.

The other man gasped and groaned, almost simultaneously. "Don't stop, I beg you."

"I won't stop, Koji-san, not until you're completely, fully satisfied." With each word, he pushed in a bit deeper and brushed the pad of his thumb back and forth across the bottom of Koji-san's balls. Damn, every inch of this guy felt like heaven.

"Ahhhh." Koji-san's rear pushed against Naoto's hand. The soft lighting in the room made the oil on the man's smooth body glisten. His moans and groans filled the air, blending with the soft music.

Naoto closed his eyes and focused all his attention on Koji-san, wanting nothing but for him to feel bliss. Koji-san needed it more than he needed food and water. He pushed his finger in almost as deeply as it would go and rubbed Koji-san's prostate.

"Ohhhh!" Koji-san's hips lifted again, pushing his whole backside against Naoto's hand.

Naoto thrust his finger in and out, never stopping the caress of his thumb on the firm sac at the same time. "How is that?" he said in a silky voice.

"Naoto-san! Naoto-san!"

Naoto's insides jumped at the sound of his name whispered so feverishly. "Do you wish to turn over, Koji-san? I can pleasure you some more that way."

"Yes. Please."

"Whatever you wish, Koji-san. I'm here to please you." He slipped his finger out of the other man's ass and manoeuvred Koji-san onto his back.

The task wasn't difficult. Koji-san practically fell over, chest heaving, large eyes wide and glazed as they fixed on Naoto. Koji-san's dragon was fully erect and jutting upward from his slim body. The member strained, thick and full, blushes of reddish colour along the veined shaft. Naoto's mouth watered at the sight. "Thank you, Naoto-san," he breathed.

"You're welcome." Naoto closed his hand lightly around Koji-san's dragon. The hard shaft fit perfectly against his palm and the massage oil made his hand slide easily up and down, from head to base.

"Ohhhhh." Koji-san's chin tilted up. His dark lashes rested against his cheeks and his head thrashed side to side on the pillow. His full lips let out panting breaths, one after the other, matching Naoto's quick strokes on his cock. "Ohhh, Naoto-san, you're...so...kind."

Naoto smiled down at him. Nothing was more pleasing than a man's release, especially a man in such need. "Enjoy, Koji-san," he whispered and increased the rhythm of his strokes.

"Ahhh." Koji-san moaned. His eyelids fluttered and his hips lifted.

Naoto leaned forward and lightly squeezed the other man's balls with his other hand as he stroked him. A quick pulse in the stalk of Koji-san's dragon and Naoto felt his climax about to erupt. He brushed his thumb over the firm soft skin of his balls and then played again around his ass, pushing the tip of his finger just inside.

A second later Koji-san's eyes flew wide open. Naoto was ready for him.

"Let go, Koji-san...let go."

Koji needed no more prompting. "Naoto-san, ahhh." Koji-san's eyes flew wide open. His hips lifted again and his shaft pulsed against Naoto's hand. In the next instant his warm, milky dragon's breath erupted onto Naoto's fingers. Naoto kept up his fevered stroking, decreasing the pressure until the other man was empty and he wilted into the futon.

Staring up, Koji-san's eyelids remained at half-mast over the glazed irises. His lips were still parted and his chest rose and fell heavily. "Thank…you…Naoto-san."

Naoto dragged in a deep breath. Heat pulsed through his body. His dragon strained almost painfully against the snug shorts. He needed release badly but there was nothing he could do about it…with Koji-san, that was, unless he was invited. "You're most welcome."

Gently, he released the man's dragon, laid it against his lower abdomen and reached for the washcloth and warm bowl of water. He saturated the cloth and began to clean his guest. "I'll continue your massage in a moment, Koji-san," he said softly, working to keep his hands steady.

"Okay." Koji's heavy-lidded gaze remained on Naoto, the dark irises clearer than they'd been earlier, yet still misty. His chest still rose and fell heavily but he lay quietly, letting Naoto wipe the warm washcloth over his skin. "That was…very good, Naoto-san. Thank you."

Naoto almost frowned. Twice in a few seconds the man had thanked him. For that paltry little hand job. As if Naoto had brought him to the heights of bliss. There was something about Koji-san that just made this ache in his chest. He worked his lips into a smile. "No need to thank me, Koji-san. It's my pleasure." He set the bowl and cloth aside and picked up the other man's right hand, which he began to massage.

Koji released a long sigh. His eyelashes fluttered and his hand relaxed between Naoto's hands. For a moment, Naoto thought the other man was falling asleep, but in the next second, Koji-san's eyes opened, pinning him with a rather intent gaze.

"How long have you worked here, Naoto-san?"

The ache tightened. It was rare that a guest asked him anything about himself. "Three years." He pressed gentle circles into Koji-san's palm.

"Three years," he repeated.

"It's not just a place I work, though. This is my home." Most people only ever came here to unwind and be fussed over for a little while. They didn't really concern themselves with the underlying purpose of the place, which was a spiritual school for the men who sought refuge with Kiku.

Curiosity slipped into the slimmer man's expression. "Your home? Really?" He seemed genuinely interested.

Naoto nodded. "Yes." He watched one feeling after the next pass through the other man's huge gaze. Koji-san's hand grew more pliant. Gently, Naoto set it down and reached for his other hand.

"How did you come to be here?" Koji-san's open curiosity could only be from the saké in his veins.

Naoto's gut fluttered a tiny bit. He wasn't supposed to spill all the troubling details of his life to a guest, but he didn't want to ignore the question either. "I went through a troubled time my life," he said carefully. "When I met the owner, he sensed it and offered me a place to go. I've been here ever since."

"Oh. Is this where you learned to give such a wonderful massage?"

Naoto chuckled. He'd learned most of the useful skills he had from Kiku. "Yes."

Koji's gaze softened. "You're very good at it," he murmured.

Naoto felt his cheeks tingle again. "Thank you, Koji-san."

"Are you…happy?"

He would have been happy had Lee not been murdered. "I'm content in this place, yes," he said, pressing down gently into the fleshy part of Koji-san's hand. There was considerably less tension in his guest now than there had been when he'd started and Naoto understood that he'd done the first part of his job well. However, Koji-san was going to need much more before they were through. Much more.

"I didn't mean *content*, Naoto-san." The slurred edge was still in Koji-san's voice and in his gaze, but the statement showed that his thoughts were coherent enough. "I meant *happy*."

Naoto looked into the other man's eyes, at the blend of mild challenge and genuine interest that now darkened his gaze. For a brief moment, Naoto considered the truth. Then decided against it. It wasn't a guest's job to listen to his troubles. "I've been told that happiness is my true nature, the true nature of every human being, Koji-san. It's our beliefs and ideas about life that are obstacles to understanding this. I'm working on understanding." He brushed his thumb over the soft flesh of Koji's palm.

He concentrated on massaging the man's hand but when he felt that gaze still on him, he couldn't help looking back up.

Koji-san was staring at him intently. "I can't imagine really being happy."

Naoto looked at him. The sadness in Koji's voice made that ache again in his chest. "It's possible, Koji-san," he said softly. "I experience happiness now, and there were definitely times I felt exactly as you feel."

Koji was silent a moment. "I want to believe you. I want to believe it's possible."

Naoto pressed Koji's hand gently between both of his while the ache inside tightened more. "It is possible, Koji-san."

He set Koji's hand down and then caressed the man's hair. He couldn't even remember the last time a guest conversed with him this way, not even while under the influence. It made him wonder what Koji-san would say next.

Koji's eyelids fluttered, as if Naoto's hand on his hair felt as good as the massage. He lay back and heaved a deep sigh, his gaze never leaving Naoto's face. "Naoto-san, you're exactly, precisely my type."

Naoto stared at him. It hadn't been what he'd expected, that's for sure. Koji's words caused a warm tingle through his middle. Nice to hear, even if it was only the saké talking. "Thank you, Koji-san. It's nice to be…appreciated."

"I hope you'll kiss me."

Naoto's insides jumped.

A kiss. The very thing he'd had wanted from the moment he'd studied the beauty of Koji-san's face. For a heart-stopping minute Naoto stared at Koji-san's full lips, pursed in an expectant way.

Then slowly, he leaned over until his face hovered an inch from Koji-san's. The aroma of saké and incense lingered in the air between them. Naoto's heartbeat rose. The heat in his body intensified. He moved closer...so close, the fanning of Koji's warm breath caressed his lips...a mere whisper away.

Koji-san's head tilted to the side.

Naoto closed his eyes and just about touched their lips together...just as a soft snore rolled into the air between them.

Naoto opened his eyes.

Asleep. Koji-san had fallen asleep.

Naoto chuckled softly and leaned back. Koji's dark lashes rested against his cheeks and his lips parted with the deep breath of slumber.

Naoto watched the other man's face for several moments, unable to ignore his own disappointment. It had been a long time since he'd wanted to kiss someone so much. There was just something about Koji-san...

He sighed. Perhaps an opportunity would present itself later, although who knew what Koji-san's attitude would be when he woke up sober.

Carefully, Naoto pulled the covers over his guest and stood a few moments, watching him. The sleeping man was quite a contrast to the basket case who'd come in just a short while ago.

Finally, disturbed by his own reluctance to leave, Naoto stepped away from the bed. He turned down the background music and lights, then slipped out of the room.

Without thinking about what to do next, he padded towards the back stairway, in the direction of his own room. The first thing he needed to do was relieve the pressure in his dragon. Hopefully then he could think clearly. Koji-san's face hovered in his mind. The man's tormented beauty made his heart pound, had made him want to strip off his own clothing, slip under the covers with him and absorb him, kiss away his agony until it had dissolved.

Thankfully, no one else was in the hallway, needing him to attend to the hotel in some way, and Naoto made it to his room unseen where he could slip back the *soji* screen and disappear inside.

The small room, on the same floor where his fellow White Tigers had their rooms, was a haven. Even without locks on the door, he didn't worry about theft because there all the guys on this floor were good friends and honourable people, and in any case, who'd want to steal some battered jeans, a few of Lee's old poetry books and photographs?

Already barefoot, Naoto undid the button of his shorts. *Ahh,* that was better already. The thick hardness of his dragon sprang free. Not that he was bragging, but the confines of the shorts squeezed his cock and balls tighter when he was hard than they did the other White Tigers. And he knew. He saw them in the baths regularly.

Pushing the shorts down to his knees, Naoto sat on his futon and leaned back against the pillows. As he did so, his eye fell on the photograph on his bedside table. Lee's sweet face smiled out at him, causing an unexpected spike of guilt. *Ay.*

Naoto turned so he couldn't see the picture and closed his fingers around his cock. The first touch made him groan softly. He rubbed, soft strokes from base to head, his palm still slick enough from the massage oil. This wouldn't take long. Sparks of heat followed the contact of his hand along his hard length and pressure swirled in his balls.

Pleasure washed through his lower body. He probably should have been retaining the yang fire Koji-san's ejaculation had emitted. The energy added to his own helped deepen his meditations, but there was just no way in hell he could hold it in now.

He stroked faster. Naoto tilted his head back against the pillows, eyes closed. Koji-san was there, in his mind, smooth skin covered with a sheen of sweat, his large dark nipples tight, erection straining. He dared to imagine what that man's dragon tasted like and he already craved the feel of it in his mouth, rubbing against his tongue. Koji-san's moans and sighs were sweet and Naoto wanted to make him utter more sounds like that. He imagined smoothing the flat of his tongue over those firm balls and feeling Koji-san's hands clutch into his hair.

Pleasure surged, filled the length of his dragon. The pressure was so tight, he erupted. Warm cum spilled over his hand and spurted onto his belly. Naoto moaned softly, stroking quickly until his climax had spiralled away and the spasms of pleasure subsided. His hand stilled on his cock and he rested, breathing heavily, his consciousness steady, melted into the world around him.

Sounds were more vivid, the soft whoosh of air through the partly open window, the gentle tick of his bedside clock, the rise and fall of his own breath. Scent, too, seemed sharper in his nostrils, the lingering incense that pervaded the entire hotel, the musky scent of his own cum and the shampoo he used in his hair.

You have long hair. Koji-san's words echoed through his mind. Koji-san hadn't said it in a classifying way, as if he'd been looking for a *lon-ge* – longhaired, a type many guys went for. At first Naoto had thought Koji was complaining, but he'd been wrong…the sweet look that had come into Koji's eyes when Naoto had pulled the tie out…and then, way the other man had run his hand down the length of Naoto's hair…almost reverent.

Naoto heaved a sigh. Time to get back to work. There was always plenty to do around here, even when there were fewer guests. And he'd need to check in on Koji-san in a while.

He reached for tissues on the bedside table. Another spike of guilt hit him when he saw Lee's picture. Naoto wiped himself off and sat up, still looking at the photograph in its simple dark frame. Throwing away the tissues, he picked up the photograph and stared at it. Lee had been bent over one of his books when Naoto approached him with the camera. He'd had a thing for taking pictures of Lee—hence, the small gallery of framed photos littering his two small bookshelves—telling him jokes to get him to laugh for the camera. He'd even loved the way Lee's skin crinkled around his eyes when he laughed.

Naoto sighed. With one index finger he traced the contour of Lee's cheek, woefully flat, lifeless. A photograph was the poorest substitute for the real person.

"*If anything ever happens to me, I want you to find someone again.*" Lee's voice now echoed inside him the way Koji-san's had a few moments earlier. Another one of Lee's prophetic statements, as if he'd sensed his impending death. It had pissed Naoto off. "*Shut up, Lee,*" he'd answered and draped his naked body over Lee's smaller compact frame, trapping the musky warmth of their combined heat between them.

With another sigh, Naoto replaced the photograph. Lee's request of him to find someone else to love hadn't mattered anyway. After three years, he still didn't want to replace him. Feeling compassion for a troubled guy and helping him relax was one thing. But having a partner, someone whose soul was entwined with yours? Completely different.

He rose from the bed and pulled up his shorts. They didn't fit quite so snugly now. Which was a relief because he had things to do. And one very troubled guest to look after.

Chapter Four

Kung fu theme music was playing in Koji's head. Playing and playing.

Koji opened his eyes. He blinked as the music played on.

An erotic drawing stared back at him from the wall opposite where he lay. Then he saw potted plants, a *soji* screen. His head swam, like it did when he drank too much. Roused by the insistent music, his memory flooded back. Three cups of saké. Long, beautiful hair. Big muscles. Incredible massage, on *every* inch of his body. A climax which made him think the top of his head would blow off. It hadn't been a dream.

The kung fu music played on. Shit! The sound came from his slacks, hanging in the closet. His cell phone.

Shoving the covers off, he lifted himself out of the bed. In a few seconds, the tune would stop playing and he'd miss the call. Surging forward, he yanked the phone off its clip. Fumbling a second, he looked at the screen. Hiru. Oh shit! He pressed the button. "*Moshi moshi.*"

"Koji, is that you?"

Koji's heart jumped. No doubt, Hiru would have all the gossip for him. "Yes. It's me."

"Hey, what happened today? I didn't want to ask you in front of everybody this morning. Are you all right?"

Fully awake now, Koji raked a hand through his hair. His throat went dry and he started to pace back in forth in front of the futon.

That's when he realised it. He was naked. His cock bobbed with his frantic pace. He halted and grabbed for his underwear, neatly resting over his slacks on the hanger, and slipped them on, as if to cover himself from Hiru. "I'm okay. Miosuke was just sending me on vacation. He was...afraid I was burning out."

"Oh, okay! When I saw the security guards, I couldn't imagine what was going on. I mean, you're one of the most straight-laced people I've ever met."

The word 'straight' sent a shiver down Koji's arms. An unbidden memory rose, of a large hand, slick with oil, rubbing it. The mere thought sent a warm tingle into his groin. Made thinking a bit difficult. "Yeah, the security guards." He cast quickly for an excuse. "They were...um...returning my wallet to me. I'd lost it. They found it and went with me to get it back." Fuck, that sounded so untrue. But if it would keep the rumours from flying in the office, so be it.

"Oh."

Koji froze. "Why? What are people saying?"

"Nothing. Just the same thing I was. That they couldn't imagine what was going on."

Though he couldn't see Hiru's expression, he could just picture the doubtful expression on the chubby guy's face. "Please, Hiru, tell them what I told you, okay? That's all it was. I'll be back in a week. You'll tell them right?"

"Of course, Koje. I'll tell them."

Koji now sank down onto the futon, heart pounding. He caught himself just before asking Hiru if he knew who'd taken over his accounts. Hiru didn't need to know he hadn't had time to make arrangements for them. He didn't want the humiliation of Hiru's knowing it had been done without his approval. "Well, thanks for being concerned, Hiru. I'm fine. Enjoying some relaxation."

"That's good to know. Just wanted to make sure. Where are you anyway?"

Koji's heart flipped. "I'm...um...in a *ryokan*...near the...airport. Comfortable room. Great baths. I've already had a nice soak." His pulse raced higher as he invented an inn quite a bit different from the one he was really staying in.

"Sounds awesome." Hiru's tone was slightly envious. "Are there any pretty attendants there?"

Koji cleared his throat. His hand shook on the phone. His legs felt suddenly weak and he sank down onto the futon. "Yeah. Mine has beautiful...long hair." True enough detail in the midst of this story he was spinning. "The food's incredible too. They make great...sushi." He raked his free hand through his hair. He often felt like an asshole, but it was worse now. Lying through his teeth to his friend. "Anyway, I'm going to get a massage now. Better go. Thanks for checking up on me. I'll talk to you later?"

"Sure, Koje. Take care. Bye."

Koji pressed the button and slumped over. His heart raced fiercely now and he felt like he was on the edge of an invisible cliff, slipping over, unable to claw his way to safety. Sitting up, he almost went to the call button to ring for Naoto.

He stopped, hand halfway to the button. His face burned as the things he'd said to Naoto while drunk flooded his memory. *Shimatta*! How humiliating! He'd let slip out every damn thought and feeling he'd had.

It didn't matter that the guy was the hottest he'd ever laid eyes on and that Koji had wanted to lick every inch of his thickly muscled body, but he'd made an absolute asshole of himself, saying things he would never say while sober, especially to a stranger. Even to a hot stranger who'd jacked him off and fingered his ass.

He had to get out of here. At least for a while. He had to try and find out who had his accounts, especially the hospital, and get them in order. Maybe then he could relax.

Quickly he threw on his clothes and grabbed his briefcase. He didn't even know what time it was, hadn't bothered to check the clock on his cell phone when he clipped it back to his belt. Not important. He just had to get to his apartment and access his office network from his laptop.

Koji rushed out, remembering at the last second to close the screen behind him. Naoto came to mind, followed by a strange tickle of guilt he felt at leaving, as if he were doing Naoto-san a disservice. Not waiting for the elevator, he rushed to the stairs, down the three flights, to the front entrance. At the shoe rack, he searched desperately for his shoes among the pairs arranged in the small cubbies.

"Koji-san."

Koji wheeled around.

Naoto stood a few feet away. *Kuso!* Just the sight of him made Koji's cock start to tighten in his briefs.

The taller man bowed. "I was coming to see if you needed anything."

Koji returned the gesture. "No, thank you. I...have to go out for a while. I'll be back later."

Naoto's brow furrowed. "Just a moment, do you have your—"

"I'm sorry. No time. When I come back." He bowed again, feeling his cheeks burn. He was in as much of a hurry to get away from the man he'd made a fool of himself with as much as he was to get home. Exposing his cock and ass was one thing. That's what he was here for. But exposing his insides during a drunken stupor? Unacceptable. "Thank you, Naoto-san."

Naoto bowed again and followed him to the doorway. "Let me get your shoes for you, Koji-san." Without waiting, he went to the rack and retrieved Koji's shoes, setting them on the floor for him.

Koji felt his cheeks burn again. He avoided the other man's gaze as Naoto straightened. "Thank you," he murmured. Damn, he'd forgotten to put on his socks. There wasn't time to go back for them. He slipped his bare feet into his shoes. "See you later."

"Yes, Koji-san."

Without another word, Koji rushed out the glass doors and hailed a taxi. He gave the driver his address and sat back. His stomach was clenched tight and he stared through the window at Ni Chome, the neighbourhood this White Tiger hotel was in. It was twilight and the bistros and bars were lit up. Soon the sidewalks would be teeming with people on their way to those bars and to the many swanky gay clubs and pick-up bath joints the area had to offer.

Koji exhaled. He'd only dared to come around here a few times himself, always afraid someone would recognise him or spot him on the streets and report back to his family. Oh well. It didn't matter now. His secret was in Miosuke's hands and he could only hope his boss had the decency to be discreet. His stomach clenched again at the thought. Calling in the security guards this morning to lead him out of the office in front of everyone had sure as hell not been discreet.

Back at his apartment building, Koji paid the driver and bounded upstairs. He flicked on his laptop and sat shivering while it booted up. Finally he was able to type in his username and password to the company's network.

Access denied.

Koji's heart lurched. What? He typed the words in again. And was denied again.

Oh shit! Miosuke had blocked his access to his work!

Koji launched from his chair and began to pace, both hands buried into his hair. He felt as if all the blood were draining from his body, yet he couldn't sit, couldn't take deep calming breaths. Not if his life had depended on it.

Think. Think. He had to find a solution to this nightmare. He halted and looked at the screen. He could hack into the system but then any changes he would make — and yes, he would find errors needing correction, no doubt — would show up and Miosuke would know what he'd done. He'd be in trouble, worse than now.

He thought about going directly to the hospital, only a few blocks' from here. No good. At this hour, the administrative offices would be closed and he didn't dare access the mainframe from a nurses' station. Interrupt their work and someone could die.

He plopped back into his chair and stared blankly at the screen. A cold sweat had erupted on every inch of his body. What the hell was he going to do? He couldn't try to go into the office. If he were caught there — if Miosuke hadn't already blocked his pass card there, too — he'd be punished.

The worst part? He couldn't even tell anyone. He could *not* discuss this with Hiru or anyone else from the office. He sure as shit wasn't going to talk to his father or sister and brother-in-law. They wouldn't understand and would only tell him to relax and stop worrying so much. If Shizuko had been alive, he would have talked to her. His stepmother had been the one true friend he'd had all these years.

He fell forward, arms on his knees, fingers digging into his scalp. He felt like the world was crashing around him, as if all the nerve endings in his body were on the outside of his skin. It had always been that way since he could remember. When he was younger and it hit him, Shizuko would rub his back and speak softly to him until it passed. But then he got older and couldn't ask her to do that. He'd then taken refuge in drawing and in the fantasy world of his mind. After college, needing to go out and work, his only escape had become the numbing world of the computer screen and a constant workload.

Only one thing had felt good to him in the longest time. Naoto. The man's touch on his skin and the soothing way he spoke. The sleek length of Naoto's hair against his fingertips. One good thing had been given to him in forever and he'd fucked that up too by getting drunk off his ass and saying one embarrassing thing after the next to the guy.

For a little while it had felt good to be fussed over even if it was the man's job to fuss over him. He hadn't had that since he was thirteen with the flu and Shizuko had nursed him. She'd died knowing his secrets. The only other person in the world. Damn, he missed her so much it ached.

Well, now there was one other person who knew…well…one of his secrets. Naoto. Of course, he wouldn't judge or go telling other people. And he seemed really…kind. As kind as he was unbelievably, incredibly gorgeous. A *long-ge no katchiri*. Long-haired, muscle man. Naoto couldn't be more his type.

Koji pulled his hands from his hair, stood up and went into the bathroom. He turned the shower on super hot, stripped his clothes off and stepped under the spray. He scrubbed shampoo into his hair and tilted his head back so the water battered his face. Closing his eyes, he turned his back to the spray, standing under the hot water until the bathroom was cloudy with steam and his skin was red. Only then did he turn off the water, grab a towel and bury his face in it for what felt like a long time.

Finally he began to dry off. For the second time today, life had cornered him, had given him nowhere else to go but to the White Tiger. Maybe Naoto was paid to care for him, but it was better than nothing. Everything came with a price. And at least he knew the other man wouldn't judge him.

Koji sighed. He had to apologise for his drunkenness. Of course, drunken babbling was as natural to life as breathing. Always forgiven and forgotten the next day by friends and colleagues. But he'd never liked that. Never. He'd just never been able to let it pass. And even though Naoto probably dealt with drunk businessmen all the time and would, doubtless, act as if it never happened, an apology was still in order. Just because other people did the same thing he'd done didn't make it more pleasant for Naoto-san.

Koji hung up his damp towel, dressed in a T-shirt, jeans and jacket, threw some toiletries and changes of clothing into a gym bag and left. He had locked the door and started for the elevator when he realised he'd forgotten to shut down his computer. *Screw it*, he thought. He just really wanted to get back to the White Tiger.

Down at the curb, he hailed a taxi. The subway was cheaper, but the subway also took much longer. He slid into the back seat, gave the driver the address and sat back, clutching his gym bag on his lap, the way he'd clutched his briefcase earlier. Only this time, thank god, there weren't two security guards on either side of him, making him feel like a fucking criminal. He didn't need them for that, he felt criminal enough. Every day.

Through the window, Koji watched the city pass by. Night had fallen and myriad neon colours splashed through the taxi window, illuminating the people on the sidewalks and in the windows of stores and restaurants. Something about the constant churning of movement made breathing difficult and he ended up closing his eyes and tilting his head back until the taxi pulled up to the curb and the driver said, "You're here."

Koji's eyes popped open and his heart sped up. He glanced out the window. Warm light glowed through the glass doors of the White Tiger. He fished out his wallet, paid the driver and got out.

However, long after the taxi chugged back into the night traffic, Koji stood on the sidewalk, staring into the glass doors. The warm light pulled him, coaxed from him his longing for what was offered inside. And yet, his shame held him prisoner on the sidewalk. What must Naoto-san *really* think of him? Not of his desires, but of the wanton way he vomited them all out, as if Naoto-san were a mindless body instead of a person with feelings. Everyone had *honne*, their true feelings, and *tatamae*, the face they showed to the world. Perhaps Naoto's *honne* shouldn't matter. But they did.

Koji sighed. Really, he wanted nothing more than to stretch out on that futon in his room with Naoto-san next to him. Nothing seemed better than the prospect of running his hands over the other man's bulging muscles and long sleek hair. Naoto-san would probably let him do that, too, if he asked. But after his drunken tirade, how the hell was he going to go back in there now?

~~~~~

Naoto sighed. From the chair he sat in, he watched Kiku-sensei type on his keyboard. Night time was when

Kiku did the books and any other administrative stuff for the hotel that needed doing, and Naoto often liked to just sit and hang out while Kiku worked. Behind Kiku, Ryu stood, his boxing gloves hung, tied together, over one shoulder, one hand on Kiku's hard shoulder.

Naoto's gaze rested momentarily on Ryu's hot pink hair and then stole over the parts of his body where his tattoos peeked out from his sleeveless white shirt. He'd just gotten back from training at the gym and sweat still gleamed on his skin. Ryu had turned pro recently and showed promise. His next fight was this Saturday night and he'd invited Naoto and Kiku. Everyone else wanted to go but Saturday night was too busy at the White Tiger to spare so many hands.

When Naoto had first come here, he'd been drawn to Ryu. The guy had that small wiry build and innocent gaze that always got him. But Ryu refused to partner with anyone else but Kiku. He'd had it for Kiku ever since Kiku had defended him from Taro Suzuki, a psychotic *yakuza* who'd had a thing for him for years and raped him when he was a teenager. Well, Kiku had come in too late to prevent the rape from happening but he'd gotten the guy off him and out of the room.

Naoto felt sorry for Ryu. Though Kiku loved Ryu, it just wasn't in the way Ryu wanted it. Naoto had to give the guy credit. He stuck around, no matter what Kiku did. Or *whom* Kiku did. Like his lover Quan Chan from the White Tiger Temple in Shanghai who was now visiting and staying in Kiku's room with him.

Kiku looked up and smiled. "I'm sure your guest will return soon," he said softly.

Naoto started. After three years, Kiku's psychic perception still got him. And Kiku was right. About an hour earlier, Naoto had started feeling true concern over Koji-san's whereabouts. Remembering the man's condition when he'd arrived, he couldn't imagine Koji-san at large, trying to get around as if he were functional. He'd even considered dialling the man's cell phone, even though it was against hotel policy. "Am I that obvious?"

The older man looked thoughtful a moment. "Yes."

Ryu also studied him with a contemplative expression. "Don't worry, Naoto," he said. "He'll come back." A grin teased the corner of his lips. "They always do."

Naoto laughed now. For Ryu, this was major humour. It had taken a while for Ryu to accept his presence, as it did with any of the guys who came to be part of the White Tiger as more than guests. Each man who entered the fold and received instruction from Kiku, forced Ryu to face his unrequited love. Yet Ryu befriended all of them eventually, even Quan Chan. Ryu was nothing short of amazing.

"Thanks, Ryu-chan."

Ryu returned the smile. "I have to go now," he said. He leaned over and kissed Kiku's shaved head, receiving an affectionate caress on his hair from the older man, then gave a friendly nod towards Naoto. Ryu was much more familiar with Kiku than everyone else was, since they'd known each other for many years. "See you."

He left and Kiku took a sip of tea from the tray Naoto had brought in with him.

Kiku's dark gaze rested a few moments on him and then understanding lit his eyes. "How did it go with your new guest?" he asked, though doubtless, his perceptive look showed he already knew.

Naoto sighed again. "Fine. I…I'm being…careful."

Kiku pursed his full lips a second and then picked up a pencil, fiddling with it between thick fingers. The loose shirt he wore gapped open in front, giving Naoto a glance of the body tattoos that had once marked him as a *yakuza*. "Perhaps I was wrong to warn you as I did. Trying to control your heart is not the spirit of what we learn here." He looked down briefly. "As you know, I tend to be overprotective."

Naoto gazed at him. Kiku *was* ultra-protective. After leaving the *yakuza*, protecting Ryu and the others, including Naoto, was the true purpose of the hotel he'd established. Kiku would try to save every lost young man in the world if he could. "You sure as hell shouldn't feel bad about that, Kiku-sensei. You saved *my* ass." No doubt, if he'd gone through with his revenge on a yak for Lee's death, he'd be dead now, or worse. And then, who would be around to take care of Lecy? Lee's mom had no one else in the world to lean on but her dead son's lover.

A smile quirked at the other man's beautifully shaped lips, though his eyes remained sad. He was truly magnificent and Naoto fully understood Ryu's devotion to him. "Thank you, friend." His gaze flickered up to the security monitor. "Ah, I see your guest has returned."

Naoto's heart jumped. He stood and looked up at the screen. There was Koji-san, dressed in a T-shirt, denim jacket and jeans now, a gym bag in his hand instead of his briefcase, slowly approaching the door. He reached out and tugged on the door. His large eyes widened and panic flooded his face. He tugged again, of course in vain since it was locked.

"He forgot his key card," Naoto said, already heading out of the office. "I tried to remind him to take it but he was in a rush."

"Don't worry," he heard Kiku say behind him. "Just let him in."

Naoto hurried to the front door and pushed it open. "Welcome back, Koji-san."

"Thank you. I'm sorry. I'm very sorry." Koji-san's eyes were sheepish and he kept bowing deeply as he stepped inside, looking like a little boy who'd been caught stealing candy and would get punished for it.

"I'm sorry I didn't give you your key card when you left, but I didn't want to detain you."

"I know. I'm sorry…I wasn't thinking…I didn't know it would be locked. I'm sorry."

That ache Naoto had experienced earlier squeezed again in his chest. "It's not a problem." He followed the other man in and took his shoes for him, replacing them with clean slippers.

"Thank you, Naoto-san."

Naoto straightened and looked at him. Koji-san's hair was damp and the scent of soap wafted from him. His plain white T-shirt hung baggy off his torso, as did his jeans on his lower body. He'd obviously gone home and showered. "Have you had supper, Koji-san?" They didn't serve an evening meal to guests usually, but Naoto had the feeling that taking time for food wasn't something Koji-san did very often.

The other man shook his head, eyes still sheepish, averting eye contact. "No. I…forgot."

Naoto smiled and reached out. He closed his hand around the other man's shoulder. Even through his clothing, Koji's muscle was pleasantly hard in spite of his thinness. "Come upstairs. You can get comfortable and I'll bring you something to eat."

What appeared to be relief flitted through Koji-san's eyes, replacing some of the little boy ready-to-be-whipped look and he nodded. "Yes, thank you."

Back in Koji-san's room, Naoto sat Koji on the futon. "I think you'll be more comfortable in a kimono, Koji-san," he said softly. "If you'll permit me?"

"Uh…yes…"

Naoto bent and slipped off Koji's jacket. Then he took hold of the hem of the man's T-shirt. He began to lift it and Koji-san raised his arms, like an obedient little boy. Only, he *wasn't* a little boy. Naoto swallowed hard as he lifted the shirt off the man's torso. Little boys didn't have the etchings of muscles in their chests and abdomens.

"I apologise again, Naoto-san."

Or a deep voice that vibrated inside him.

Setting the shirt aside with the jacket, he turned back and knelt down in front of Koji-san. He sat, slumped over, looking nearly as miserable as he had earlier today.

"Please, don't apologise. You're a guest, not a prisoner." He touched Koji-san's shoulder.

Koji looked up, making eye contact for the first time since coming back to the White Tiger. "I just had to go. I…needed to…try to work." He fell silent, as if waiting for a reprimand.

Naoto rubbed his shoulder a bit. Poor Koji really seemed to believe he was going to be punished. "I know you were worried about something happening at work in your absence. Did you go back to your office?" Naoto tried not to dwell on the flexing of lean muscle under his hand.

Koji-san shook his head. His eyes flooded with guilt. "No. I went to my apartment and tried to access my work from there. But Miosuke closed me out." He raked a hand through his hair. The tiny movement made Naoto remember how soft and luxurious Koji-san's hair had felt against his fingertips.

Miosuke. Must be his boss.

Without thinking, Naoto dropped his hand to Koji-san's knee, over his jeans. "There must be something important there if you needed to work so badly," he said. There probably wasn't. Workaholics worked whether there was something urgent to do or not, but he was following the flow of Koji's words.

Koji-san heaved a breath. "Yes, there is. I'm worried they'll die while I'm gone. Die." He put his head in his hands, seemingly oblivious to Naoto's touch.

Naoto's gut tightened a notch. "Who will die, Koji-san?"

Koji lifted his hands away from his face. The dark circles under his large eyes only accentuated his haunted appearance. "The people in the hospital. I'm responsible for all the computers in all the stations. If something goes wrong…" Koji-san fell silent. His bottom lip trembled and his dark eyes misted with a pained, faraway look.

Naoto stared at him. That ache in his chest intensified, along with spirals of guilt. Perhaps he'd misjudged the other man's work. Maybe there was more to his problem than workaholism. He squeezed Koji-san's knee and rose up, inching closer to him. "Do the people there, the nurses and doctors, have a way to reach you if there's a problem?"

Koji nodded again. "Yes. They have my cell phone. It's just that…it can happen so fast." He was staring into Naoto's eyes, as if searching for something inside them.

Naoto sighed. Yes, it could happen goddamn fast.

"That's why I need to be there all the time, watching."
Koji's lip still trembled. Worry radiated from him like a
vapour. The poor guy felt responsible for the lives of
hundreds of people. No wonder he was a wreck. But even
someone with that level of responsibility had to be relieved
from it for a bit, otherwise he'd go mad.

"Koji-san, I'm positive your boss arranged things so
that there will be someone to fix any problems. He must
understand how serious it is." He reached out and brushed a
thumb across Koji-san's cheek. "They know you need time
off. They won't let anything bad happen."

Bad things happened whether you were watching or
not. But he didn't say this to Koji.

He nodded and heaved a deep sigh. "Yes. Miosuke said
my accounts would be cared for. I just worry."

Damn, Koji was beautiful. And the clean scent of his
skin wafted in the air between them.

Naoto's heart fluttered. He wanted nothing more than
to end Koji's suffering. "I have no doubt your boss is good
on his word. Perhaps tomorrow, after you've rested, you can
go there, to the hospital, and check for yourself."

A small light now burned in the haunted depths of
Koji's eyes. "Yes...maybe I can do that." His deep voice was
nearly a whisper. He reached up and raked a hand through
his hair again. "Thank you, Naoto-san."

Naoto smiled. "You're welcome. Now, you need to get
comfortable." He reached for the button of Koji's jeans,
feeling his own hands begin to tremble. "May I?"

Koji stared at him a moment then nodded. He leaned
back and let Naoto undo the button and fly. No sooner had
Naoto pulled open the material than that delicious-looking

bulge with the obvious beginnings of an erection, poked through, covered only by the thin white briefs.

Naoto swallowed hard. Koji lifted his ass again, letting Naoto pull the jeans off. Did the guy realise how tempting he was? Rising, Naoto folded the jeans and went to hang them with his other clothes, bringing back the white kimono.

As before, Koji had slipped off his underwear and now stood, looking at him.

Heart beating, Naoto opened the robe and held it so Koji could slide his arms in and then let Naoto wind and secure the sash. "That must feel better, Koji-san." He averted the slimmer man's gaze and pulled back the futon cover.

"Yes. Much better." Koji lowered himself onto the mattress and slid in. The kimono rode up, revealing a sinewy thigh.

Kuso. Naoto pulled his gaze away. Now his shorts were getting tight in the front again. "Please, rest now, Koji-san," Glad for the distraction, Naoto pulled the cover over Koji's lap. "I'll be back soon with your supper." He crossed the room and reached out to slide back the soji screen.

"Naoto-san."

The pleading sound in the man's voice made Naoto turn back immediately. "Yes?"

Koji-san was watching him from the bed. The sheepish look had returned to his eyes. "I also...want to...apologise for my behaviour today." His voice was soft and full of remorse. "I almost never drink and today I fear I embarrassed you. I mean, I understand this is what people do. But it's always bothered me. Had I been sober, I would have kept my thoughts and feelings to myself, not spilled them out onto you."

So! Koji-san *did* remember what he'd said. Naoto's shorts tightened another notch. The warm pressure emanated through him, curled around in his middle and spread, a pleasant warm tingle down his arms and legs. He suppressed a wildly pleased grin. It wasn't every day a man told him he was beautiful, exactly his type, and *meant* it. At least, he hoped so. He bowed. "Sincere praise is never something to be sorry about."

Koji-san's eyes clouded. "But I..." He looked down. "It was rude."

"To praise me, Koji-san? Heartfelt praise is rude?" He waited, stomach tight, for the other man to deny his sincerity.

Koji looked up, eyes still sheepish yet, also, relieved. "I suppose not. I...didn't think of it that way."

Naoto felt a surge of warmth through his chest. "I was never embarrassed Koji-san," he said softly. "Only flattered." Perhaps in a while, he'd have a chance to show Koji just how flattered he'd really been.

His words were rewarded with a smile. A beautiful smile that almost erased the darkness hovering over his guest. A small dimple folded the man's left cheek and...the skin crinkled around his eyes in that sexy way.

Naoto cleared his throat. He worked his lips into a smile, a smile to hide the sudden pounding of his heart. "It's time for you to eat something. I won't be long."

Chapter Five

Naoto stared into the open refrigerator, one giant stainless steel door held aside. His heart was still pumping and his mind blurred. He was so worried about putting together the perfect meal for Koji-san that he couldn't choose anything at all.

"Need some help?"

Naoto turned.

Ryu was grinning at him from behind the large table where he stood, chopping vegetables for the next morning's soup. Miso soup was a standard part of the breakfast they served. "You seemed a bit overwhelmed. Thought I'd ask." He set down his knife and came around the table.

Naoto stood aside to make room for him and felt his cheeks tingle. "Thanks, Ryu-chan. I don't know why I'm having trouble here."

Ryu looked at him. His grin had faded and his large eyes looked a bit pained. "Don't worry. I know."

Naoto's heart jumped. For a second he thought Ryu might be jealous, but as he watched Ryu's pink dyed head turn towards the contents of the fridge, he understood. Ryu wanted to fuss over Kiku like this and Kiku wouldn't let him.

He watched Ryu pick and choose storage containers from the shelves. "Don't worry," Ryu said as he carried an armful of containers to the huge stainless steel table they used to prepare food, "We have plenty of good stuff in here, as you well know." Ryu began pulling the tops off. "See?" His grin had returned and when he looked like this, it was hard to picture him in a boxing ring punching another guy's brains out.

Naoto returned the smile. In moments like this he was especially glad to live here with such friends. "Yeah, thanks." He got a tray ready and made a pot of green tea, deciding against bringing Koji-san another decanter of saké.

Fifteen minutes later, Ryu stepped back and waved at the loaded tray with a flourish. "Fit for an emperor."

Naoto smiled again, looking at the finished product. Plates of pastry, cheese, fruit, sushi, bean salad and some fried fish from supper covered the surface of the tray. "I'll be lucky if I can haul this upstairs myself."

Ryu laughed. He had a really sweet laugh and every time Naoto heard it, he wished that Ryu would find someone to love him the way he wanted.

"I have faith in you, Nao-chan."

Naoto slid the tray off the table and balanced it on his shoulder. He'd had plenty of practice carrying heavy stuff this way from when he'd worked at Lee's parents' store. Some days he'd haul a truckload of full crates into the place. Of course, then, he'd also been trying to impress Lee the only way he knew how…

He headed for the door. "Thanks, again, Ryu-chan. I appreciate it."

"No problem. Good luck."

At the door to Koji's room, Naoto quietly announced himself, hoping that his guest hadn't fallen asleep again.

"Come in," he heard.

Naoto's heart fluttered as he manoeuvred the *soji* screen open and the heavy tray into the room. He managed to slide the screen closed still holding the tray.

Koji was reclining just as Naoto had left him. He sat up. "Do you need help?"

Naoto swung the tray down and set it on the foot of the bed. "No, thank you, Koji-san." He smiled and proceeded to remove the covers on the plates, ridiculously pleased at the way his guest's eyes widened.

"Wow, that's all for me?" Koji sounded like a kid.

Naoto suppressed a chuckle. He hadn't felt this way since serving Lee breakfast in bed on his birthday, a sweet feeling, kind of…like someone was tickling his insides with a feather. "It is."

Koji continued to stare down, eyes wide. "It's…amazing." He looked up. "But you'll have to help me, please. I'll never finish all this."

Naoto wasn't really hungry, but Kiku always said it was better to accept a guest's invitation for company, as long as the person didn't make you uncomfortable. Koji-san sure as hell didn't make him uncomfortable. "I'll help you then." He picked up the chopsticks. "I only brought one pair."

A shy look flitted through the other man's eyes. "We can share."

Naoto's insides jumped. Considering Koji had wanted to kiss earlier, the hygiene of sharing chopsticks wasn't really an issue. "Good idea." He plucked up a small bite of the fried fish. "Open up."

Koji's eyes widened a moment then he obeyed. His soft full lips parted and Naoto slipped the morsel of food between them. Koji's tongue flickered as he accepted the food, making Naoto's cock tingle.

Koji-san closed his mouth and began to chew. "Mmm."

Naoto watched Koji's lips move. Dusky pink and delicious looking. Tiny muscles worked in Koji's cheeks and then in his throat as he swallowed.

Naoto's shorts tightened. *Kuso.* Just watching Koji-san eat was getting him hard. He fed Koji another bite, watched him chew and swallow, and then gave him some tea.

Koji swallowed the tea and set the cup down. His lips curved in a smile and Naoto could swear that the dark circles under his eyes had lightened. A shy look flitted through Koji's eyes followed by what appeared a decision. "Your turn, Naoto-san." He held out his hand. "Chopsticks, please."

That tickle in his insides intensified. Silently, he handed the chopsticks to Koji.

Koji's large eyes surveyed the plates. "What would you like?"

"I'll have the fish, please." This was turning out better than he'd expected.

With another shy smile, Koji lifted a bit of the fish and held it up, close to Naoto's lips. The fish trembled between the chopsticks. Naoto steadied Koji's hand with his. Warm skin met his fingertips, sending a thrill through him. He held Koji's gaze as he took the fish into his mouth.

The delicate flavour rolled on his tongue. He chewed carefully, aware of the other man's gaze on him, shy but steady.

Koji-san's breathing grew noticeably heavier. "Would you like another?"

Naoto bowed his head, working to restrain the swelling in his cock. A fruitless task. "Yes, please, Koji-san." No matter how full he was, he wanted the simple pleasure of Koji feeding him.

He watched Koji retrieve another bite of fish and lift it upwards. Again, Naoto caught his hand and steadied it, ridiculously flattered by the other man's nervousness. He gave Koji a quick smile just before closing his lips over the morsel of food.

Now, Koji-san stared at his lips, his own lips slightly parted, lids heavier over his eyes, as if in an erotic trance. When Naoto swallowed, Koji blinked as if coming back to life. He reached for the small teapot and poured some of the yellowish liquid into his cup, which he raised up towards Naoto in both hands. "For you, Naoto-san."

Naoto accepted the cup with a bow of his head. Again, his fingertips brushed Koji's as the cup exchanged hands. His heartbeat rose as he sipped the tea, every movement he made still under Koji's wondering gaze.

And so they continued — Naoto making certain that Koji ate well over half of what was on the tray — until Koji's aroused breathing matched his own and Naoto was certain that his dragon would tear its way through his shorts to get to Koji-san.

Koji collapsed lightly against the pillows and heaved a breath, hands on his stomach over the soft kimono. "That was so good. I haven't eaten that much in…" He trailed off and looked down, shoulders sagging. "I barely eat."

Naoto's heart squeezed. Poor guy. Couldn't even enjoy a meal. Quickly he neatened the tray so that he could lift it away and set it just outside the door. Someone would come by later and remove it. Then he returned to the futon and knelt down.

Koji looked up and his bottom lip worked slightly. "I feel like I'm drowning…Naoto-san," he said in a near-whisper. His large dark eyes misted, as if the words themselves had induced such a response. "Drowning."

That last word sent a shiver through Naoto. The force of Koji-san's whisper spiralled in his mind, like a stick in a muddy pool, stirring his own memories of grief...making him remember what that drowning was like.

And he did remember. Had felt that way for months and months after Lee's murder. Until Kiku had reached out to him and helped him through the worst of it. *"I promise you won't drown, Naoto,"* Kiku had said. At first, Naoto hadn't believed him — had thought Kiku might even be lying. But he hadn't been and Naoto had survived, grown stronger...

"I promise you won't drown, Koji-san," he heard himself say.

Koji-san's eyes widened and the look in them made Naoto feel as if he were gazing into a clear pool. Everything Naoto needed to say and do was reflected in those beautiful eyes.

Without thinking, he slipped off his vest and dropped it aside on the floor. "I've felt that way too, at times," he went on. The clarity gathered, made him understand that his intense arousal was not simply rude lust for Koji-san, but a tool to help him. "I'm here with you. You can hold on to me." He undid his shorts and slid them off also, tossing them aside with his vest. Then he stood before the bed.

The sound of Koji's ragged breathing filled the room, blended with the gentle tones of the *shamisen* and flute music piped into the background. His gaze roved slowly down Naoto's naked body, and finally came to stop on his tight erection...Naoto could feel it growing heavier under Koji's stare.

Naoto felt Koji's gaze follow him around to the other side of the futon where he started to pull the covers back. Wait... Koji-san hadn't actually invited him into the bed.

I don't want Tomoko. I want you. Koji's earlier words during his massage came back. *I want you,* he'd said. Naoto's dragon tightened at the echoes of those words. Invitation enough.

He finished pulling the covers back, waiting to see if Koji would say something to stop him.

But the other man's eyes still appeared riveted on his naked body.

He slid in beside Koji-san.

Koji's lids now half-covered his eyes in a sensual gaze, as they'd been while watching Naoto chew his food. Naoto observed him, making certain his presence in the bed was not unwelcome.

Didn't seem to be, if the erection tenting Koji-san's kimono was any indication.

Naoto slid closer, and then pulled the tie out of his hair, letting it flow over his shoulders for Koji-san's pleasure. The slimmer man's gaze went immediately to the ebony fall and he pulled in a soft breath.

Naoto smiled at him and then reached out and took one of Koji's hands. "See, Koji-san?" he crooned, rubbing the soft flesh of the man's palm in gentle, massaging circles. "No drowning, only skin against skin."

Koji's breathing grew even more ragged and he sank lower, closer to Naoto, still watching him with that fascinated, mesmerised look that made Naoto feel totally…completely…desired.

Still smiling, Naoto brought Koji's hand to his lips. Koji's index finger brushed his lower lip and Naoto licked the pad of it with the tip of his tongue.

"Ooohh." Koji's whoosh of breath conveyed nothing but enjoyment.

Naoto licked again, pulled the digit a bit deeper into his mouth, and massaged the sensitive pad with the flat of his tongue. Mmm. Koji's salty flesh was delicious and Naoto's eyelids fluttered closed, as if were savouring one of those fancy French pastries Kiku provided for the guests.

Koji's tiny moans and whimpers guided him and Naoto took each fingertip, in turn, relishing, licking, tasting, until his own dragon stretched past the point of painful. The tension of fullness had spread deep into his balls, demanding satisfaction, wanting a long, languorous rub against Koji-san's body until it coated him with its cloud of release.

He lifted his mouth from his feast on Koji-san's fingers and looked at the man's lips. Soft and full, they moved with each panting breath Koji-san took. "I hope you still want me to kiss you, Koji-san," he said softly.

Koji nodded without hesitation. "Yes." His answer was breathless.

Sweet.

The quickness of it made Naoto's insides jump in a pleasant way. He leaned into Koji and brushed his lips across Koji-san's. Ooohh, so soft, like cherry blossom petals, only a million times better.

Closing his eyes, Naoto kissed him again, lingered this time, enjoying the velvety softness and tickle of Koji-san's breath on his own lips. Koji was unmoving, only panting. Not seeming to know how to kiss back. He obviously didn't kiss much…if ever.

Naoto filed that bit away in his mind, along with the few other insights to Koji's psyche their interactions had revealed. Kiku said you could learn so much about a man from his kiss. What was he learning now about Koji-san?

Naoto pressed down a bit more, flickered the tip of his tongue along the yielding softness of Koji's mouth.

Koji groaned softly and leaned in closer. His hand moved down Naoto's loose hair in a trembling caress.

Inexperience. Need. Coiled up passion. Sweetness.

So many things from this tiny kiss.

It was such a little taste...such a small glimpse into Koji's inner world. But it only made Naoto want more...

I am *drowning*, Koji thought. Only this wasn't bad. Not at all. He was drowning in a world made of Naoto. Naoto's able, large hands undoing the sash and unwinding it so that his kimono opened. That large muscular body, warm and male, sinking down on top of his. Naoto's broad chest fused to his, the muscles rubbed his nipples, made his whole chest tingle with incredible sensations. The larger man's lips were warm and soft, yet commanding. Each little nip and lick he gave brought another shimmer of bliss through Koji's body, all the way to the tip of his cock.

Naoto's scent, male musk and incense, filled Koji's nostrils, like a vapour that travelled straight into his brain and made him drunk. Drunk on Naoto.

Long hair tickled his skin, fell over him like the most incredible fan. Without thinking, he palmed Naoto's back. Large muscles bunched and shifted with the tiniest movement.

And then, that thick cock slid against his. Hard yet silky. He groaned into Naoto's mouth.

Naoto nipped at his bottom lip then lifted up slightly. "How's this, Koji-san?" His voice was an erotic whisper.

"Good. So good."

Naoto slid their cocks together.

Bliss shot through Koji's whole body, made his balls vibrate with it. "Yes! Yes!" His voice slid from a whisper to full sound.

Naoto thrust against him, elbows propped on either side of him. Male heat and scent permeated the air.

"Yes! Naoto-san." Koji couldn't stop himself from shouting. The pleasure exploded like a storm, winds so powerful he could no longer withhold them. "Yes!"

Naoto's lips came down on his. A velvety moist tongue slid along his teeth, danced with his tongue, the warm cave absorbing his moans.

Eyes closed, Koji clutched at Naoto's back. Sparks of the most intense pleasure seemed to tingle over every inch of his skin, right to his toes. For years he'd dreamed of a handsome samurai who grabbed him up and took command of him, just like Naoto was doing now…

Koji slid his hands down to those powerful buttocks, followed the sliding motion as Naoto thrust against him. Powerful, raw, male. Every inch of Naoto was beefy, strong, thick with muscle…beautiful.

Naoto's mouth stayed on his while he rocked his hips against Koji's. Each thrust made the pressure build. Harder. Faster. Koji screwed his eyes shut as heat spiralled through his entire lower body.

Naoto lifted away from their kiss and stared down at him. He slowed the rhythm of his hips to a teasing slide.

Koji panted. "So…good…so…good."

The larger man smiled. "I'm glad, Koji-san. Enjoy."

"I…am." His eyes shuttered closed and he tilted his head back, feeling Naoto's breath pulse warm and sweet over his skin.

For what seemed so long, Naoto teased him, speeding up, then slowing down, bringing him closer until the pressure in his balls was so tight he felt like he'd explode.

Naoto brushed a hot kiss across his lips. "Are you ready, Koji-san?"

Koji squeezed Naoto's ass, loving the feel of power under his hands. "Yes," he breathed. In the shadowy light he saw Naoto smile down at him then thrust, harder, faster, as if milking his seed up to the top.

"Ohhhh!" Koji shouted. His cum spurted out, bringing with it the most intense, blissful release.

Again, he felt Naoto's lips close gently over his, absorbing the sounds. Koji couldn't stop moaning, as his fingertips dug into Naoto's hard ass cheeks. Naoto still slid against him, slick now from cum. The sensation was intense and Koji thought the climax would never end. He pulled on Naoto, urged him to rock faster. Naoto had given him such pleasure, he deserved some too.

He kissed Naoto back now, slid his tongue against the other man's in a fevered way. Wow, kissing felt so good, and tasted so incredible. He'd barely done it. Not even with…

Naoto groaned into his mouth. The larger man's cock surged, hot and full and Koji felt the splash of Naoto's climax on his chest and stomach. He held on to Naoto's ass, clutched it, pulling him to keep rubbing until he was completely satisfied.

Naoto seemed to understand and answered with small quick thrusts of his hips until he was empty and collapsed lightly on Koji, a delightful crush of large muscular body on his, fusing them together.

Naoto's ragged breathing crashed in Koji's ear and his body pinned Koji down into the futon so that he could only move his hands.

Perfect.

Koji wanted it to never end.

After resting a while, Naoto eased away from him. "Everything all right?"

Koji heaved a sigh and tilted his head back, hands resting on Naoto's ass cheeks. "Naoto-san," he whispered. "Thank you so much."

The larger man lifted slightly on one elbow. Sweat gleamed on his forehead and upper lip. His wide cheeks were flushed and his lids heavy over his eyes. One large hand passed over Koji's hair. "You're most welcome, Koji-san." He lowered his face to Koji's and pressed a soft kiss on his lips. "I'm glad you enjoyed it. That was only the beginning."

A ripple passed through Naoto's body at his own words. He continued looking down into Koji-san's large captivating eyes. Though the dark circles were still there underneath, the other man's skin was flushed, gleaming with sweat and his eyelids lowered halfway down, in a contented look.

His lips were slightly parted, his breathing still a bit heavy, even after resting for several moments. Finally, Naoto rolled gently off of him. "I'll be back in a moment, Koji-san," he said softly. Before they could do anything else, he had to clean them up. It was part of the whole thing.

He went to the bathroom, washed himself off and returned moments later with the customary bowl of warm water, cloth and towel. Koji-san still lay on his back, breathing more normally now, the satisfied look still on his face. The soft music continued to play in the background, imparting a sense of peacefulness even to the mundane act of wiping Koji's dragon cloud off his torso.

Koji seemed to enjoy even this part and Naoto caught himself wondering again about the quality of the man's life. He seemed honourable and decent enough. His concern over the people's lives in the hospital was admirable, if not somewhat hyper-responsible. Koji-san was also definitely inexperienced with sex. Hard to imagine, as good-looking as he was. Then again, just because a man was handsome didn't mean he automatically had an easy life. Here at the White Tiger, he was surrounded by handsome men like Kiku and Ryu. They'd all been through hell.

Anyway, inexperienced or not, Koji-san sure as hell had enjoyed the sex. No doubt, his pleasure cries had carried through the entire hotel, small as it was. No one would dare tease Koji directly about it, but Naoto was certain that one of his fellow White Tigers would rib *him* a bit about the noise when he ordered his guest's breakfast the next morning.

"Naoto-san?"

Koji's voice pulled him from his musings. He wiped Koji's stomach and set the towel and bowl aside. "Yes?" He remained kneeling by the futon.

Koji gazed at him, still content, though also with that sweet wonder, as when he'd first asked to touch Naoto's hair. "I was...hoping...that I haven't kept you from...other guests."

Naoto smiled at him, moved by the other man's shy tone. If Koji-san only knew how much he didn't need to worry...

He shook his head. "Not at all, Koji-san," he said. "I'm very happy to remain here with you as long as you wish me to."

His answer was rewarded with a smile. Koji-san's eyes lit up in a shy yet luminous way that almost made the dark circles seem to vanish. "Thank you, Naoto-san. I...don't want to burden you."

"You're never a burden, Koji-san." Naoto reached out and touched Koji's cheek. He loved the smooth texture of the slimmer man's skin and traced the faint outline of beard at the edge of his jaw. Koji-san probably shaved once a month at most. "I'm truly enjoying this time we have." More than he should be, probably. He rose, padded to the other side of the bed and slid back, stretching out alongside Koji-san. "May I hold you?"

Koji looked at him, his dark eyes showing a relaxed satisfaction for the first time. "Yes, please."

Naoto shifted in closer and gathered Koji against him, spooning the back of the man's slim body to his front. Koji-san heaved a sigh and Naoto felt him settle more snugly against him.

Closing his eyes, Naoto breathed in the other man's clean scent. A pleasant feeling passed through him. It had been a really long time since he'd done this, just lie with someone quietly, holding him after passionate sex. A small spike of guilt struck him. He'd spent the last three years wishing for what he couldn't have and here he was, enjoying someone who wasn't Lee. But Lee wasn't coming back. Ever. How could it be wrong...especially when Lee had *wanted* him to have this again?

Naoto slipped one hand over Koji's and laced their fingers, holding him close, their joined hands against Koji's chest. Koji-san heaved a deep breath and pushed back even more snugly against him. The movement made Naoto's lips slide against Koji's hair. That hair was so soft. And smelled so good. The scent flooded him, made his body tingle. Well, at least he could enjoy these moments. It wasn't like they were...together.

"Thank you, Naoto-san," he heard the other man whisper. "I have not felt this calm in the longest time."

"You're welcome," he answered, though he certainly had as much to thank Koji-san for at this point as the other way around. Koji-san had come on Monday with his troubled soul and his physical beauty, and so doing, had helped him get through another Monday in the best way possible.

He found himself wishing that every Monday could be like this.

But it wasn't.

Chapter Six

They were dying. All of them. One by one.

Had…to…stop…the dying.

Koji's heaving breath burned in his lungs, but he kept running. The heat was overwhelming. Sweat poured from every inch of his naked body and wet leaves squished under his bare feet with each step.

They were dying.

He could see the hospital through the trees of the forest in which he ran. He was almost there. One more step —

A giant tree fell on him. The trunk, heavy, hot, as if it were on fire, pressed him into the forest floor, pinned him, helpless and flailing. The soft ground absorbed his weight.

Oh no! They would die now. He couldn't get to them…

Koji's eyes popped open. Sweat beaded on his face, dripped down his temples. His body was hot, damp, against the bedding. He tried to move. Couldn't. Something…

He looked down. Someone…Naoto…was on top of him. The tree from his dream.

Koji let his head fall back on the pillow and sighed as best he could under the weight of Naoto's brawn. Naoto's soft breathing penetrated the ghostly remnants of his dream, blowing them away, as if even in his sleep, Naoto meant to comfort him.

The enjoyable sensations of Naoto's weight and breath tangled with the anxiety of his dream, the subconscious carryover of what he worried about all the time when awake.

He wanted to call the hospital, needed to make sure everything was all right. But he was also remembering Naoto's assurances the night before, the man's certainty that everything would be all right. And then, he also didn't want to disturb Naoto. Naoto had been so kind, so comforting…so passionate.

Naoto's presence was pleasant, soothing, and with each rise of Naoto's breath, his long hair brushed Koji's side. The ebony strands fanned over him like a sleek black ocean and Naoto's muscular body exuded raw male heat.

For a second he tensed with that post-sex-supposed-to-throw-on-your-clothes-and-run-out-before-anyone-finds-you feeling. It had first hit him last night after they both came, but then he'd remembered he was surrounded by men who were here for the same reason and he didn't have to go anywhere. And then Naoto had wanted to hold him. He couldn't resist *that* offer and had sunk willingly into that safe feeling Naoto gave him. Even then, he'd felt that habitual need to leave…but Naoto's hard warmth against him had won out and he relaxed so much he'd fallen asleep.

And woken up like this! A whole night! He'd often wondered how it would feel to spend a whole night with someone. Not just to visit a guy in his hotel room while he was giving a talk at a conference, have a few drinks with him, fast, hard sex and then go back to his own room to sleep it all off.

Now he knew.

Koji resisted the urge to caress Naoto's hair. That incredible, magnificent hair. Naoto was so amazing, Koji wondered why the man wasn't a model or an actor.

Naoto stirred. The heavy stubble on his cheek rubbed Koji's chest. Several soft whimpers escaped the larger man, as if he were having a bad dream, and then he lifted his head, eyes open, blinking, seeming to focus. "Koji-san," he murmured. More blinks of his eyelids and he seemed to become aware of his position. "I'm crushing you. So sorry." He rolled to the side, leaving cooler air in his wake.

The absence of his weight left a disappointed feeling. "You weren't crushing me at all."

Naoto pulled strands of hair from his own eyes and looked down at Koji, as if assessing his condition. "How are you, Koji-san? Did you sleep well?"

Koji's heart sped up a bit. He wanted Naoto to lie back down and hold him the way he had last night as they fell asleep. That had been one of the most incredible experiences he'd ever had, the *most* incredible being the sex just before that. He nodded. "Yes. I slept very well, thank you." He wished he could ask Naoto for what he wanted, but surely, the man had other guests to worry about. He'd already monopolised Naoto enough.

Naoto's hand came out and several fingertips brushed Koji's cheek. The touch sent a pleasant tingle through Koji, all the way to his toes.

"Perhaps you need breakfast, Koji-san?"

Food? His stomach was so tight, Koji couldn't imagine even a sip of tea. He never ate breakfast anyway. He shook his head. "Not yet, thank you." He sighed then averted his gaze. "Please, Naoto-san. I feel as if I'm dominating your time. Don't let me do that…if you have other guests."

Did Koji-san want him to leave? Naoto couldn't tell. His listening skills seemed to be failing him. Not because he was sleepy, but because his feelings had somehow gotten so damn blurred. First, his recurring dream about Lee had woken him up. That dream always left him with a strange feeling, as if Lee were trying to tell him something. When he'd told Kiku about the dream, Kiku had said it would be revealed to him when the time was right.

And then, the first thing Naoto had seen was Koji's gaze, those large, beautiful eyes, staring back at him, shy and sweet. Guilt clawed at him, warred with the sweetness of Koji's presence in the bed. He'd never spent the night with a guest...hadn't spent the whole night with anyone in his life but Lee. He hadn't meant to fall asleep with Koji-san. He'd only meant to hold him a little while until the other man fell asleep. And then...

Kuso. He needed time to sort out all the strands of emotion running between his heart and mind. Koji-san was his guest. This man's enjoyment and pleasure should be his only concern. The fact that Koji was so beautiful and delicious *shouldn't* matter.

Sweat gleamed on the other man's smooth skin and the look in his wide eyes was difficult to read.

Naoto cleared his throat and brought his attention fully to the man next to him. "Koji-san, you're not dominating my time at all." He glanced away briefly. "The truth is, yesterday, when you made your reservation, Kikuchiya, the owner, assigned me to you. He felt I would be able to help you. And now..." His heartbeat sped up, especially at the widening of Koji's eyes. "I'm enjoying your company very much." He looked down again. "I would rather be here with you." The simple truth seemed to be the best choice.

Silence. And then a small catch of breath.

Naoto looked up.

Koji-san wore a shy smile. The corners of his lips turned slightly up and that sheepish, yet glad look brightened the dark irises. "Thank you, Naoto-san."

Relief prickled down Naoto's arms. His guilt dissolved for the moment as Koji filled his consciousness. He remembered Koji's wretched condition of the day before. Koji was already in better shape thanks to a little bit of care. How could he allow his personal turmoil to interfere with the man's recovery? He reached out and touched Koji's hand. "Now, did you wish to call the hospital as you'd planned last night?"

Koji nodded. "Yes. I should do that."

"I'll get the phone for you." Naoto slipped out of the bed, retrieved Koji's phone from its clip on his jeans and turned.

Koji had sat up and perched on the edge of the bed, giving Naoto an eyeful of his fully-hard erection. The sight stirred his own loins and he knelt down, handing his guest the phone with both hands.

Koji accepted the phone, his eyes locked on Naoto. Suddenly the man blinked as if shocked from a trance. His cheeks coloured and he bowed. "Arigato, Naoto-san," he said softly.

Naoto bowed, then rose and went into the bathroom, listening to Koji-san's side of the conversation. For a second he tensed, realising he'd taken on Koji's fear for the patients there as his own. However, Koji's voice remained calm and from what Naoto could gather, everything was fine at the hospital.

Quickly Naoto brushed his teeth with one of the disposable toothbrushes that were always stored conveniently under the vanity, using some of that flavourless toothpaste Kiku bought from Korea, the kind that freshened the breath but didn't leave the minty tingle that could be irritating to the sensitive parts of the male anatomy. He looked at his reflection and scrubbed a hand over his heavy stubble. He needed to shave but didn't have his razor or time to use one of the disposable razors also stored underneath. After washing his hands and face and smoothing some water over his hair to tame it, he went back in.

Koji-san had ended his call and set the phone on the bedside table. He was watching Naoto come towards him, eyes widely appreciative. His gaze dipped down to Naoto's partially erect dragon, following the movement as Naoto knelt back down in front of him.

Koji sighed. "Everything was fine, as you'd assured me."

Naoto smiled. He moved in closer and laid his hands on the tops of the other man's hard thighs. Koji-san's erection still jutted up, straining and ready, deliciously blushed skin and light veins along the shaft. Naoto's mouth watered. A brief memory of his recurring dream flashed through his mind. A spike of guilt, then the invasion of Koji-san's clean scent, blurred it all again in his mind...

"Naoto-san, I can't thank you enough." Koji's gaze remained on Naoto's eyes. The huskier tone of his voice showed Naoto the effect he was having on him. "I...don't feel as...crazy this morning."

Naoto moved in a bit closer, insinuated his broad form partway between Koji-san's spread thighs. "You're most welcome, Koji-san," he said softly and skated his touch up the other man's hard thighs, towards his hips. Koji still needed more release. Naoto sensed it in the way the other man's *yang* force swirled in the air around them.

Koji's breathing deepened. His gaze was riveted, dusky, yet his hands remained at his sides, as if afraid to reach out.

Naoto craved the feel of those hands on his skin. "You can touch me, Koji-san. If you'd like." He brushed his thumbs over the smooth skin of his hips, teasing light strokes that went deeper each time towards his groin.

A sharp breath escaped him and Koji reached up. His hands came to rest on Naoto's shoulders. He fanned his fingers over the rounded hardness and slid down, tracing the lines of definition between each muscle. A lock of Naoto's hair had fallen forward and Koji stroked that too as his touch glided down.

Koji's touch was like being caressed with feathers, leaving a tingle in its wake. Yet the trembling underneath it conveyed sheer appreciation, wonder and awe, as if Koji had never touched anything better in his life.

Naoto slid his hands around to Koji's lower back. He moved in closer and nuzzled Koji-san's chest. Mmm, he smelled so good, like musk, light sweat and soap. Wanting more, he pressed his lips to the warm skin and feathered his tongue over the hard muscle.

Koji-san pulled in a breath. One of his hands slid into Naoto's hair, fingers burrowing until he cradled the back of Naoto's head.

A thrill travelled through Naoto's whole body. Emboldened, he kissed his way over to one nipple and tongued it. Koji groaned and arched his back. Naoto took the dark tip between his tongue and upper lip, bathing it sensuously, feeling it harden. Damn, it tasted as good as he had imagined the day before when he'd first taken Koji's shirt off. Closing his eyes, he feasted on it, licking, sucking, in all the ways Kiku had instructed him that brought out the most pleasure and made a man's yang force swirl inside him.

"Naoto-san," Koji whispered. "Oh, Naoto-san." With each repetition, his voice rose in volume.

Naoto heard it crash in his ears. No matter. Everyone in the White Tiger had probably heard Koji-san's pleasure cries by this time. He lifted his mouth away and kissed a path over to Koji's other nipple. With his fingertips pressed against the ridge of muscle along Koji's spine, Naoto licked and teased the other disk into peaked hardness, savouring, taking his time. The longer he took, the better Koji-san would feel.

Koji's fingers agitated against Naoto's scalp. The touch, feverish yet light, conveyed his pleasure, as did his long, loud groans.

Naoto continued to tease with his mouth while one hand ventured downward and closed lightly around Koji-san's thick dragon. The shaft throbbed and jumped in his hand. Koji-san was already close to exploding again. The poor guy, so pent up.

Lightly, Naoto stroked the entire length, head to base. Koji-san groaned with each stroke, up and down. His hands clutched at Naoto's hair and his chest heaved under Naoto's mouth. "Yes! Yes!" He was practically shouting now and Naoto could feel the pressure of Koji's climax building against his hand.

Pulling away from Koji's chest, he bent over and took the head of Koji's cock in his mouth.

"Ohhh!" Koji's hands slid through Naoto's hair and back to his scalp again. "Yes!"

Koji tasted as good as he looked and Naoto gathered the small drop that had seeped out and swallowed it. Mmm, salty-sweet. He took Koji in deeper. The velvety skin and hard muscle slid against his tongue and filled his mouth as only a cock could. Better than any pastry in the entire world.

With his thumb and forefinger around the base, Naoto slid up and down, bathed Koji's cock in languorous strokes with his mouth while his other hand rested on the top of Koji-san's thigh. Eyes closed, he savoured the man's taste, the sound of his loud groans and the squeeze of Koji's hands in his hair.

As Naoto sucked, his own body relaxed, moved into the flow. His mind softened and tiny lights twinkled behind his closed eyes. Heaven! He was reaching closer…the merging of mind and body, the flow of life…

Koji groaned. A long, velvety sound that pulled Naoto back. The shaft twitched and the first warm gush hit his tongue. He lifted away and let the spray of Koji-san's release coat his neck and chest. Men liked to see their seed erupt and land on the flesh of the one who'd pleasured them.

Well, it was a pleasure to have Koji's seed on his skin and hear Koji's groans of release spiral in his ears. Koji's yang force swirled in the air, the smell of it potent and musky.

When Naoto finally opened his eyes, he saw Koji-san's eyes glazed with the obvious enjoyment of watching his own climax erupt and hit Naoto's skin, drip down his muscles. Naoto smiled at him. Without speaking, he leaned forward and caressed the tops of Koji's thighs again, feeling him relax a bit more with each slide of his hand along the smooth muscles. Koji's shoulders slumped and his chest rose and fell heavily.

His gaze never left the sight of Naoto's torso and something about the wonder in the man's eyes gave Naoto the sense that this was all new for him. He couldn't imagine that Koji was a virgin. He appeared to be in his late twenties, thirty, maybe. That was kind of old not to have had any experience.

Just wondering about it stirred Naoto's curiosity. Something about Koji-san was deep and mysterious, made

Naoto want to understand him in a way he hadn't wanted to understand someone in a long time.

He reached for Koji's hand. "Would you like to shower, Koji-san?"

Wide-eyed, Koji nodded. Something passed across his eyes, a question, perhaps, but it remained unworded as he let Naoto lead him into the small bathroom and waited quietly as Naoto adjusted the shower knobs to a comfortable temperature and pressure.

"Come in, Koji-san," he said when the shower was ready. The other man seemed content to let Naoto guide him around.

In the shower, Naoto detached the showerhead and gently wet Koji-san down, noticing, of course, the way the water darkened the man's flawless skin and made his hair gleam. When that was done, he gave himself a quick spraying off and replaced the head so he could wash his guest.

Lathering up a washcloth with soap from the dispenser on the wall, Naoto rubbed gentle circles over Koji's back.

The slimmer man's eyelids fluttered closed and his body grew pliant under the soapy massage. "Naoto-san, that feels so good."

Naoto smiled even though Koji wasn't looking at him. "I'm glad." In silence, he moved the washcloth lower, followed the ridge of Koji's spine down to his butt cheeks, which he wiped gently...slowly...his look riveted on the angry-looking white slashes. What the hell had happened to—?

"Naoto-san."

Naoto looked up. "Yes?"

Koji-san was leaning his palms against the wall and gazing down at him. "You don't need to be so concerned about the scars. It's not like they hurt."

Naoto's cheeks tingled with heat. "I didn't mean to —"

"It's all right." Koji lifted away from the wall and turned to him. "When I was eight, I stole some Pocky from a store near my house. A neighbour was in there and saw me do it. She told my father and he punished me."

Naoto's blood froze in spite of the hot water. What kind of bastard whipped an eight-year-old kid that hard? And for stealing some candy? That kind of whipping went beyond teaching a lesson about not stealing. That was taking out your rage on a weaker being. Shit. Beating a guy like Koji was like abusing a puppy or a deer. *Unforgivable.* "I...I..."

Koji's brow furrowed. "It was a long time ago. He didn't mean to harm me."

Bullshit.

Those large soft eyes widened. "I angered you. I'm sorry."

Only then did Naoto feel himself wearing the expression he used to get when the yaks hounded Lee for the money he owed them. *Fierce.* "*You* didn't anger me, Koji-san." Of course, Koji wasn't the one who was making his blood heat with rage. Given half a chance, he would have wanted to thrash the shit out of Koji's father. The guy better hope Naoto never met him.

He pulled in a deep breath, fully aware that his emotions were going way out of bounds. Kiku wouldn't approve. Yet, Naoto felt powerless to stop. He smoothed Koji's wet hair back. "It's just, you're...you seem so gentle. I hate to think of anyone hurting you."

As before, Koji's liquid gaze rested on Naoto in a way that made Naoto feel...transparent. As the seconds passed, the look shifted to something else, something more velvety. Koji's lids seemed to grow heavier and his lips parted with deeper breaths.

Naoto felt the tentative press of fingertips on his chest, just below his collarbone. The dappling of touch made his dragon, forgotten during Koji's revelation, now resurge. Under Koji's exploring caress, the shaft rose, tingling to life.

Koji-san pressed in closer, making the shower spray surround them both. He tilted his chin upwards, lips slightly parted. Water beaded off them and ran down his chin.

Damn, if anyone could be clearer about wanting to be kissed without actually *saying* it, Naoto couldn't imagine. Unable to resist, Naoto leaned in to the wet warmth of the other man's body and kissed him. And immediately tasted heaven.

Koji's lips were soft and melty from the water. Delicious. He slipped his arms around Koji and pulled him closer, feeling the protectiveness surge in him. No one would ever harm this man while he was around.

Invisible waves of feeling cascaded through him, one after the other, shivering down his back and ass, spreading all the way to his toes. Koji's yielding response to his kiss was intoxicating, the way Koji sagged against him, hands pressed on Naoto's chest, made his brain feel like it was melting away even as his body hardened, cock erect, pushing against Koji's.

In the next second, that invisible something inside him crossed a line. Koji was no longer his guest, not in his mind, not in his heart, and *not* in the possessive way he held Koji against his chest. Not in the hungry yet sweet way he slid his tongue against Koji's, as if tasting Koji's very essence.

If Koji were merely a guest, he wouldn't taste like plums and chocolate, honey and ginger…everything good.

A sudden zing of pleasure up Naoto's dragon made him realise Koji's fingers were closed around his thickness, pumping it in unskilled yet eager strokes.

Kuso. Koji was making him lose control.

No more White Tiger, guiding his guest's pleasure, using his erotic strategies on the man to make his yang churn with heat yet also relax him. The feel of Koji's hand on his cock took it all away. There was no stopping himself from pulling back and turning Koji in his arms so he could slip his straining cock between Koji's perfect ass cheeks.

Hands on the slimmer man's hips, Naoto rocked against him while the shower spray battered his back and thundered in his ears along with his own blood. Koji's hips were narrow, perfect, smooth, under his hands and he pushed Koji's buttocks tighter around his dragon.

Koji's back heaved and through the thunder of water Naoto could hear Koji's harsh whisper of *yes, yes* over and over again.

Slipping one arm around Koji's front, Naoto pulled Koji back firmly against him. Koji leaned his head back against Naoto's chest, hands still pressed to the tiles in front of him, then pushed his ass back against Naoto's cock.

Without thinking, Naoto grasped Koji's hand and guided it down, bidding him to stroke himself and the man's harsh breathing mingled with the other sounds. Naoto took hold of Koji's hips again and slid against him. The building pressure stole all thoughts away, made Naoto unable to think of anything else, to worry about anything but Koji's wet body sliding against his, the overwhelming pleasure, the warm wet flesh. He leaned forward and gathered the droplets off Koji's warm skin…just as the pleasure exploded.

His fingers tightened on Koji's hips, anchoring him as his climax erupted onto Koji's skin, only to be washed away by the shower as it spurted out. With the power of release came the torrent of feelings. *Want. Need. Desire. Koji's eyes. The scars. Naoto's protective anger. His possessive embrace.*

He slumped against Koji's back and held the man against him, lips pressed to Koji's shoulder. He wanted to stay just like this and never have to move.

No.

He had to stop. For so many reasons, not the least of which was he still wanted Lee. Why else would Lee be calling to him nearly every night in his dreams? Wasn't that dark passageway Lee always tugged him towards, leading to the place they could be together?

He let out a deep sigh and then felt Koji's hand slip over his. Koji's body was pliant in his embrace, in the way a man relaxed after he came. The shower still battered them and Naoto imagined it washed away everything that had just passed and everything he'd felt.

Better that way.

Pulling gently away from Koji, he finished washing them both then turned off the shower. He reached for a towel, unfolded it and began to dry Koji off.

Koji stood still, arms at his sides, eyes averted as if he too, had felt that…whatever it was…pass between them and had thought the better if it.

Naoto got them both dried off then dressed, leaving Koji wrapped in his kimono while he went down to the kitchen to get Koji's breakfast.

Basho, who did all the cooking, grinned at him when he walked in. "Good morning, Naoto-chan. You need a tray for your guest?"

He nodded, coming to a standstill by the large stainless steel table in the centre. On the other side, Ryu stood chopping green onions, with Tatou and Mod on either side of him, chatting in English. Their chatting stopped and all three men looked up, ginning at him, eyes sparkling.

Naoto pinned them with a look. "What?"

"Oh, nothing," Tatou said.

"Nothing, my ass," Basho said in English, ladling soup into a bowl. His eyes, too, glittered with mischief, which was a miracle, considering how sullen he'd been for a long time. A man of mysterious origin, he'd not even shared his story with Ryu who was the one person he trusted. The only thing evident was that, like the twins, Basho had lived a long time in England because of his accent when he spoke the language. Not even Kiku knew his whole story. Well, not from being told. Kiku's psychic visions had told him enough to urge him to the White Tiger, the way he'd done with Naoto. "Tatou here was saying he didn't know you were auditioning your guest for a choir."

Naoto looked at him. He couldn't help grinning in spite of the heaviness he was feeling inside. "Is that right?"

Tatou shrugged. A sideways grin curved his lips. "No big deal, mate," he said. "It's just that he has a healthy set of lungs, that one."

Ryu chuckled but put his head down, making an obvious show of concentrating on his work. "Just ignore them, Nao-chan," he murmured.

Naoto smiled at him. "No problem." Normally he didn't hesitate to banter back and forth with them, but this morning couldn't think of anything to say. Koji haunted his mind. He couldn't get enough of the man's scent, the feel of his skin, his wide-eyed look and his pleasure cries. So intoxicated was he, he was still tending to the man on his day off. Tuesday was his day of the week to sleep later and relax before visiting Lee's mother and his own parents. And yet, here he was, looking after Koji.

Sooner or later he'd have to get out for a few hours. The space away from Koji-san would help clear his mind.

Maybe.

He knew all too well how unpredictable life could be. And the more you tried to control it, the more out of control it became.

Chapter Seven

Koji's cell phone rang. His heart sped up when he saw his boss's name in the ID window. Shit, it was as if Miosuke had a telescope trained on him. Reluctantly, Koji pressed the button and put the phone to his ear, turning guiltily away from the computer screen. "*Moshi moshi.*"

"Watanabe-san?'

"Yes, hello."

The older man cleared his throat. "I just wanted to see how you were today. I was…concerned."

Koji breathed a sigh of relief. It didn't seem that Miosuke knew he was in the hospital's administrator's office. The one place he should *not* be. "That's very kind of you. I'm much better, thank you. I'm having an excellent…vacation."

Pause. "Good. Very good. Well, I won't keep you. I'm glad you're all right. See you next week, Watanabe-san."

Koji nodded, even though Miosuke couldn't see him. "Thank you. See you next week." He clicked off and let his shoulders sag. That had been too close.

Exiting the program he was working on, he returned to the hospital's working mode. He sighed as he watched the screen change. As Miosuke had told him yesterday, his work only needed a minimum of supervision. When Koji had gotten to the hospital, he'd already made certain that every station on every floor had his number should there be a problem. Now it was nearly five in the afternoon, and truthfully, there really wasn't anything else he could do unless he just wanted to sit there and stare at the monitor.

Rising from the swivel chair, he left the administrator's office and started down the corridor towards the main lobby. Had it been a normal work week, he would have walked back to his apartment a few blocks away, showered and then returned to the office where he'd stay until at least ten. After all, there was no on to go home to.

His stomach did a small flip. Today that wasn't true. Koji picked up his jacket, slowly slipping it on while inside he savoured the feelings that passed through him. The anticipation, the incredible sensations and pleasures that he was free to have just for these few days...

Koji sighed and pulled his mind back to the present. Naoto said he'd be out until about eight in the evening, visiting his parents. That left a few hours to fill.

Feeling aimless, Koji walked through the sliding glass doors of the hospital entrance and stood on the sidewalk, hands in the pockets of his windbreaker. For several minutes, he watched the traffic go back and forth on the street in front of him.

A breeze passed over, rustling the leaves on one of the sidewalk trees. He looked up and let his attention dwell on the tiny green leaves as they fluttered against the wind.

That's when he remembered. The *sakura,* the cherry blossoms, were in bloom. Now was the peak time and *hanami* would be in full swing down at Ueno Park. A pang squeezed in his chest. Had Shizuko been alive, the two of them would be there right now, sitting on their blue plastic sheet, sharing barbecue and listening to the karaoke singers while they watched the petals of the cherry blossoms fall in the breeze. Like last year.

He started walking, his path taking him to the train for Ueno Park...

~~~~~

"Naoto, is something bothering you?"

Naoto looked up at Lee's mother. Lecy smiled at him as she poured him some tea.

"You're unusually quiet today," she added.

He sighed, still unable to shake the image of Koji-san's scars from his mind. Truthfully, that wasn't the only thing about the man he hadn't been able to shake since they'd parted earlier, but some things were inappropriate to discuss, even with someone as close to him as Lecy. "There's a guest I'm taking care of who has these scars. His father whipped him when he was little." Anger surged through him again.

Lecy was quiet a moment. Her brow was drawn together in the same way Lee's used to when he was deep in thought. The image made his heart squeeze. "That's terrible," she said softly. She reached out and covered his hand where it rested on the table. "You've always been so protective."

Those words seemed to hover in the air between them. There was no interaction he and Lecy ever had that wasn't somehow full of Lee's memory.

She cleared her throat and took a sip of tea. "You've never mentioned a guest before." Her gentle tone conveyed understanding.

He said nothing and held his cup. The hot porcelain felt like a brand against the pads of his fingertips. Sometimes he felt like she was as psychic as Kiku. "No, I haven't."

Lecy squeezed his hand gently then released it. "Naoto, I have something to tell you."

He looked at her, alarmed at first. But she was smiling.

"I'm seeing someone."

He raised his eyebrows. "Really?" Lecy had been widowed most of the time he knew her and she'd never been with anyone since then. "Who?"

"Mr. Park who rents the store from me. His wife died almost two years ago and I've been helping him downstairs, as you know." She gave a small shrug. "It...developed...recently." Her smile faded. "I wanted you to know. It doesn't change anything." She touched his hand again. "You understand?"

He continued to stare at her. Many things passed through her dark eyes. She was not only telling him about her new relationship.

Her hand tightened on his. "Do you understand, Naoto? My precious son."

He did understand. "Yes. Thank you, Lecy." He picked up her hand and kissed it. "Precious mother," he added softly.

She smiled at him.

~~~~~

Koji wandered around the edge of the park. The interior too littered with people to walk among the trees, but it didn't matter. He preferred to stay on the edge anyway, watching while he sipped a beer. At this hour, many people were already singing and laughing raucously, beer bottles in hand, dancing around, while others were passed out and probably wouldn't wake up until after nightfall when the weather had turned colder.

Nearby on a blue sheet, a woman sat with a little boy. She was young, twenty-five, perhaps, the age Shizuko had been when she'd married his father. The woman's long hair was pulled back off her face and she smiled as she handed the child a cup full of something to drink. Juice, probably. Koji watched them, the scene hauntingly familiar. He'd never cared about the cherry blossoms really. The pink flowers were pretty and the festivities lively, but he'd only ever gone to *hanami* to be with Shizuko, first with the family, and then, when he got older, and Gina and his father had lost interest in the cherry blossoms, he'd gone to have Shizuko all to himself, if just for a little while.

The woman with the little boy looked up, her gaze on some *sakura* petals wafting down around them. A wistful look crossed her face just before she returned her attention to the boy.

Unable to watch any longer, Koji moved on. By the time he reached the area near the station, he'd had enough food off the vendors' carts that he felt stuffed. Damn, he hadn't even noticed how much he'd actually eaten, only that a short while ago he was suddenly starved and everything on every cart looked delicious. It was the first time since Shizuko got sick that he could remember actually feeling hunger.

Tossing his empty beer bottle into a nearby trashcan, he left the park and went back to the station. The image of the woman with the boy haunted him the entire ride back to Shinjuku, especially the sweet sad look that had crossed her eyes as the petals floated around her.

With still some time to kill, he got off at Shinjuku station. Back in the neighbourhood of the hotel, he wandered the streets, peering in shop windows and watching people pass as they overtook his meandering pace. He still had well over an hour before Naoto would be back. Somehow, the thought of seeing Naoto made him feel brighter, made the ache in his chest a little less sharp.

A bit farther down, he passed an art supply store. And halted. Slowly, he turned and stared at the window display, letting his gaze rove over the array of drawing pads, coloured pencil sets, and other various items such as *origami* paper, stationery and book bags. Guilt flared through his chest, made the back of his neck tingle as if he were looking at some sort of illegal substance.

Well, for many years, drawing *had* been illegal, an activity he made sure to do when his father wasn't around and then hid the papers away in various stashes around his bedroom.

He dared to step closer, gaze riveted on the pads and pencils.

Please, Tashiro-chan, let Koji draw.

Koji remembered overhearing Shizuko. She'd sounded hysterical. He'd peeked around the corner and seen his father pacing, a crumpled sheet in his hand. Koji had broken into an icy sweat. The one time he'd been careless and left one of his drawings on his bed. Thankfully it hadn't been one of his samurai drawings. Every fantasy he'd ever had made it into a drawing. He'd have gotten a beating for *that*.

The boy has his head in the clouds, his father had answered, thrusting the paper closer to Shizuko's face. *He's thirteen now, almost a man and he'll never amount to anything if he doesn't study more. You coddle him, woman.*

Please. He's a good boy. He'll do fine. Carefully she'd retrieved the drawing from his hand.

Koji remembered his father's scowl, the hand he'd pointed accusingly at Shizuko. *Fine. But if he gets one low grade…*

Koji had pulled in a breath, partly of relief that Shizuko had gotten her way and partly in fear.

Thank you, Tashiro-chan. Thank you.

Koji sighed as the memory faded. She'd never known he'd overheard them but he'd made sure to get high marks in every class that year.

Standing there, in front of the store, the realisation hit him. He still believed he'd get caught and punished for doing the activity he loved.

But it wasn't true.

A flutter stirred in his heart. He hadn't drawn in years, not since his last year of high school, the year he'd made the album for Shizuko's birthday. Once he'd started college, he'd given it up, knowing he had to pursue a real career.

Well, now he *had* a real career. And yet, the desire to draw had resurged. Or…maybe it had never left him but had just gotten pushed to the side. He grimaced inwardly, disgusted. Nearly thirty years old and he still behaved like that frightened boy. *Shimatta.* He was on vacation anyway, what could it hurt to pass the time drawing a bit? He'd have to put it aside again anyway once he went back to work. Turning sharply, he went in, bought a sketchpad and some pencils then headed back in the direction of Ni Chome.

On the next block, however, another shop display caught his eye. He stopped and stared through the glass. His pulse rose. It was the kind of thing he would never, ever have thought to buy, especially as a gift for…someone. *No.* He couldn't. It wasn't right. It wasn't…proper. Naoto-san would get the wrong idea.

Koji started to walk away. He got two blocks down yet felt the item pulling at him with an invisible force. It gnawed at his consciousness, made him feel…daring.

He came to a standstill, torn between two directions until one feeling grew stronger than all others and tugged him back to the store.

~~~~~

After leaving Lecy's, Naoto went home and found his mother in the kitchen, standing over a pot of steaming soup. His father sat at the kitchen table in a cloud of cigarette smoke, reading his paper. A familiar scene he'd grown up with. And yet, today…different.

He kissed his mother's cheek and sat down at the table.

His father looked up and folded his paper before setting the cigarette in the ashtray. "Naoto, how are you?"

"Hi, Dad. I'm fine." Naoto looked at him.

His father smiled, but under Naoto's steady gaze furrowed his brow. "Something wrong?"

Koji flashed in Naoto's mind for the thousandth time that day. Those scars…

He sighed. For much of his life he'd resented the attention his brother had gotten, the way his parents had spent their whole lives working to make sure Shin's special talent was cultivated to the fullest. But today, it didn't matter. "No. I mean…" He glanced up at his mother but her back was to the table as she worked. "I need to ask you something."

His father picked up his cigarette and took a drag on it. The movement made his tattooed arm muscles flex and Naoto caught a splash of colour and watched. Though Take Shimura wasn't a yak, he had the same full markings that many working class men had. "What's on your mind?"

His mother set down her spoon and came over to the table. She touched the back of his hair. "Do you feel ill, Nao-chan?"

He looked up at her. "No. I...do you feel like I'm a failure?"

Both his parents' eyes went wide.

"What the hell are you talking about?" his father said.

Naoto felt his mother's hand on his shoulder. "Of course not. Why do you have that idea?"

Tears stung his eyes. In his mind all he saw were the angry white marks on Koji's ass. He couldn't imagine that Koji would have a conversation like this with the man who'd hurt him that way. "Because of...the difference between...me and Shin," he managed to say past the lump in his throat.

His father tapped out his ashes and leaned forward. "Listen, Naoto, you're like me. I ran wild when I was younger than you. For a long time. But I didn't work, like you did. I didn't settle down and care about people the way you did. You know why? Because my parents hounded me. The more they hounded me the more I said, 'Fuck you.' I was going to show *them*."

Naoto stared at his father. The man had never spoken to him this way. He tried to think of his father as a teenager. Naoto's grandparents had passed away when he was little so he didn't remember them, but the family photos showed stern, demanding people.

"Don't put a tiger in a cage," his father said. "It'll never be a cat and you'll destroy its soul." He took a puff on his cigarette, watching Naoto through the cloud he exhaled. "Your brother is a cat."

Naoto bowed his head. "Thank you, Dad. I wish I'd asked you sooner." He felt his mother kiss him on the head and then she squeezed him in an embrace.

His father still looked at him and took another drag. He blew out the smoke. "I wish I'd told you sooner," he said softly.

~~~~~

Naoto's heart beat a bit faster as he unlocked the back door to the White Tiger. This day had been surreal somehow. From the moment he'd woken up on top of Koji-san to the conversation with his parents.

Something had changed and he couldn't say what it was. But it had definitely changed.

He had changed. Been freed inside from certain ideas, feelings, beliefs about his unworthiness as a man that had covered his heart, had made him unhappy for so long, even when he'd been with Lee. He wasn't unhappy now. In fact, the word joy wasn't exactly an inaccurate way to describe how he felt in this moment. The very kind of happiness he'd spoken about to Koji-san the day before, was happening to him now. Sheer, sweet joy.

The sensation gave him such fullness in his heart he wanted to share it.

And there was one person he really wanted to share it with in this moment.

Naoto went up the back steps, resisting the potent urge to go immediately to Koji's room. Back in his own room, he stripped off his jacket, T-shirt and jeans, showered and put on his uniform. It was only a few minutes past eight when he rapped gently on the door to Koji's room.

"Yes?"

"Koji-san, it's Naoto."

"Oh!" he heard behind the door, followed by a hasty shuffling sound.

Naoto furrowed his brow. Did Koji have someone with him? The thought made a sudden uncomfortable heaviness in his chest.

"Please, come in."

Pulling in a deep breath, Naoto slid open the door.

Koji stood at the foot of the bed, wearing his kimono. Barefoot, he took several steps forward and bowed. "Naoto-san. Welcome back." He straightened up, a smile stretching his lips. In spite of the still haunted look in Koji's eyes, the other man seemed genuinely happy to see him.

It was mutual.

A quick glance at the small bathroom revealed no other person in the room. Relief shivered through him and Naoto returned the smile. "I'm the one who should be welcoming you."

"Come in, please. I was just resting a bit until you got back."

Until you got back. Sounded like Koji-san had been waiting for him. A warm tingle spread through Naoto's middle. He followed Koji' s lead over to the bed where he knelt in the customary way in front of Koji who sat on the edge of the bed.

Koji frowned. "Naoto-san, you don't have to kneel like that." He slid over and patted the bed next to him. "Please, I invite you to sit with me."

The warm tingle increased to a flush. Damn, that's what used to happen to him when he first met Lee.

Wordlessly, Naoto rose. The cover was pulled back and rumpled and it was then Naoto noticed a large sketchpad and a box of pencils. "I didn't know you drew, Koji-san."

Koji's cheeks coloured and he looked down. "I haven't drawn in a long time, not since high school. I just thought since I'm not working, I'd try my hand again." He lifted his gaze then. "Did you have a nice visit with your parents?"

Naoto looked at him, touched by the thoughtful question. His visit had been better than nice. The words his father had said to him were worth more than any gold and diamonds. That conversation had changed his life, had made him appreciate things about his parents he'd not truly considered before, clouded as he'd been by his jealousy of Shin.

They'd always been respectful of Lee and very supportive when Lee had been killed. And neither of his parents had *ever* whipped him or his brother. They'd yelled at times and once in a while his father had given him a light cuff on the head for tracking in dirt or something like that, but nothing that had done worse than muss his hair a bit.

Of course, he couldn't say any of this to Koji-san since Koji's experience had apparently been vastly different.

Koji frowned. "Did it bother you, my asking that?"

Without thinking, Naoto reached for Koji's hand. "Of course not." Koji must have taken his hesitation for offence. "I had a very good visit with my parents. Thank you for asking."

"Good." Koji's expression turned thoughtful. He said nothing though Naoto sensed that Koji was curious about him and trying to be polite.

"Koji-san, how did things go for you today?"

Koji's gaze, suddenly sheepish, rested on his. "Things were just as you'd said they'd be. No chaos at the hospital, systems shutting down because I wasn't there. Everything was fine. So I left and went to *hanami*...in Ueno Park." His smile faded and he looked down. "I used to go every year with my stepmother, since I was a kid. She loved it." When he looked back up, his large eyes were misted.

Naoto's heart fluttered at the vulnerable look in them and it was a moment before he realised he was brushing his thumb back and forth across the top of Koji's hand, still in his.

"She died of cancer last summer," Koji said softly. "She hadn't been sick that long but it was too late to do anything. It spread so quickly." The words seemed to tumble out, as if unlocked from a place deep inside. "She was so young. Only forty-five."

Naoto gazed at him. "I'm sorry, Koji-san." From the sound of his voice, Koji must have loved this woman very much and his own chest ached as if the other man's grief passed directly through it. With it, a light seemed to come on in his mind, clearer now from his own personal realisations. Koji's obsession with the hospital, his overwhelming fear that people would die if he wasn't working every single second...

Koji's way of dealing with his grief. An emotion Naoto understood only too well.

Without thinking, Naoto lifted Koji's hand and pressed it to his lips. There was nothing he could say in a moment like this. Koji had to feel what was inside himself or he'd continue to be a workaholic mess. The only thing Naoto could do was comfort him while he was here.

Koji's eyes widened. Naoto kissed his hand again, brushed his lips across Koji's skin in a way he meant to be sympathetic but which blurred with his desire.

He glanced up in time to see Koji's eyes go dusky, his lids lower a bit. "Naoto-san, you mentioned the bath today before you left."

Naoto lowered Koji's hand, still holding it. His stomach tightened a bit and he hoped that he hadn't embarrassed Koji-san somehow. "Do you wish to go down there?"

Koji nodded, his eyes still heavy-lidded yet also a bit shy. "Yes. As long as...you can come with me."

The warm flush through Naoto's middle returned. The way he was feeling now, he'd do whatever Koji wanted, always. "Of course."

A smile curved the other man's sensual lips.

Naoto caught himself staring at them, as if his body suddenly realised it had been too many hours since he and Koji had been naked together. He tugged Koji's hand and rose to his feet. "Now's a good time. The bath is often empty."

Koji pushed his feet into his slippers and Naoto let him out and down the elevator.

On the ground floor, Ryu passed them, leading Mr. Hamura, an elderly man in a kimono, towards the massage rooms. Ryu shot Naoto a grin and bowed his head courteously at Koji as they passed, as did Ryu's guest.

Naoto returned Ryu's smile just as Ryu slid back the door to a massage room and assisted the elderly man inside. Mr. Hamura was one of only a few handpicked regular guests that Ryu took care of. Kiku only left Ryu with men who were older and completely non-threatening. Delivering punches in a boxing ring surrounded by people was one thing. Being naked in a room alone with someone who was bigger and stronger than Ryu was a different matter for him.

In the shower room, Naoto adjusted the shower to be pleasantly hot then approached Koji and unwound the sash of his kimono. The second the other man's robe fell open, Naoto felt his cock tingle to life. He tried not to leer like a lust-crazed teenager at the Koji's slim, graceful musculature, especially at the delicious trail of hair beneath the other man's belly button. He concentrated on slipping Koji's kimono off his shoulders, but the bloom of colour in Koji's cheeks showed Naoto he'd been caught.

He then stripped off his own uniform and hung it up with Koji's robe. Turning from the wall peg, he caught Koji staring at him now, an undisguised stare that travelled up and down Naoto's physique. If Koji's eyes had been hands in that moment, Naoto would have found himself being completely fondled.

Well, it was mutual.

Smiling, he held out his hand and gently tugged Koji into the shower. With his bare hands, he soaped Koji's sleek body, loving the dark golden sheen of Koji's wet skin, and forcing himself to hold off from touching him lower. Water beaded off Koji's lean muscles and dark nipples, a sight that made Naoto's mouth water.

When he'd rinsed Koji off, he pulled aside his own hair, still loose, and held it up so that he could rinse off too. He felt a pair of soapy hands on his back and looked over his shoulder.

Koji was looking at him, his eyes velvety yet also shy. "Let me…wash you, Naoto-san," he said just above the noise of the spray. "That way, you don't have to get your hair wet."

Just the sweet look in Koji-san's eyes sent a ripple of heat straight into his dragon. "Thank you," he said softly and lifted his hair out of the way.

Koji's touch explored his body in a tentative way. Naoto felt Koji's suppressed excitement in his hands as they slid, soapy over his chest, around to his back muscles and down, over his hips. Sweet. No guest had ever offered to wash him in return...only Lee, and that had been so long ago. The sensation of slippery yet gentle hands over his wet skin made his nipples tighten, as did his balls, especially when Koji reached down and began to lather each thigh. A pleasant jolt shot through him each time Koji's fingers grazed his balls. How he wanted to beg Koji to knead them, but bit his lip to keep silent. Instead, he leaned his head against the tiled wall, allowing Koji access. Koji's inexperience came through his touch and Naoto once again wondered at the man's innocence.

Glancing down at the top of Koji's dark head, he almost smiled at the serious look of concentration on Koji's face. He could just picture him in front of his computer at work, so conscientious. Koji slid a soapy hand up Naoto's thigh, to his hip. Ohh! Naoto stifled a moan as a current shot through his dragon at Koji's sudden lightning quick touch on it. Instinctively, Naoto thrust his hips outward towards Koji, whose face was...so...close...

Remembering they were in the common showers where anyone could walk in, he sucked in his breath, easing his hips away from Koji. If they'd been in a more private place, it seemed that Koji, with his tendency to want to reciprocate the pleasures given him, might have wanted to take Naoto's cock in his mouth and suck it to release.

He cleared his throat. "That's good, Koji-san...thanks." Best to get into the bath before he lost control and did something embarrassing. In spite of the fact that this was a love-hotel for men, Kiku did have certain standards of conduct for his White Tigers. Public sex in the shower or bath was on the list — however short — of things not allowed.

With a hand on Koji-san's shoulder, Naoto drew him up. He rinsed both of them off then gave Koji his towel to wrap around his hips as they went to the bath. The towels tented out with their erections, but at least there was no one else around to see them.

No one else was there, Naoto noted, ridiculously pleased to have this private time with his guest. Normally it didn't matter to him, but it did now. He set their towels to the side and descended to the bath, a very small swimming pool with built-in seating all around the sides. "Come here, Koji-san, I'll rub your shoulders for you, if you'd like." He sat in the corner, arms out.

Koji's eyes still looked dusky, as they had in the shower and his smile still charmingly shy. He settled on the bench between Naoto's thighs, his back dangerously close to Naoto's erection. Naoto lifted his hands to the slimmer man's shoulders and started to rub them, noting with satisfaction that the knots in his lean muscles were considerably less tight than the day before.

"You are so good at that, Naoto-san," Koji murmured. His body grew pliant and moved easily under Naoto's hands.

"Thank you, Koji-san. Though truthfully, the pleasure is all mine." It was true. Koji's skin was flawlessly smooth yet masculine and just touching him, feeling his surrender to the care offered, was blissful.

Koji turned then and stared at him, the way he'd done the day before after the three cups of saké, only tonight, the man was sober.

Koji's sensual expression sent a thrill through Naoto, right to his toes. Before he knew what he was doing, he'd sat up, leaning in towards Koji, wanting nothing but to taste those soft, slightly parted lips.

Sudden voices made him pull away. He leaned back against the side and tugged Koji-san closer, to sit in front of him, the back of Koji's body spooned to his front and ignored the thrill of his cock sandwiched against Koji's back, just as Ryu and Quan Chan walked in from the shower room, towels around their hips.

"Mind if we join you?" Ryu asked, politely leaving his towel on until Naoto nodded, realising he and Koji must have been cuddling in the bath longer than he'd thought. Ryu had been with a guest only moments ago, or so it had seemed.

Only then did Ryu and Quan Chan pull their towels off and descend into the bath, Ryu a splash of colours as always, between his electric pink hair and body tattoos. Both men sat a respectful distance away and lounged, arms along the edge of the bath.

Naoto made introductions and then returned to rubbing Koji's shoulders, loving the heat that collected between their wet bodies so close together and the light brush of Koji's backside against his still-hard dragon. Koji sank down a bit lower and rested his head back against Naoto. The tiny gesture conveyed a sense of affection and trust that struck Naoto down to his toes. Without thinking, he closed his eyes and nuzzled the other man's damp hair, soft and sleek against his lips.

For a while, they all sat in companionable silence and then Quan Chan turned to Ryu. "Do you feel ready for Saturday, Ryu?"

Ryu grinned at Quan Chan. "I guess so. This guy has been at it a year longer than I have and has way more wins. He's from Seoul."

Naoto shifted his body a fraction to ease his cock. "Ryu is a boxer," he said to Koji. The conversation helped to pull him from his erotic trance. "He turned pro recently."

"I see." Koji sat up a bit and the tiny movement put his ass back against Naoto's cock. Naoto let out a silent breath, wondering how much longer he'd have to hold himself in check. Only his years of training at the White Tiger allowed him to restrain himself from rubbing feverishly against Koji. Aside from their interrupted kiss, *that* was something else that would have to wait a while longer.

"That's really great," Koji told Ryu. "Congratulations."

Ryu bowed his head. "Thank you, Watanabe-san."

"Please, call me Koji."

Ryu smiled and gave a nod.

"I wish I could say I've seen you fight," Koji said softly. "My father probably has, though. He'd an avid fan of the sport."

Naoto bit back a retort about Koji's father and concentrated on his massage, now sliding his touch down to Koji's biceps, luxuriating in the feel of the smooth contours of his graceful musculature.

"His favourite of all time was Naboru Miyazaki."

Naoto's gaze shot to Ryu who visibly tensed.

Ryu's gaze dropped. "He's...my father," he said softly.

Koji nodded and bowed until his face was just above the water line. The depth of his bow showed an apology. "Ah, I see. Well, I wish you all the best for your match." The sound in Koji's voice also showed he'd picked up on Ryu's tension and Naoto resisted the compelling urge to close his arms around Koji and shower grateful kisses on his neck. Which he would have done anyway had they been alone. And would as soon as they reached their room.

Their room. Naoto's thoughts stopped in mid-track. When it had started to become their room? He forced his attention back to the conversation.

Koji's sensitivity was rewarded with one of Ryu's star smiles, quite a feat considering Koji had unknowingly hit Ryu's biggest emotional button. "Thank you, Watanabe-san. I...have an extra ticket if you'd like to come to the match. Naoto is going. You can be his guest. Right, Naoto?"

Naoto saw the quick look Ryu gave him and nodded. "I'd like that."

Koji sat up and turned around to look at him. "Are you sure? I wouldn't want to intrude."

Naoto smiled at him, resisting the urge to touch Koji's lips with his fingertip. "No intrusion at all. Your company would be most welcome." A warm flush fanned through his chest at Koji's smile.

Koji turned back to Ryu and bowed again, almost as deeply as the first one. "Thank you. I'm honoured." He fell silent and settled back against Naoto, resting in a familiar way, as if they'd been lovers for a long time instead of guest and attendant, which is what they really were. Even though, somehow, to Naoto, it didn't completely feel that way.

Koji shifted and the movement made him slide against Naoto's cock again.

Naoto pulled in a breath and held Koji in place with firm hands on Koji's upper arms. He managed to be subtle enough that Koji didn't seem to notice. Yet, a glance over Koji's shoulder, down his front, revealed that their bodily contact was getting him hard too. Koji's knees were raised, hiding the evidence from Ryu and Quan Chan who were both now engaging Koji in polite conversation.

Damn. Not since Lee had Naoto wanted to be alone with someone so badly. Behind Koji's back, Naoto managed to catch Ryu's eye. Ryu nodded, imperceptibly enough that a guest would never catch it but which conveyed his understanding. Naoto watched Ryu end their chat in his customary graceful and charming way, so subtly, that no one would guess he was giving Naoto the perfect lead-in to get Koji back upstairs.

Chapter Eight

Naoto frowned as he and Koji ascended the stairs. Since they'd left the bath, a heavy air seemed to settle over Koji. Was Koji hesitant about going back upstairs with him? His doubt dampened his arousal. Koji had seemed to be enjoying their time. It didn't make sense. "Koji-san, are you all right?"

Koji looked at him. Worry lines crinkled his brow. "About Ryu-san, I think I said something wrong to him. About his father. He looked upset when I mentioned his father's name. I...didn't know."

"Of course you didn't, Koji-san." There was no way in hell Koji could have known about the tension between Ryu and his father. Naboru Miyazaki had joined the Suzuki crime family when his boxing career was finished and worked his way into an exalted position. Koji could not have known that Ryu and Kiku colluded to keep his rape a secret from his father for fear the man wouldn't believe him. Worse, that his father, completely loyal to the Suzuki crime family, would have punished him for accusing Taro Suzuki, the son of the family's leader, of such a crime. Koji could not have known any of this. "However, you were so sensitive to him. So kind."

When Koji's worried look remained, Naoto stopped on the step and turned to him, at once aching to relieve the man's worry and relieved that it wasn't about going back upstairs with him. "You don't understand what you accomplished this evening, Koji-san." Naoto smiled at the blank look the other man gave him.

"Accomplished?"

He nodded. "Yes. You won Ryu over in a matter of moments. Something no one else has ever done." He glanced back to make sure they were alone. "Ryu is wonderful with guests and is a good friend to us here, but he doesn't warm easily to people. He did with you. And I know it was because you showed sensitivity to him." He fell silent and watched feelings pass through Koji-san's eyes as his words sank in.

Finally, Koji nodded. "I see." That shy smile returned, so charming it made Naoto's insides flutter. "I'm glad."

Relief cascaded through Naoto. He ushered Koji up the rest of the stairs and down the hallway to Koji's room. Koji still looked thoughtful as Naoto slid the door open. "I think I understand," Koji said. "The hair, the tattoos, the nose ring. They say much about him." He walked in ahead of Naoto, sank down on the side of the bed and sat, looking up. The soft lighting in the room glowed off his hair and skin. Naoto had meant to ask him to explain his thought about Ryu, but found himself unable to speak. Only able to look.

He slid the door closed and approached Koji. Now that he knew the reason for Koji's worry, his arousal began to resurge. The erection that had faded earlier now began to rise again and pushed against his shorts. He knelt down and looked at the other man. Koji-san's kimono had opened, revealing one side of his chest. The mere sight of a dark nipple made Naoto itch to yank his kimono off and lay him onto his back.

"Naoto-san?"

Naoto's breath hitched. "Yes?"

Colour fanned through Koji's cheeks. "Could I...would you...pose for me? I'd love to draw you."

Naoto felt an intense flush of pleasure at the request. It wasn't what he'd had in mind, but...well...perhaps posing for Koji could be erotic too. He nodded. "Yes, of course. Right now?"

"Yes." That shy look slipped through Koji's eyes, just before he reached for the drawing pad and pencils on the nightstand.

Without thinking, Naoto rose and slipped off his vest and shorts. When he turned, Koji's large gaze rested on him.

Naoto felt his cheeks heat a bit. "I'm sorry, I assumed you meant...nude."

"Y...yes. Nude is good." Koji's eyes widened and his gaze rested on Naoto as he slipped his shorts off too and set his uniform neatly on the floor at the foot of the bed. "Should I sit here?" He indicated the bed.

"Yes. And don't worry about the pose. Just something comfortable for you."

Naoto slid onto the bed and lay on his side, head propped in his hand, leaning on one elbow. "How's this?"

Koji swallowed hard. Looking at Naoto filled him with awe each time. The man was all broad muscle, smooth skin and long sleek hair. Yet there was also that look in his eyes, a misty softness in the dark irises that made him appear as if he were feeling love for the whole world...

"That's perfect," he murmured, then flipped back the cover of the pad and took out one pencil. Damn, it had been more than ten years since he'd sketched and well, Naoto was probably an ambitious subject. But truthfully, there was no one or nothing else he could imagine more beautiful.

Naoto was respectfully quiet as Koji sketched and the room filled with only the sound of the pencil lead scratching across the paper. At first, his hand trembled and he needed to erase several lines that were out of proportion, but after a while, he found a rhythm, a flow under which a likeness appeared that showed Naoto in all his muscular glory, completely alluring and delicious with his brawny physique lounging on the bed, his long hair like a beautiful fan over his shoulder.

With longer strokes of the pencil, he sketched Naoto's hair then moved right into the lines of definition on his broad chest. One part led to the other, carved abdominals, the small indentation of his navel, the soft trail of hair below that ended in his pubic hair. Koji swallowed hard. A thrill travelled the length of his body, making his cock tighten. Naoto had a full erection. His cock was very thick and as powerful-looking as the rest of his physique. Koji sketched that part of him too, including the firm, heavy sac underneath. Naoto's masculine beauty heated his blood, made his pencil scratch faster across the paper. Almost effortlessly now he sketched the contours of Naoto's strong thighs and sloping calves, all the way to his feet with rounded toes and clean neatly trimmed toenails. Even the man's toes made his mouth water.

Finally, when there wasn't a part on Naoto left to draw, he lifted the pencil away. "I've finished," Koji murmured. Truly he just wanted to put the pad aside and taste that thick erection. But he'd never been forward, like the day before when he was drunk. That had been embarrassing enough. Better just to let Naoto lead. He hesitated, pad in hand. The only other person he'd ever voluntarily shown his work to was Shizuko. Yet, somehow, it seemed wrong not to show Naoto the picture he'd taken his time to pose for. "Would you...like to see it?"

Naoto nodded. A soft gleam came into his eye as he sat up and leaned over. Koji put the sketchpad in front of him and watched Naoto's face for a response.

When Naoto looked up, his eyes had that misted quality and were wide. "Koji-san, I can't believe it. That's me." His voice had a hushed wonder in it.

Koji grinned even as a flush of heat travelled down his body, warming his body inside his kimono. "I'm glad you like it. I was worried I wouldn't do you justice."

"Thank you, Koji-san. It's beautiful. I'm…honoured." He leaned in and kissed Koji's cheek, a shy sweet peck.

Skin tingling from the kiss, Koji set the pad back on the table along with the box of pencils. "You can have that drawing, as long as you let me do more of you."

Now Naoto was grinning and his large hands reached out, unwound the sash of Koji's kimono. "It's a deal." Naoto pushed the robe over Koji's shoulders, then leaned in and brushed a kiss over his lips. Koji's eyes fluttered closed, head tilted back as he let Naoto slip the robe off and drop it to the floor. He slid closer to Koji and Koji surrendered to the raw male power enveloping him. He had found in the last two days that there was nothing on Earth that could equal being made love to by Naoto-san.

A while later, satisfied and sweaty, Naoto cleaned them up, turned the light off and then settled back into the bed. He pulled Koji into his arms and moulded their damp bodies together. With a smile, he breathed in the musk of Koji's skin and sex, as powerful a sedative as having savoured every inch of the other man's sleek body with his tongue. First his chest, a long time spent on each nipple, then down his stomach, his thighs, balls, cock, getting Koji hot and panting before sliding up on him and rubbing their cocks together until they both reached bliss.

Koji's scent filled him, like a soothing cloud. Not long until his eyelids grew heavy…

Let me love you…

The feverish words made Naoto's eyes pop open.

I've wanted you for so long.

Warm breath tickled over his face. A weight pressed on his chest and slipped between his thighs, spreading them apart. Then something hard poked into the crevice of his ass. He certainly knew what that sensation was. But…

Consciousness slammed him awake. *Nande?*

Koji was hovering above him, breathing heavily. "I've wanted you for so long," he whispered. He punctuated his words with the push of his hips. A full erection nudged Naoto's hole.

"Don't worry, Shizu-chan," Koji said, his voice feverish, husky. "He won't find us. I won't tell anyone. Ever."

"Koji-san." Naoto clasped Koji's hips. In the shadowy light, he couldn't see Koji's face, but the strange energy he emitted made Naoto sense he wasn't completely awake. Shit, Koji was *dreaming*.

"It's all right," Koji whispered. "I love you." Koji leaned down and brushed his lips across Naoto's. A small groan vibrated in Koji's throat and Koji deepened the kiss, sought Naoto's tongue with his in hungry swirls of heat.

The slide of Koji's cock against his balls made them tighten, tingle with heat and Naoto's body unclenched, powerless to try and shake Koji from his dream.

Kiku had once told him that he might experience this with a guest at some time. He'd said that men often felt free to release pent up longings or secret desires once they were in the care of a White Tiger who'd been gently harvesting their yang and touching them in ways that loosened his energy and unlocked their secrets. Not that it was deliberate.

It just was a natural effect of stimulating the life force the way they did.

Kiku had also said not to worry if it did happen, that it was healing for the person. And Naoto certainly wanted Koji-san to heal.

Eyes closed, Naoto surrendered to the other man's kiss, letting Koji live out whatever dream was going on in his mind. It was weird, but kind of…kinky…and even if it hadn't been, Naoto wanted to do anything to help Koji.

Koji pulled away from their kiss yet still undulated his hips against Naoto's. "I've loved you for so long," he whispered again. "Do you love me too?" One hand slid over the side of Naoto's chest, cupping the muscle in a strange way, almost as if he were touching…a woman's breast. The pad of Koji's thumb brushed over the nipple, making the small disk harden. Naoto's breath caught. Koji's touch was amazing…sweet. "Yes," he whispered and lifted his hips against Koji's.

The response worked. Koji let out a sharp breath and lowered his mouth to Naoto's again. This kiss was quick, a deep lick of his tongue against Naoto's before pulling away again to kiss a trail down Naoto's throat.

Naoto's hands slid up Koji's back, amazed at the passionate way Koji licked and devoured him, swirled his tongue over each nipple. This wasn't the same passive Koji he'd been with the last couple of days. This man was wild, a tiger unleashed, taking possession of someone he wanted so badly. It explained Koji's grief, why it seemed so familiar, a man who's lost someone precious to him, so deeply entwined that losing the person was like losing a piece of his own soul.

Had Koji-san actually been with Shizuko, or was this wish fulfilment?

Not that it mattered. He sure as hell didn't judge Koji.

Koji slid further down Naoto's body and now crouched over his cock. The moist heat of Koji's tongue feathered along Naoto's shaft and over his balls, his hands splayed on Naoto's hips.

Naoto gripped the bedding as his body tightened under Koji's incredible tonguing. If Koji kept this up much longer, he was going to get woken up by the hot spray of cum on his face.

In the next moment, though, Koji crawled back up Naoto's body and nested his hips between Naoto's thighs again. The head of Koji's cock bumped against his opening, pushed in repeated tiny thrusts. "I want you so much," Koji whispered.

"I want you too." With one hand on Koji's arm, he reached with his free hand to the drawer of the nightstand and pulled out the small tube. As quickly as he could he squeezed some out and smeared it up and down Koji's cock.

Koji groaned at the contact. "Yes," he whispered, "You're so wet."

Kuso! The man thought he was inside her. Naoto tossed aside the tube and guided Koji's cock to his opening. He pulled in a breath as the head penetrated him the first inch. The only guy who'd ever gotten on top of him was Lee, yet he couldn't deny the pleasurable shudder that rippled through his body as Koji pushed deeper in.

Koji groaned. "Yes," he whispered.

Naoto grasped the man's ass and pulled. One hard slide and Koji was buried in deep, so deep, their bodies met.

"Koji." Naoto pulled his legs back, let out a sigh at the sensation of fullness and tingling that Koji's thick hard dragon made inside his tight passage.

"You feel so good," Koji said and lowered his mouth to Naoto's again. Koji's kiss, the chafe of his lips and heated swirl of his tongue were both tender and commanding, making Naoto melt in surrender. His body relaxed, unclenched a bit around Koji's cock and their bodies fell into a rhythm. Koji sank down lower on top of Naoto and each inward thrust he made with his hips rubbed Naoto's cock against Koji's stomach.

Naoto's fingers tightened on Koji's ass. The hard round muscles flexed under his hands and he let his fingertips slide inward, into the crevice of Koji's ass.

Koji groaned into Naoto's mouth. He thrust faster, harder, his kisses wild…hungry. That's when Naoto saw them. The blinking lights. They twinkled gently in his mind, dots of light against black velvet. Brighter and brighter they grew, as hot as the sun on his face, then exploded. Thick creamy seed spilled onto his stomach as his climax unleashed itself. Then he wilted, offering his sated body for Koji's pleasure.

Koji groaned again. His body stiffened and Naoto felt the other man's climax fill his passage. He caressed Koji's slim hips and rocked against him until Koji collapsed on top of him, breathing heavily. He held Koji gently, wondering if the sensations had woken him, but then Koji slipped out and rolled to his side, cuddling up to Naoto, one hand caressing Naoto's hair where it spilled over the pillow. "Don't worry, Shizu-chan," he murmured, his face nuzzled into Naoto's neck. "I'll protect you, always. You'll never feel unloved anymore." He fell silent and Naoto listened to his breathing slow into a peaceful, even rhythm, the steady quiet of sleep. Naoto's breath hitched softly. The words hadn't been meant for him, yet the way Koji said them went like arrows on fire to his heart. Damn, there was a whole world of emotions going on in the other man that probably no one else knew about…until now.

He lay quietly, listening to Koji breathe. His own body still tingled, especially his ass, which now felt the absence of Koji's dragon. Carefully, without disturbing the sleeping man, he reached for tissues and cleaned himself off as best he could, then lay still, enjoying Koji's body, warm and hard, curled up against his. Koji's erection had subsided and he seemed back in a deep sleep. He wondered if Koji would remember this when he woke up.

Not that it mattered. Awake or asleep, Koji was intoxicating. Beautiful. Complex. Amazing.

All the things Naoto had seen in Lee.

When he'd been falling in love with him.

~~~~~

Naoto opened his eyes. His usual dream of Lee, beckoning him towards the dark passageway, spiraled away. He blinked, becoming aware of Koji's warm body still curled up against him, face pressed into the curve of Naoto's neck.

With his free hand Naoto rubbed his eyes, wondering what time it was. Judging from the grayish light filtering through the window, it was barely dawn. His cell phone with the clock on it was back in his room and he didn't want to disturb Koji-san by getting up. The man seemed to be sleeping especially heavily this morning.

No matter. Naoto was content to hold him as he slept and to remember the night before. How wild and fiery Koji had been, how tenderly yet hungrily he'd made love.

Before Naoto could decide what to do, Koji stirred and lifted his head up. His dark eyes appeared unfocused and he blinked several times before he seemed to realise where he was. "Naoto-san," he murmured. He heaved a deep sigh.

Naoto touched Koji's cheek. "How are you?"

Koji blinked several more times before his head sank deeper into the pillow. "I feel as if my entire body is filled with lead. So tired."

Naoto pressed his lips to Koji's forehead. No fever. Perhaps he was crashing, finally letting himself get the rest his body and soul craved.

"Just rest, Koji-san."

Koji looked up at him. His dark eyes looked heavy with sadness. "Naoto-san."

Naoto cupped his cheek. "Yes?"

A strange look clouded the man's eyes. "I had this dream. About...her." He didn't offer the name but Naoto knew whom he meant. He also recognised the look in Koji's gaze. Guilt.

"It's very erotic," Koji went on. "I've been having it for years."

A shiver passed up Naoto's spine. He knew firsthand how erotic the dream was.

More guilt darkened Koji's eyes. "It's only a dream. I swear. Nothing ever happened between us. Ever. I promise. My father married her not long after my mother died. She was a young woman and so pretty. He wanted someone to take care of me and my sister. She protected me from him. He never loved her." The words seemed to tumble from him, a desperate confession.

Naoto's heart squeezed and he smoothed back Koji's hair. "I wouldn't think anything bad of you if something had happened, Koji-san. You're a good man."

Koji's eyes misted over and Naoto could see the gratitude in them. "Naoto-san...Please...don't tell anyone. I've never told anyone but you."

Naoto pressed a kiss to Koji's forehead. He'd heard men's secrets before, but not one that touched a deep place inside him the way Koji's had. "I won't, I promise. Just rest now, okay?"

Koji nodded. "Thank you." Before Naoto could say, "You're welcome," Koji had fallen back asleep.

Naoto lay awake, listening to Koji breathe. No doubt he should get up and tend to other things while Koji rested, yet couldn't bring himself to leave. As if something would happen to Koji while he slept. As if Koji needed protection.

He just couldn't leave. So when his own eyelids grew heavier, he succumbed...

~~~~~

"Naoto, please, come. I have something important to show you." Lee wasn't smiling. His eyes looked desperate...haunted now, like Koji-san's eyes. Naoto made the comparison even as a shiver raced down his spine. Lee's hand was outstretched, waiting.

Naoto pulled in a deep breath. He had to go. He had to risk it. He reached out, towards Lee's hand. Just as their fingers touched...Naoto began falling...

"Huh!" Naoto's own voice and the jerk of his body woke him. The soft bedding under his back, the daylight filtering into the room brought him slowly from the spiralling terror of falling.

Worried that he'd woken Koji with his cry, he turned.

Koji had rolled away from him and was on the other side of the bed. His eyes were closed, one hand on the pillow by his face. Koji's breathing was soft, a barely there kind of sound. He slept like a man who'd been drugged.

Naoto recognised that kind of sleep, the sleep of grief, of being drained, resting so your very soul could heal. It had happened to him after Lee died. Once the funeral was over, he'd crawled into the bed he'd shared with his lover for years and slept for days, until he needed to help Lecy open the store again.

There was nothing he could do for Koji except to let him rest.

Resisting the urge to kiss Koji's head, Naoto climbed softly from the bed, slipped on his clothes and left the room. He checked back on Koji every hour, only to find him still asleep, which was how he stayed most of the day and into late evening. Only then did Naoto find Koji sitting up in the dark room, just staring ahead, not moving. Before Koji could see him, Naoto slipped away, down to the kitchen and returned with some food and tea for him.

"Naoto-san, what's wrong with me?" Koji sat, propped up against the pillows, watching Naoto pour tea into a cup. Koji's large eyes were sleepy looking and his short hair stuck up at odd angles. Indentations from the sheets had left crease marks on one cheek, the result of having slept the entire day and much of the night.

In a word, Koji-san was adorable.

Naoto cleared his throat and lifted the cup to the other man with both hands.

Koji-san accepted it with both hands and bowed his head in thanks.

Naoto watched him sip, let his gaze drop down to watch Koji's throat work as he swallowed. "I think you're just getting the rest you've needed for a long time."

Koji lowered the cup, eyeing him in that assessing way he'd done the first day when he'd asked Naoto if he was happy. "How do you understand all these things, Naoto-san? I think you're close to my age, but you're so wise."

Naoto chuckled. He couldn't help it. 'Wise' would never have been a word he'd use to describe himself. Then his humour faded. Perhaps now, telling Koji more about his life could be useful to him, rather than a burden.

He leaned against the side of the bed, easing out of his kneeling position. "I don't know. It's just that…well…I've been through it."

Koji sat up a bit straighter, gaze intent. "You have?"

He nodded. "Yes. My partner, Lee, we were together for almost five years and he was murdered. Shot while he was closing his parents' market."

"Naoto-san, no!" Koji's hand shot out and landed on his shoulder.

Naoto covered the other man's hand. It wasn't necessary to tell him the killer had been a yak coming for money Lee owed him. "We wanted to be together for the rest of our lives."

Koji's fingers tightened on his shoulder. "I'm so sorry."

He nodded, acknowledging Koji's obvious heartfelt sympathy. "Thank you." Speaking about it made the memories vivid. He pulled himself together, remembering that he was sharing them to help this man. "Shortly after the funeral, I crashed, just like you did. I slept for days." He looked up at Koji. "I promise you, it does get better. You feel your grief because it's there. You loved someone very much. It's not a bad thing. It's…good to love somebody so much."

Koji was still staring at him. "No wonder you're so…kind."

Naoto looked down. "It's easy to be kind to you, Koji-san." He sat with Koji until the other man had finished the tea and pastries Naoto had brought him. Koji was turning out to have quite a sweet tooth and Naoto had made sure to bring several extra pieces for him. He needed it, the poor guy.

When he'd set the tray outside the door, he returned to the bed, seeing that Koji had moved aside and pulled back the covers.

The un-worded invitation sent a ripple of warmth through Naoto. Stripping off his uniform, he slipped in and gathered Koji against him. He sensed that Koji just wanted to be held...at least for the moment. And he was happy to oblige. Whatever Koji needed.

"Naoto-san?"

"Yes?"

Koji tilted his face up. "How did you know him? If I may ask."

Naoto sighed and smoothed his hand over Koji's hair. "His parents had a market in Little Asia. They were from Beijing originally."

"He was Chinese?"

"Yes." He tensed a second even though Koji's question hadn't sounded hostile. As gentle as Koji seemed to be, you never knew what prejudices a person could harbour, especially in Tokyo where many people still didn't like Chinese.

But Koji only nodded, his look understanding, the way it had been with Ryu earlier. "I see," he said softly. "Please...go on."

Relieved, Naoto took a breath. "I was passing down the sidewalk and saw him. He was unloading crates of vegetables from a truck. So I…helped him." Naoto chuckled. "He caught my eye." He savoured the image of Lee, small and wiry muscles flexing through his thin sleeveless shirt, sweat glistening on his skin. And those eyes. Strange how Naoto had also noticed Lee's eyes in that moment of lust. "Anyway, he thanked me and offered me a job. He was studying at the university and his father was ill so they needed help." He looked down briefly. "It didn't matter to them that I was Japanese. And anyway, I needed a job because I wanted to save up money to move out of my parents' home. It worked out."

Koji rolled to the side and propped on his elbow, looking up. His large gaze was now full of undisguised curiosity. "How did it…happen? I mean, that you were together?"

Of course Koji would want to know such things. Someone as suppressed as Koji needed to know freedom through someone else.

Again, the memories rolled through Naoto's mind. "Well, I was there for a long time, day after day. Lee's father passed away from illness and I helped them a lot. At one point, Lee started to get annoyed with me often and snap at me. He told me I was making mistakes all the time that I wasn't making. At first it got me upset, but I was so taken with him I let it go each time." He laughed softly. "Then one day, after he'd closed the store, we were in the stock room and I dropped a can of something on the floor. He started yelling at me. Really yelling, saying mean things. I started to get angry, so angry I wanted to hit him. But then for some reason I stopped. I just watched him and listened. And then I understood. He wasn't upset about me dropping the can. It was something else. It was…desire. Suppressed desire coming out sideways."

Koji blinked. "You mean he was angry at you because he...*liked* you?"

Naoto smiled. "Yes. That's when I realised it was mutual."

Koji stared at him. "Naoto-san, you don't mind telling me all this?"

"Not at all." Truthfully, it felt good to speak about that special time in his life. He bowed his head. "I'm glad to share it with you, Koji-san." When he looked back up, the other man's gaze had not left his. Naoto remembered Lee's face, the sweat on his brow, the wild look in his eyes, all his sexual energy channelled into yelling, into pretending. "I grasped his shoulders and kissed him. I didn't think about it. I just reacted." The moment came back. The surge of heat through his body just before he grabbed Lee. The touch of their lips. The way Lee had gone silent and fisted Naoto's shirt, pulling their bodies together. Like in a movie or something.

"Wow." Koji glanced away. "That's amazing." He was silent. Emotions seemed to churn across his beautiful face. The man was so readable. Naoto touched his cheek, brushed his thumb along the rounded contour of Koji's cheekbone.

Finally Koji looked back at him. "Naoto-san, wasn't it difficult, hiding all that time?"

Naoto's heart squeezed. "Yes. But actually, we didn't end up hiding for so long. At first, I would bring him around here, to Ni Chome, to a *hattenba* and get a room for a few hours after closing the store. But as time passed, we started sneaking up to his bedroom at night to be together, after his mother had gone to bed. I always left before morning, but then, one night, accidentally, we both fell asleep. His mother found us the next morning." Naoto paused, remembering the way Lee had vaulted from the bed, a sheet wrapped around his waist to hide his nakedness and fallen to his knees in front of Lecy in terror. He described the scene for Koji whose eyes widened more than Naoto imagined eyes could. "She was…to our shock…very accepting, as if she'd somehow known all along what had been going on." He shrugged. "Maybe she did. But it didn't matter. We were free to be together. Not long after that, I moved in there with them. And we were happy…until…"

He fell silent and looked down. A hand covered his, making him peer back up. Koji's eyes were misted and what appeared swirls of emotion, sadness, surprise, envy, sympathy, passed through them. "That's amazing," he said again, as if there were no other word that could possibly describe Naoto's story. "I can't believe Lee's mother."

Naoto nodded. "She's like a mother to me. I went to see her also today, before my parents. We're close." Then he realised what he'd said. "I'm sorry, Koji-san. I didn't think."

But Koji squeezed his hand. "Please, don't be sorry. I'm…honoured that you told me such important things." He sat up and bowed, so deeply his face almost touched the bedding. When he straightened, he wore the same churning look.

Without thinking, Naoto reached out and pulled Koji to him. Until then, he hadn't felt his tension, his worry that Koji would judge him. But Koji's arms were around him too and he felt one hand smooth along the fall of his hair down his back. "Thank you, Koji-san."

He felt the answering caress on his hair, which he'd taken to wearing loose because he knew it brought the other man pleasure.

"Naoto-san?"

"Yes?"

"May I ask you another question? If...it's all right."

"Of course. Please ask." Naoto found himself wanting to share so much with Koji. Koji's willing acceptance was irresistibly sweet.

"After...Lee...died, did you come here?"

Naoto took a deep breath. "Well, not exactly. After Lee's death, I wanted to take revenge on whoever killed him. I was pretty sure it had been a *yakuza* because a long time ago when Lee's father was ill, Lee had borrowed money from one of them. Lee's mother began to rent the store shortly afterwards to a Korean family. They ran the place and so neither of us worked there anymore. I had nothing but time on my hands to plan revenge." He paused. "I'm not proud of having felt that way."

Koji's hand closed over his. "It's certainly understandable that you did, though, Naoto-san."

Koji's words sent a wave of affection through him, softening the ache. "Thank you," he murmured. "Kikuchiya felt the same way. When our paths crossed, he saw something in me and asked me to come here." Naoto decided to skip the psychic part and went on. "Kiku begged me not to take revenge and risk getting myself killed. I've been here ever since. This is my home now."

Koji sighed and Naoto felt the other man sag a bit in his arms. Koji-san was still exhausted and Naoto felt a spike of guilt for keeping him up. Gently he pulled back. "Koji-san, I think you should rest some more. You've been through a lot." He eased the slimmer man back down and pulled up the covers.

"Naoto-san, I'm relieved that Kikuchiya brought you here. I would...never have met you."

Naoto stared at him. Truly, that was one of the kindest things anyone had ever said to him. "Thank you, Koji-san. I...I'm honoured. And I feel the same way."

"Are you leaving now?" There was a note of worry in Koji's voice.

"Of course not." Naoto pulled the covers over them and settled in, gathering Koji back against him as he had before Koji questioned him. "Are you comfortable, Koji-san?"

"Yes, very."

A pleasant shiver passed through Naoto. There seemed to be a double meaning in the statement. At least what he *hoped* was a double meaning.

"Just rest now," he said to Koji and lay quietly with the other man's solid warmth against his. No, Koji didn't have to worry about him getting up and leaving. Not at all.

If he'd had what he wanted, he'd hold Koji for a very long time.

Chapter Nine

On Sunday morning, Koji stared at his reflection in the bathroom mirror. The man who looked back at him was not the same man who'd come to the White Tiger nearly a week ago. The dark circles under his eyes had faded. He'd put on a bit of weight and his complexion had colour in it now.

All thanks to Naoto.

The last few days had been like a kind of heaven, not that the first few days hadn't been either. After he'd arisen from his crash of sleep, Naoto had spent plenty of time lounging around with him, pleasuring him, bathing him, as well as posing for a million drawings. Naoto had told him much more about this place and about the Way of the White Tiger, taking plenty of time to show him all the techniques of caressing, licking, sucking and kissing, the path taught a practitioner. They'd also soaked in the bath and gone to Ryu's fight the night before, holding hands in the cab back to the White Tiger, then celebrating Ryu's win with champagne.

There was truly something magical about Naoto and about this place. He'd thought he was just going to stay at a hotel to relax. The White Tiger was the first place Koji had ever felt really comfortable and free. The thought of leaving and go back to the world made his heart ache.

Sadly, there was nothing he could do about it. He had to go back to his life.

With a sigh, he went back into the bedroom. His heart thumped when he saw the tissue paper wrapped gift he'd bought for Naoto. Of course, he'd put a generous gratuity in the discreet envelope provided, but that couldn't possibly be enough. Nothing he could give or do would repay Naoto's kindness to him this week. Naoto had probably saved his life.

Sinking down onto the bed, he picked up the gift and stared down at it.

"Koji-san?" Naoto said from the other side of the door, "It's me."

Koji rose. "Come in." His heart sped up as Naoto slid back the door and walked in.

The larger man's eyes looked distinctly sad even though he wore a smile. "I came to help you pack your things."

"No need. I did it a minute ago. Would you like to sit down?" He gestured to the bed, making himself aware of the object in his hand. He had to give Naoto the gift now, before he lost his nerve. "This is for you."

Naoto's eyes widened. "A gift?"

"Yes." Koji held it out with both hands.

"Koji-san, that was so kind of you." Naoto accepted it and smiled at him. "Should I open it now?"

Koji's cheeks burned. What would Naoto think when he saw it? He had to know. After he left the White Tiger, he might never see Naoto again. "If you'd like."

Naoto sank to a kneeling position and Koji sat in front of him on the bed. Koji watched Naoto's thick fingers pull at the tape on the tissue paper and unwrap the item. He held it up, staring. His eyes misted over at the white jade tiger, meticulously carved in a running position. "Koji-san, it's beautiful." He leaned over and pressed a kiss to Koji's lips.

Koji closed his eyes, savoured the last velvety touch he might ever have of Naoto's kiss.

"You didn't have to do this."

"I wanted to, Naoto-san. This has been the best week of my life, thanks to you."

Naoto looked down. "I'm honoured, Koji-san. For myself, I've not had such a nice week since Lee was alive." He cleared his throat in a way that made Koji sense he was nervous. "Koji-san, um, you're always welcome here."

Koji's gut tightened. So many times over the last few days he'd thought about coming back. Then he thought of his family and knew he couldn't. Koji laced his fingers with Naoto's. He so didn't want to leave, but really, what else could he do? "Thank you," he murmured. He looked into Naoto's eyes just as an image of his father rose in his mind. His heart jumped. "I want to come back here and see you, more than anything, but I...have...family pressures." His father had recently started in on him about finding a woman. "If I can't come, it's not because of you."

Naoto's fingers tightened on his. "I understand."

"But I pray you'll let me return your kindness if it's ever needed." It was the best he could do, as paltry as it was. Naoto had probably saved his life.

A look of sadness passed through Naoto's eyes. Silently, he leaned forward and embraced Koji. Koji melted against him. If there was anything better than being in Naoto's arms, he couldn't imagine what it was. *I love you.* The words hovered on his lips, made him tremble. He could never say them. And besides, how was it possible? He'd known the man barely a week.

When Naoto pulled away, he furrowed his brow. "Are you all right, Koji-san?"

He nodded. "I have to get going. I'm due at my sister's house soon." He sighed.

Naoto cupped the back of his neck and kissed him. His lips lingered against Koji's for several sweet moments. Then he gently released Koji. "I'll walk you down."

~~~~~

"Koji, is that you?" Gina's voice echoed from within as it did every Sunday night when he came for supper.

Koji set down his gym bag and slipped off his shoes. "Yes. I'll be right in."

"All right."

His heartbeat pounded. Carefully he set his drawing pad underneath his gym bag. Just looking at the cover reminded him of his drawings of Naoto on the pages within. Naoto's bulging muscles. Naoto's long sleek hair. His kind eyes. And erotic touch.

A pang shot through Koji's chest. The sensation felt as if it travelled into his throat and caught there, making it difficult to swallow. Slowly, he went up the steps into the main part of the house and went down the polished hallway to the dining room.

And froze.

His stomach tightened past the point of pain. Bad enough his father sat at his usual place.

Etsu, Gina's friend from high school, was there. Etsu, who Gina used to tell him all the time had a mad crush on him all through school. Etsu, whom, Gina had made a point of telling him not long ago, had gotten divorced recently and was moving back to Tokyo from Kyoto where she'd been for several years. *Kuso*, he'd been in such a fog then and hadn't registered the pointed sound in Gina's voice when she'd mentioned that. No mystery why Etsu was here.

"Koji!" Gina shuffled up to him and kissed his cheek. She pulled back and drew Koji into the room. "Look who's here. She just moved back to Tokyo. Remember I told you last week at supper she'd be here?"

Koji stared. Tiny lights danced in his eyes now, but not the pleasant ones he'd seen when Naoto was making love to him. "Of course. He...hello." Slowly, he bowed, barely straightening before Gina tugged him to a seat. Shit, of course she was putting him next to Etsu.

Etsu turned to him, smiling. She was older now, of course, at twenty-seven, but still as pretty. And she had long hair. "How've you been, Koji?"

He cleared his throat and pulled in his chair. If his heart raced any harder he feared he'd pass out into his soup. "Good. And you?" He glanced at her then down at his place, where a bowl of miso soup steamed up towards him.

"Hello, Koji."

Koji looked up at the sound of his father's voice at the foot of the table. "Hi, Dad." It was getting worse each second. The only modicum of relief was his brother-in-law's presence. Jiro had sympathised with him more than once over a beer about Gina's and her father's insistence on getting Koji married. Not that Jiro hated marriage, but he always made a point of telling Koji that his single status wasn't a bad thing *at all*. One glance at his brother-in-law confirmed the man's support. Jiro gave him a quick wink then took a sip of his beer.

Gina finished serving and sat down. "So, Koji, you seem better today. Did you work less this week?" She turned to Etsu. "Koji works so hard."

Etsu nodded but didn't say anything. The soft lighting in the room shone on her hair. Like Naoto's hair.

Heart aching, Koji picked up his spoon, habitually waiting for his father to take the first taste of soup before he tried to eat. "I…had a vacation."

"Oh, wonderful! Where did you go? I didn't even know."

Koji glanced again at Jiro. Only his brother-in-law's sympathetic look enabled him to say anything. "To…the Crown. The company reserves rooms there. They make you rest." He heard his father's slurping sound and then took a spoonful of his own soup.

"I'm glad, Koji. I was concerned about you." Gina smiled, looking all around before tasting her soup. She set her spoon down and patted at her lips with her napkin. "Etsu's very glad to be back in Tokyo, aren't you, Ei-chan?"

Koji's stomach tightened several more notches. Gina had always been quite a little busybody and she was putting that delightful quality to full use now.

"Yes, I am. There's so much more culture here, and well, the publishing industry opportunities are better."

"Koji, Etsu is a publisher. Well…" she giggled. "She's a big fish in a company that publishes *manga*, of all types, right?"

Koji's cheeks burned. His mind flew to the drawings in his pad. Naoto's naked body, every single, delicious inch of him in pencil. If they all only saw those…

"Yes, that's right." Etsu glanced shyly at Koji, as if to see whether he was impressed or not, then concentrated on her soup. He didn't know how she interpreted the way he looked away from her and down, as if he'd found a frog swimming in his soup bowl and needed to study it.

When he dared a look back up, Gina's cheeks darkened and her eyes went sheepish. She looked quickly at their father, as if just realising she'd revealed Koji's secret adolescent passion. Of course, that was because her snooping into her brother's room had revealed all his hidden *manga*. At least she'd never told on him. Though Shizuko would have defended him anyway.

Koji forced himself to eat and not appear as miserable as he felt. After all, the sooner they finished, the sooner he could escape. He endured Gina's constant attempts to engage them in conversation until all their plates were empty and Koji knew she could no longer put off going into the kitchen. Fortunately, when she did, Etsu went with her, carrying some empty plates.

Unfortunately, Koji's father remained where he was and pinned Koji with a look. "Etsu's a nice girl," he said, sitting back and putting his napkin on the table.

Koji looked down. In his lap, he gripped his napkin in both fists. It went without saying what would come next.

"Why don't you offer to take her out?"

"Dad," Jiro said gently, "Koji's just getting back from vacation. Maybe he needs some time to get back to his routine."

Koji gave his brother-in-law a grateful glance.

"Koji is nearly thirty. He's had enough time for a routine." His father shifted and Koji saw the older man turn fully to him. "Koji, I don't know what goes on in your head aside from work. No one *only* works. But it's time to do the other important things you must do with your life."

Koji looked up, hating the way he shivered inside. He always had. Such a contrast to how he'd felt only hours ago in Naoto's arms. To how he'd felt the entire week with him at the White Tiger. As if the hotel had been his home and Naoto his real lover.

His father glanced towards the kitchen and then leaned in closer, lowering his voice. "You think I don't know how much time you spent doodling as a kid," he went on. "But I know it was a hell of a lot more time than you spent on the violin. Who knows how great you could really have been had you stayed with it." He shook his head. "Your stepmother was soft on you. I should have never allowed her to talk me out of forbidding you to draw." He fixed Koji with a look, a look so hard it sent a shiver right down Koji's spine. "You can at least do *this*."

Koji swallowed, fighting back the urge to jump up and run out. Was that edge in his father's voice telling him he knew the truth about Shizuko? Or was Koji imagining it through his guilty conscience? His gut tightened and he wiped his palms on his jeans, resisting the urge to look at Jiro. Aside from a sympathetic look, there was nothing the man could really do for him.

A vision of Shizuko rose in his mind, a memory. He'd come home from the dorm during college to have dinner with them. No one else was home yet but Shizuko. She'd been standing at the living room window, staring down. When he walked in, she'd turned and smiled at him, her eyes sadder than when she watched the *sakura* blossoms fall. He'd gone and stood next to her. What had possessed him in that moment to put an arm across her shoulder he never knew. It was something he never dared. And then he knew why. She'd leaned into him just a bit, enough for him to sense everything she felt...

Another pang of guilt stabbed Koji and he nodded slowly. "All right, Dad."

~~~~~

Naoto stared up into the darkness of his room. With his hands clasped behind his head, he sighed for the thousandth time. Was this sleepless, restless empty feeling what he had to look forward to every night now?

So many nights after Lee died, he'd tossed and turned, aching for the warm solidity of Lee's body against his, the feel of the smaller man in his arms. Only in the last year or so had he begun to reconcile the aloneness and actually start to feel okay about the empty space in the bed beside him.

Not now. Not after sharing a bed with Koji. Koji's body moulded to his, the warmth of Koji's smooth skin and hardness of muscle, Koji's soft breathing, the scent of his hair, the way he blinked when he first opened his eyes in the morning and then smiled at Naoto as he came more awake…

The more he remembered these things, the more he ached for them.

Even though the week had been about Koji's need for comfort and not his, Naoto had found comfort with the other man, comfort he'd thought he didn't need anymore. Not the first time he was wrong about something important.

Was it really only a few hours since Koji had left the White Tiger?

The late night city sounds filtered through the window opened a crack to let in the balmy spring air. The alleyway his window let out on was removed enough from the traffic fumes to allow fresh air in.

Another sigh and Naoto turned on his side, crumpling up the covers around him.

That's when he heard the voice.

"Suzuki-san, *nanitozo! Nanitozo!*"

Naoto sat bolt upright.

Ryu. He was having one of his post-traumatic episodes. Even though Suzuki's violation had happened nearly ten years ago, Ryu sometimes lived it out in the middle of the night through his subconscious, the way Koji had lived out his inner pain.

"Please, Suzuki-san! I promise, I won't tell your father. Please, let me go!"

At the continued breathless, desperate sounding pleas Naoto threw back the covers and vaulted from his bed. Sliding back his door, he jogged down to Ryu's door and opened it just enough to see in.

He'd expected Kiku to be there. Kiku had a method of bringing Ryu back from the visions, something he'd told Naoto about in absolute confidence just in case Naoto was ever there and he wasn't.

Another second and Naoto realised Kiku wasn't coming. He was probably downstairs, entertaining a late night guest or sharing the bath with Quan Chan.

Slipping into the room, Naoto pushed the *soji* closed and approached Ryu's bed. Ryu's head was thrashing back and forth and his covers were thrown back, revealing his tattooed body wearing only a pair of body hugging boxer briefs, in a prone position, as if he were being restrained.

Naoto's blood went cold.

Ryu was reliving what had happened to him.

"Ryu, it's okay," he whispered. "I'm going to keep them away from you."

Ryu didn't seem to hear him. His pleas to Suzuki continued to tumble from him in fevered whispers.

Naoto slid into the bed next to him, a hand on Ryu's shoulder. Gently, he bid Ryu onto his side. To his surprise, Ryu turned easily, even though he was still begging Suzuki to go away. Naoto moulded his body to Ryu's back and held him close, being careful of Ryu's bruises from his fight the night before. No doubt the guy was still stiff and sore. In spite of that, Ryu's wiry form trembled in his arms and his back heaved against Naoto's chest. "I'm keeping them away, Ryu. They're gone. They can't hurt you now." Without thinking, he reached up and caressed Ryu's hair. "You're safe, Ryu," he murmured.

Ryu let out a sharp breath, as if his consciousness had shifted. "It hurts so much."

Naoto held him a bit tighter. Tears stung in his own eyes. He couldn't imagine what it had been like for Ryu in the moment it happened. Another gentle person like Koji who'd been preyed on by an abusive prick. Thank God Kiku had been there at the time. He'd been too late to prevent the crime, but at least he'd been able to comfort him. "I know it hurts," he whispered.

The smaller man let out several short, sharp breaths and then grew calmer. His shivering died down and his breathing grew normal. Soon, Naoto realised, Ryu had fallen back asleep.

Just to be sure, he stayed a little while, his hand still moving over Ryu's hair. With the crisis past, Naoto became aware of how Ryu felt in his arms. His physique was compact, wiry, like Lee's had been, and Ryu was about the same size. Holding Ryu this way increased the ache he'd felt since Koji left. Ryu was his good friend, but it wasn't the same. Ryu wasn't Lee.

And he wasn't Koji.

When more time had passed and Ryu continued to sleep quietly, Naoto released him and carefully slid out of the bed. He pulled the covers over Ryu and padded out of the room. Ryu didn't remember these episodes in the morning, but if he happened to remember this one, he'd probably be embarrassed and it was better if Naoto wasn't there.

Back in his bed, Naoto found himself staring up at the ceiling once again. For a second, he almost reached for his cell phone, then resisted. Better not to talk to Koji. Hearing his voice would only make it worse. And even if Koji responded positively, it wouldn't be fair to him to pursue a relationship when Lee would always be there in the background, haunting his dreams, beckoning to him, making him feel guilty for falling in love with someone else.

Naoto sighed again. Well, if he never saw Koji-san again, at least they'd had this week together.

Small comfort in the wee hours as he stared at the dark ceiling above his head, listening to the sounds of the city filter through the open window.

Chapter Ten

Monday morning. Nine o'clock. Nothing had changed. The office was exactly the same.

Koji walked down the centre aisle that separated the sea of desks. Everyone who was already there greeted him, eyes a bit wider than usual, before they looked back down at their work. Well, after leaving between two security guards days before, it was no wonder they were surprised to see him there.

Hiru wasn't at his desk. He was either in the men's room or in the break room, flirting with whichever female co-worker happened to be in there.

Reaching his own desk, Koji set down his briefcase and turned on his monitor. Why he was so tense, looking for all the devastating changes that had occurred in his absence, he didn't know. The place was exactly as he'd left it. His desk was exactly as he'd left it. Considerate co-workers hadn't even put order to the piles of paper around his keyboard or replaced the caps on his pens. Life seemed to have moved right along while he was at the White Tiger.

Come to think of it, life had always moved along, with or without him. He'd just been too busy working to notice.

What had he expected?

Looking up, he saw Tomoko at her desk, talking on the phone. She smiled and waved when their gazes met.

He waved back and then turned his attention to the computer screen.

"Hey, Koji."

Koji looked up at the sound of Hiru's voice. It was really good to see a friendly face. "Hey, how are you?"

The chubby man was grinning down at him. "Not as good as you, Koje. *Someone* at that *ryokan* breathed life back into you. You look like a new man."

An image of Naoto, wet from the shower, lathering his back with a washcloth flashed in his mind and Koji's cheeks burned. He shuffled a few papers into a pile. "Yeah, I guess you could say that."

"You'll have to bring me to this place on the next break."

His cheeks felt even warmer as he pictured Hiru being led by the hand by one of the attendants at the White Tiger. "Uh, I don't think you'd like it, Hiru."

Hiru frowned at him. "Why not?"

Koji shrugged. The casual gesture belied the churning in his middle. "I know you. Trust me. They're not your type."

"Okay. If you say so. But I want to hear about it anyway. How about I take you to lunch and you can tell me all about your revival?"

Koji grinned in spite of himself. Maybe it was time to tell his friend the truth. If they were such good friends, it shouldn't matter. Besides, after a week spent in such openness, he didn't think he could bear the torture of being out in the world and always keeping to the superficial, *safe* layer. He had to tell *someone*. Might as well be someone who called himself a friend. "Okay, sounds good."

Hiru went back to his desk and Koji stared at the monitor. Life really had a wicked sense of humour sometimes. Here he was, in love with a man he couldn't be with, and had a date for Friday night with a beautiful woman he had absolutely no romantic interest in whatsoever. And there was Hiru, a decent, hard-working guy who had lost a girlfriend he'd adored back in college when they'd been in a car accident. Hiru would probably really appreciate another chance at romance with a woman like Etsu. It was all so fucked up.

For a second, he entertained the idea of setting Hiru up with Etsu. But just as quickly dismissed it. It didn't seem right to pawn her off because he wasn't interested. She was a human being after all.

He glanced at Hiru who was now bent over his keyboard, tapping away. His heart lurched at the thought of telling Hiru about Naoto. But at least he'd get to talk about him.

Maybe talking about Naoto would help get the man out of his system. After all, it was ridiculous to think of a future based on a few days of bliss. The circumstances were so controlled, so contrived. He had to remember that Naoto was trained to comfort guys like him. He couldn't let himself think that the way Naoto had looked at him and touched him was unique to him. No way.

Maybe if he talked enough about Naoto, he could talk himself out of how in love with the man he was.

~~~~~

Tuesday...

"Naoto, please, come here." Lee's huge, soulful eyes beckoned him with a force all their own. Behind him, the darkness of the hallway looked so deep and inky black, Naoto was sure it could swallow them both up forever.

'Lee, we shouldn't go in there. It's so dark. Something bad will happen.' Naoto stared at him, praying silently he'd change his

mind. But he knew how stubborn Lee was. He'd always been so stubborn. Though Naoto was physically larger and stronger, Lee's will had far greater strength than Naoto's brawn. And they both knew it.

Lee stared at him a moment longer, then turned, heading towards the blackness.

Naoto lunged forward, grabbed at the sleeve of Lee's jean jacket, the one he wore all the time, but missed. Lee was already fading into the dark. "Lee! No!" Naoto took off after him, but his feet stuck on the floor. Losing his balance he fell forward…

Naoto sat bolt upright. His chest heaved and sweat poured over him. Only the daylight coming through his window told his fevered mind that he'd been dreaming. Clutching both hands into his hair, he raised his knees and rested his elbows on them until his breathing calmed.

Finally, he threw back the covers and swung his legs over the edge. His eye fell on the bedside photograph. He picked it up as he did so many mornings after waking from that dream and stared at Lee's face. "What are you trying to tell me?" he whispered.

Then he sighed and put the picture back. No use asking. He asked all the time, but had never gotten an answer. Why he expected this time would be different…

Rising, he made the bed and dressed. Later today he would go visit Lecy, but would spend the morning after breakfast meditating and helping with the usual hotel chores.

At least he didn't have a guest to attend to right now. Kiku-sensei was considerate about that, giving him time away from physical contact with guests. Naoto didn't see how he'd be able to attend to anyone else now, at least in a giving frame of mind. How could you wait on a guest wholeheartedly, bring him erotic pleasure and harvest yang force when you felt a hole blown through your middle?

Before leaving the room, Naoto's gaze fell on the white jade tiger. He went to the shelf and picked it up, rubbed the pad of his thumb along the carved surface. So beautiful, the attention to detail. It couldn't have been cheap. And it had been so thoughtful. So...Koji-san.

He sighed and set it down on the shelf. It would have been easier if Naoto hadn't felt what was behind the gift.

Well, at least what he'd *sensed* was behind the gift. It he was right, then Koji was feeling the same thing he was.

And neither of them could say a damn word about it.

~~~~~

The moment Naoto walked into Lecy's apartment, his heart thumped. Something wasn't right.

Lecy's drawn face was chalky looking and her shoulders hunched over.

"Lecy, what's wrong? Are you ill?" Naoto rushed to her, his hands on her shoulders. That's when he saw it. In her hand was an envelope.

"I'm fine, Naoto." She lifted it between them. He looked at her, noting how much Lee had resembled her in his sharp cheekbones and delicate lips. And how much she'd aged in the last three years. "I'm so sorry."

A cold sweat erupted in his armpits. "What is this?"

"I feel terrible," she said. "I only found it a few minutes ago."

Naoto looked at the envelope. *To Naoto* it said in Lee's handwriting. His heartbeat sped up.

"It must have blown behind the dresser long ago when you and Lee kept the window open all the time. I...finally worked up the courage to go back in there, to clean. I'm so sorry, Naoto. He must have meant for you to have it so much sooner." She put a hand on his arm and drew him in, towards the kitchen. "Come, have some tea. You can sit down to read it."

"Yes, thank you." Naoto let the older woman lead him to a chair at the table. He sank down down, grateful for the support he was now missing from his knees. When Lee had been alive, the three of them had spent quite a bit of time at this table, eating her cooking, laughing, enjoying each other's company. Hands shaking, he tore open the envelope and pulled out the piece of folded paper.

Dearest Naoto – Now that I'm gone, I wanted you to know the truth.

Nande? Naoto pulled in a sharp breath. He glanced over his shoulder. Lecy was at the stove, her back to him, filling a teapot from the kettle. Heart racing, he turned back and re-read that first line. What the fuck? He almost crumpled the note in his fist, but a mere glance at Lee's handwriting, words done by Lee's own hand, urged him on.

At the time of writing this letter, I've recently gotten some test results from the doctor I couldn't bring myself to tell you about. Remember that time I fell down? We thought I must have tripped, but it was something else. A cancerous tumour on my spine. The doctors told me they could operate on it, and that I would probably live, but I would be paralyzed for the rest of my life, at least from the chest down. If I didn't operate, I would be completely paralysed within months and blind as well. Either way, the beautiful life we had together was over.

I couldn't tell you at the time because I knew if I did, how you'd react. You (and my mother) would have wanted to take care of me. That would have meant a lifetime of feeding me and cleaning up after me, and for you, not even the pleasure of sex. It would have been a living nightmare for all of us and I just couldn't do that to anyone, especially you, Naoto, the love of my life.

My dear love, obviously since you're reading this, I'm gone and the way that I died was not an accident, not a cold-blooded murder. I arranged for it myself at a time I knew you wouldn't be there. It would be quick, hopefully painless as possible and was something I couldn't do myself, the physical coward that I am. Even by the time my death drew close, my vision was blurring and I could feel my strength draining rapidly.

Please, Naoto, don't hate me for this. I had the best life possible because you were in it and I only want you to be happy. I pray that you'll honour my last request of you to love someone if you find someone special. Don't do the one thing that I tried to prevent through dying. Love, forever, Lee

"Naoto, are you all right?"

The concern in Lecy's voice made him realise how hard he was breathing, and the way his hands clutched the piece of paper, practically crumpling it. He looked up, into her face etched in worry lines. Their gazes locked and he saw her eyes mist. She'd already suffered so much, losing her husband and then her son. He couldn't give her another moment's suffering by not telling her the truth. If he didn't, she'd know he was lying and that would torment her.

Rising from his chair, he dropped to his knees in front of her and put the paper in her lap. He bowed his head as she picked it up and sensed her churning emotions as she read it.

Steam curled from the teapot, ignored, and Naoto heard the woman's breathing grow harsh. Her hand, note clutched in it, dropped to her lap. "Oh, my god. Oh my god. My son."

Naoto grabbed her hand and pushed his forehead to it. His own emotions churned, his heart ached. How could Lee not have let them choose?

Lecy sobbed quietly for what felt a long time then quieted. In the moment that followed, Naoto felt a soft hand on his hair, caressing it. "It's all right, Naoto." Her hand moved gently over his hair, so sweet, so motherly. Strangely, her touch felt calm. "This is better. You'll see."

The serenity in her voice made him look up. Though her dark eyes shimmered with tears, she smiled. "I love you as my own son," she said.

Tears stung in Naoto's eyes. "Thank you." He bowed his head and she resumed her soft caress. "Naoto, I want to leave you this apartment. I hope you'll let me."

Naoto looked up at her. "Thank you. Of course I'll let you." He certainly wasn't in need of a place to live, but he understood perfectly her reasons and wouldn't have refused her gift.

A tiny smile played at the corners of her lips and she continued to look at him, her hand resting on his head.

Lightly, he grasped her wrist and held her hand to his cheek. He loved her so much. "Are you all right?" he asked.

She nodded. "Yes, I am." Her gaze seemed to study his. "Thank you for letting me read that note."

"Of course." Naoto's heart squeezed painfully then.

"Naoto." She squeezed his hand. "The heart is made to love. But it doesn't mean that the love we had for Lee isn't there too. It always will be."

He nodded. "There is a part of me that will never stop missing him."

"I know. I really do know."

The grief washed over him, seemed too much to bear in that moment. The second he closed his eyes, he saw someone else's face in his mind. Big sweet eyes, shy smile. So much like Lee's, yet different.

And alive.

The only person he wanted to see right now, to hold in his arms.

I hope you'll let me repay your kindness, Naoto-san, Koji had said.

Naoto thought of the jade tiger on his shelf. That gift had been more than a polite gesture, hadn't it? A symbol of feelings that couldn't be expressed openly? People in Japan often invited a person over to visit, but they didn't mean it. It was polite.

But Koji had meant his words, hadn't he?

Naoto sighed against Lecy's hand. He lifted his face and pressed a kiss onto her skin before releasing her. His heart was pounding, his body burned with a need only one person could soothe. He needed to leave yet he didn't want her to be alone.

As if reading his mind, Lecy patted his hand and stood up. "Mr. Park is coming up to have supper with me in a little while. You're welcome to stay, but I think you have somewhere to go."

"Yes."

"Good. You'll come back soon, I hope."

He worked his lips into a smile. "Of course I will." He squeezed her hand gently. "Thank you, Lecy. For everything."

She returned his smile and then rose. When they were both standing, she pulled him into an embrace.

~~~~~

Koji's heart jumped the second he saw the caller's name on his cell phone. He pressed the button and turned away from the computer screen. Thankfully, the hospital administrator had left his office for the moment.

Hand shaking he held the phone to his ear. He hadn't expected this call. "*Moshi moshi*. Naoto, hi." His heart beat so fast his voice came out as breathless.

"Koji-san, is it all right that I called you?" Naoto's voice trembled with a choked sound. Had he been crying?

Koji hunched over the phone, as if that gave him more privacy. "Of course, Naoto-san. Are you all right?"

"No. I...hoped...to see you." A sniffling sound came through. Damn, Naoto *was* crying.

If Naoto hadn't sounded so upset, Koji would have felt joy burst through him. He stood up quickly from the swivel chair. "Yes, definitely. I'm just finishing up in the hospital. Wh...where are you?"

"Little Asia. At Lee's mother's."

Koji's heart leaped. Sad or not, he'd thought of nothing and no one else for the last forty-eight hours but Naoto. Well, mostly Naoto. He'd also thought quite a bit about the date he'd agreed to take Etsu on this coming Friday. He could deal with that later. "That's not far. Can you meet me in front of the hospital? Meiji Memorial. Main entrance. I'll be there and we can go to my apartment. How's that?"

"Good, Koji-san. I'll be there in twenty minutes."

"See you then."

"Koji-san?"

"Yes?" In the background he heard cars going past and people's voices, and pictured Naoto somewhere on a busy sidewalk in Shin-Okubo, walking past Korean groceries and Vietnamese take-outs.

"Thank you."

Koji frowned. Naoto sounded so sad. "You're welcome. I'm going to wait for you outside."

"Okay. Bye."

Heart pounding, Koji turned back to the computer and exited the program he'd been working on. The system was running smoothly so he packed up his briefcase and made his way to the main entrance of the hospital where he spent the time walking back and forth on the sidewalk in front of the doors, watching for Naoto and wondering what had happened to him in two days to upset him so badly.

He spotted Naoto immediately. Tall and broad, with that long hair, Naoto stood out in the crowd of people bustling past. "Naoto-san!" Koji went towards him, working on putting one foot in front of the other so he wouldn't fall flat on the sidewalk. Looking at Naoto, white T-shirt hugging his thick muscles, long hair loose about his shoulders, made his legs feel as if they were made of noodles instead of flesh and bone.

Up close, however, Koji forgot his lust, alarmed by the redness of the other man's eyes and the lines around his mouth. A cloud seemed to hover around Naoto, shadowing the leap of joy every cell in Koji's body felt as seeing him.

"Naoto-san." Without thinking, he reached out and clasped Naoto's arm. His fingertips closed over hard muscle, warm and thick underneath the thin layer of cotton. "Come with me, okay?"

Wordlessly, Naoto nodded, letting Koji lead him like a child.

"Koji-san, thank you so much for this," he heard Naoto say after several moments of walking. The larger man sounded lost and frightened.

Koji looked at his profile as they went along. "There's nothing to thank me for. I was glad you called me."

"You…were?" Naoto sounded surprised.

"Of course." Koji looked away again and cleared his throat. "I've…missed you." Even though revealing the truth to Hiru and Hiru's calm acceptance had relieved his loneliness somewhat, it hadn't made him stop missing Naoto.

"You have?"

Koji met his eyes once more. Emotions swirled within him as the two gazed at each other.

He was jostled by someone on the street. "Oh, excuse me." Any more words would have to wait until they reached his apartment.

He concentrated on getting Naoto to his building, which was, thankfully only a few blocks away.

The questions whirled in his mind. What the hell had happened to upset Naoto so? And how was he going to help him? He'd never directly helped anyone like that in his life, the way Naoto had done for him last week.

Koji didn't speak again the entire walk and Naoto didn't seem inclined to say anything else. He led Naoto through the front entrance and up the three flights of stairs to his apartment. "It's a mess, I'm sorry," he said as he opened the door. Damn! He'd never imagined that Naoto would be here to see his place. No one ever did except for Hiru occasionally, and his friend was a bigger slob than he was so Koji never cared.

"It's all right, Koji-san," Naoto said as he slipped off his sandals. "I only wanted to see *you*. I don't care about anything else."

But Koji threw down his briefcase, kicked off his shoes and rushed ahead to clear his drawings off the small sofa. Not only wasn't there space to sit, but he realised at the last second that Naoto would see certain things…

"Make yourself comfortable." Koji piled up the papers and sat them by his stacks of violin sheet music on the surface of his desk just behind the sofa. He wanted to go about hiding them, but in his cubby hole of an apartment, that would just be too obvious.

"You've been drawing some more, Koji-san?" Naoto had sat down and was looking up at him. The look in his eyes did not reveal whether he'd seen the content of the drawings.

Koji's heart lurched as he came around to the front of the sofa. "Huh? Oh, a bit."

Naoto nodded, a faint smile on his lips that did not reach his eyes. "That's very good. I'm glad. You're an artist."

He bowed his head. "Th…thank you, Naoto-san." When Naoto didn't answer, Koji searched his mind for the next step. "I'll get you some tea, if you'd like." He turned towards the kitchen.

Naoto caught his wrist. His eyes were pleading up. "No, thank you. Please… just stay here?" A gentle tug made Koji realise Naoto wanted him to sit.

"Of course." Koji sank down next to Naoto, just close enough that his knee almost touched Naoto's.

As soon as he did, Naoto slipped his hand around so that their fingers laced.

Koji nearly shivered with the warm pleasure. Damn, he'd missed that feeling so much! The longest two days of his life. "Naoto-san—"

"Just Naoto. Please?" Naoto's dark eyes were misted over. "I want to think of you as a friend. Is that all right?"

Koji's heart flipped over. It was more than okay. "Perfectly all right. I...want to think the same way." He looked down, mind swirling. "You don't have to tell me anything...if you don't want, Naoto. We can just sit here."

"No."

Koji's gaze whipped up at the seriousness of the word.

Naoto's eyes were misted. "I could never have come to you if this happened while you were my guest," he said softly. "A guest should never be burdened with another's problems."

Something about that made Koji's heart squeeze. "It's not that way with friends," he murmured.

The other man nodded and his hand tightened a tiny bit around Koji's, as if gathering strength from him through touch. "It was a lot just to tell you at the time that my partner had died." He paused and his bottom lip trembled slightly. "He was murdered...I'd thought. Shot down three years ago in his parents' store in Shin-Okubo. I thought it was the *yakuza* he'd borrowed money from to pay his father's hospital bills."

Naoto heaved a deep breath. "Today, when I visited his mother, she'd found this..." He paused and pulled a crumpled-looking paper from his jeans pocket. "She hadn't gone into his room all this time and today, when she did, she found this note. He'd written it to me, but it had fallen behind some furniture and I never saw it. Until now." Naoto held the paper out. "I can't say anymore. But this will tell you what happened."

Koji pulled in a breath. "Are you sure?"

"Yes. Positive."

Wordlessly, Koji took the paper. Naoto released his other hand so he could unfold it and then read.

Naoto watched Koji's face as he read Lee's letter. He could tell the moment Koji read the part about Lee's planned murder.

Koji looked up at him, his large beautiful eyes widened in his customary way and the golden skin of his face paled.

"Naoto," he breathed. "Oh no." He sank back, letter loosely in his hands, which floated to his lap. He looked up. Sympathy radiated from his gaze. "No wonder you're so upset."

"Yes." His shoulders slumped. His heart felt like a bleeding lump in his chest as one emotion after the other passed through him, so quickly, so raw, he could barely distinguish anger from grief, from betrayal, from relief. "All this time! All this time!" The tears began to leak and run down his cheeks. "How could he have done that? I thought he really was sending me on a delivery." A lump formed in his throat as the reality poured in, bigger and more shocking even than when he'd first read the confession.

"He'd asked me to deliver a box of groceries for someone who lived about ten blocks away. I saw the person the things were for out on the street, not too far away and he took the delivery into his car. So I was able to go back sooner." Naoto stared down at his hands. "He...he didn't think I'd get back so soon." He shoved a hand through his loose hair. Part of him wanted to get up, to run around, anything to absorb the rising hysteria inside him.

He gripped Koji's arm. "Koji, he *knew*. I can't believe he knew. He sent me away, knowing what was going to happen." Naoto heard the hysteria and shock in his voice, but couldn't stop himself from repeating the phrases several more times.

Koji appeared about to cry himself. "You don't know all of it, Koji. I thought the yak murdered him because of his debt. I was going to take revenge. That would have gotten me killed, no doubt, but I didn't give a shit." The curse felt harsh in front of Koji who'd never heard him swear, but Koji didn't seem to notice.

In fact, Koji reached out and put an arm across his shoulders, then moved in closer.

"It was Kiku-sensei who stopped me. He said he saw the potential in me. Would I come with him he asked. He had been a yak for a long time and was clean several years. The White Tiger was still pretty new. He begged me not to do what I was planning and come help him run his place." Kiku had changed his life. Taught him about service, dignity, meditation, gave him direction so he wouldn't lose his mind. The *way* Kiku had done some of it, through sex, had been unconventional, but that had never mattered. There was no way to convey to someone else the full force Kiku had had on his life after he'd lost Lee and wanted to die. To kill and be killed.

Koji's hand slipped from his shoulder and passed over his hair. The touch was so gentle, so kind, Naoto couldn't speak, only give way to the tears. Without thinking, he fell against Koji.

And felt the other man's arms close around him. Koji's hand passed down his hair, one sweet caress after the next. All Naoto could do was allow the emotions to run through him, raw and painful, while images of Lee passed through his mind. Cradling Lee's dying body. The bleeding wounds. The wide-eyed gaze as Lee's life passed out of him. Naoto had cried out, yelling for help. Lecy had come running downstairs and screamed. But she'd kept her head and called the ambulance. Of course, it had been too late.

Naoto clutched a fistful of Koji's shirt. He felt Koji pull him closer, bringing with the clean scent his skin and hair, of starch in his shirt. Somehow, it all made him feel safer. Koji's hand on his hair, and Koji's warm, hard leanness against him.

Naoto heaved several breaths, felt his tears sink into Koji's shirt, darkening the white cloth. A long time seemed to pass before he could look up. "I'm sorry, Koji. So sorry."

"Don't be." Koji smoothed back his hair, his own large eyes misted. "I'm sorry that happened to you." He paused, his gaze scanning Naoto's face. "Let me get you a tissue or something." He rose quickly and came back with a large wad of toilet paper. "I'm sorry this is all I have." He sank back down and handed the paper to him.

"Thank you." Naoto wiped his face and sat back, still looking at Koji. "I only wanted to see you," he said softly. "I...didn't know if it was right. I just thought...that beautiful tiger you gave me. It made me think I could call you."

Koji's cheeks darkened and his eyes took on that sheepish look Naoto now recognised as shyness. "You were right." Koji paused and Naoto saw him preparing to speak. He remembered how Koji had been about to say something earlier in front of the hospital, before someone had bumped into him.

"Naoto, I don't know how to say this without seeming strange. It's only been a week...but..." He paused again and that shy look slipped through his eyes.

Something *was* different in Koji. Hard to say exactly. But he was stronger, less able to remain underneath the weight of his fears and guilt.

"...I never thought I could have another friend like you...after...Shizuko." Koji spoke the words quickly, as if forcing them out before he lost his nerve. He looked down. "I know it's strange after only a few days. But it's the truth." He fell silent and glanced away briefly before his gaze rested evenly on Naoto's.

Naoto watched him for several moments, enjoyed the subtle play of emotions across Koji's beautiful face. "It's not strange, Koji. I feel...much...the same about you."

Koji's eyes widened. "Really?"

He nodded. The words had slipped out. He'd never meant to say them out loud, but now that he had, the smile on Koji's lips made him know he'd been right to.

Koji's smile deepened and Naoto kept gazing at him. He didn't know when the energy shifted, darkened into desire, but the longer he stared into Koji's eyes, listened to his breathing, the deeper his yearning for him grew.

Koji's lips parted slightly, as if he were thinking the same things.

Naoto leaned forward and pressed their lips together. His body felt strangely clean, melting and warm from crying. He closed his eyes and breathed in Koji's scent, savoured the velvety softness of his lips. Warmth flooded him. He reached out and closed his hands over Koji's shoulders. The hard lean muscles twitched under his hands and he felt Koji's hands on his triceps.

A small murmur echoed in Koji's throat, a tiny sound that shivered right through Naoto. In one movement, he leaned in closer and pressed Koji back against the cushions, covering him so they were chest to chest.

Naoto's mind swirled as he deepened their kiss, licked across Koji's lips and tongue in hungry strokes. Koji was kissing him back with equal fervour and each touch of that moist warmth fuelled Naoto's hunger for the man. These last two days without Koji had been torturously long and slow. He used to miss Lee that way, unable to bear even a few hours away from him, even just from the chance to look into his eyes. Koji had been his guest for one week, but somehow, in that short time, something inside him had claimed Koji as a lover, something invisible, beyond his control. He was helpless in its grasp.

And then Koji had agreed. They were friends. And more.

Before he knew what was happening, he'd pulled back enough to get his hands in front of him, frantically working open the buttons of Koji's shirt. He loved how Koji didn't wear an undershirt, all that smooth warm skin open to his touch as he unbuttoned the shirt. Yanking the tails out of Koji's slacks, Naoto pulled it open and dipped his face immediately to that expanse of leanly muscled flesh.

Like a hungry man at a feast, he licked and kissed every inch he could find, swirled his tongue wildly around each nipple, making Koji groan and arch his back, sift a hand through his long hair, like Koji loved to do.

Naoto slid down, kneeling on the floor so he could get lower. Koji's breath thundered in his ears and he licked at the man's belly button, while his hands worked open the belt and slacks.

They'd done this part so many times in only a week that Naoto felt Koji move with him so naturally, lifting his ass up so Naoto could slide down the slacks, taking his briefs with them.

Koji's erection sprang into his face. Naoto captured it in his mouth as if it were precious food. The taste of that hardness, Koji's moans filling the air, the scent of his skin and musk...all were like a healing balm.

Hungrily, Naoto took Koji's whole length in, slid up and down, sucking with the amount of pressure he knew made Koji wild. Pushing Koji's slacks down around his ankles, Naoto pulled back and tongued Koji's balls, licking in that feathery way that made Koji's hips rocket off the cushions. "Naoto!" came the harsh whisper.

Uh oh. Now was close to the time Koji started shouting. Time to kiss him, to absorb the sound so they didn't alert the neighbours. A gay couple wasn't something you advertised.

Naoto sat up, tugged his shirt off and sucked off his jeans as fast as he could, seeing Koji work his own slacks off his ankles and then lie back, legs spread, staring up with that glazed look that said, "Fuck me now, I beg you," even though he didn't say it out loud.

Naoto wet his hand with spit and slathered it the length of his cock. No ounce of training he'd ever done enabled him to wait long enough to get oil or lube. Who even knew if Koji kept that stuff around? He'd seemed so unprepared for life. But he was still so sweet...so wonderful. Who cared?

Kneeling down between Koji's thighs, Naoto pushed two gentle fingers into Koji's ass.

"Ohh, Naoto." Koji's eyelids fluttered and his hips lifted up a bit. Damn, he loved this so much, even the way he said *Naoto*, so affectionate and wanting...

Naoto pushed in deeper, worked Koji's tight hole open, massaged the soft insides in gentle strokes.

"Now, please!"

Koji's fevered command shuddered through him and he pulled his fingers out, replacing them with his wet cock.

"Ahhh." Koji threw his head back, eyes rolling up. His hands clutched Naoto's hips.

That alone made Naoto feel wild, possessive, as if Koji were being claimed. Naoto pushed, slid in deep. Koji's ass swallowed his cock with its own hunger until their bodies met.

"Oh!" The sound was nearly a shout and Naoto leaned over Koji and claimed the man's lips so the sound vibrated through him, instead of through the air.

Koji's hands clutched at his back and his inner thighs pressed into Naoto's hips. Damn, Koji was luscious. How was he going to enjoy this feast, Koji's flavour, sounds, passions, the way Koji looked at him, and then leave? Not see him until God knows when?

Even as he rode Koji in hard strokes, the questions rolled through his mind. As he slid his tongue hungrily against Koji's, all he wanted was to taste him every day.

Pleasure tingled through every inch of his cock, sparks that seemed to dance wherever his hardness slid against Koji's tight passage, and then into his chest as it rubbed Koji's chest, their torsos sandwiching Koji's hard cock, rubbing it as they fucked.

Naoto felt his breathing slow, match the rhythm of their bodies moving together. His mind softened. The questions and unfulfilled desires melted down, leaving only Koji's scent, the feel of his hands on Naoto's ass, his fingers clutching, the scent of their sex and sweat diffusing in the heated air. Tiny lights danced in his mind and then faded.

Naoto dipped his tongue languorously against Koji's. Time seemed to stop and Naoto could no longer feel where his body ended and Koji's began. Even the groan that vibrated against his lips and the splash of hot cum against his chest could have been his and not Koji's.

If it was Koji's, it was his. No matter what else happened between them.

Pressure built in his cock…he was pretty sure it was *his* cock. The slippery warm pool between him and Koji was Koji's…his lover's…and his own climax was building. The pressure surged in his balls. He thrust long hard strokes into Koji's ass.

"Yes, Naoto, yes." Koji's voice was a fevered whisper now and he was squeezing his muscles around Naoto's cock. The intensity made Naoto burst. He groaned and pushed deep into Koji, emptying into him, then collapsing gently.

"I'm not crushing you, am I?" he whispered.

Koji shook his head. "No." His hands rested on Naoto's back, still squeezing the muscles as if he were afraid to let go. "I'm fine. It's you I'm concerned about."

Naoto lifted his face and brushed a soft kiss on Koji's lips. "I'm much better now." He stared down into Koji's eyes again and in seconds, that *feeling* slipped through him, the one that had made him see Koji as a lover, not a paying guest.

With a sigh, he sank back down into the haven of Koji's arms. He could only hope Koji felt the same way. Not that it mattered. He remembered all too well the pressure Koji was under to get married. Love or not, he would have to accept what Koji could give him.

Naoto blinked. Since when had he felt quite this way? Ready to devote himself to Koji, the way he'd once devoted himself to Lee? Holy shit! The force of revelation almost propelled him right off Koji's resting body.

Free. His heart felt free. That burden, the pressure holding him back…it was gone. Lee's confession must have freed him, made him understand the chain that had kept him from fulfilling Lee's dying wish. *Dying wish.* That's what it had been, really. Not some strange fancy that Lee had had in his head.

I couldn't have saved him. Kuso! That had been the bond, the chain around his heart. Well, not completely. There really hadn't been someone until now that he'd wanted to love. Yet, now that there was, Naoto realised the truth. All those years of blaming himself, of believing he could somehow have prevented Lee's murder…there was nothing he could have done. *Nothing.*

Lee had made certain of it.

Naoto pulled in a breath. The flood of understanding brought fresh tears. His back heaved under Koji's hands and he felt Koji's answering caress on his skin. What a sweet man Koji was, so kind. So good.

His tears were not as forceful as they'd been earlier and soon he was resting quietly, listening to Koji's gentle breathing and simply enjoying the man's touch, the feel of Koji's naked body underneath his.

"Do you need anything?" Koji's voice was soft, concerned.

"No, Koji-chan. Just this."

Koji's hand passed over his hair. "Let me know when you're hungry. I'll get you something to eat."

"Okay." Naoto nuzzled the warm smooth skin of Koji's neck. If he always felt the way he did right this moment, he'd never need food again. Finally, however, enough time had passed that he needed to call Kiku and tell him what was going on. Reluctantly, he levered himself up and rolled to the side. "I need to tell Kiku where I am," he said. He really just wanted to curl up with Koji and never move. He cleared his throat. Just because *he* felt that way, didn't mean it was mutual. "Koji, I'm not…keeping you from anything, am I?" *Or anyone.* He so didn't want to leave, wanted to fall asleep with Koji in his arms. The need made him ache.

Koji was gazing up at him. "Not at all. You can…stay…tonight…if you want."

Naoto's insides leaped and he couldn't help the huge grin. If anything else could have made him more joyful, he couldn't imagine what. "I'd like that."

Koji sat up. "In that case, I guess we should shower, but I need to clean the bathroom before you come in." His sheepish look slipped into his eyes. "It's not terrible, but still."

"You don't have to do any—"

"Yes, I do, Naoto…-chan." Koji touched his arm. "I want it to be nice for you." He leaned over and pressed a soft kiss on Naoto's lips. "It's your turn to be cared for. I won't be long."

Naoto watched Koji cross the small room. Even in a little over a week, he'd already put on enough weight that the physique Naoto had guessed him to have, was now emerging. His back was perfect, v-shaped, tapering down to slim hips and an ass that couldn't be more perfect. Even with those scars.

Koji disappeared into the small bathroom and then Naoto heard the sink running. Fishing his cell phone from his jeans, Naoto dialled Kiku.

Kiku answered on the second ring and Naoto rose, pacing in front of Koji's desk as he told Kiku what had happened.

A deep sigh sounded over Kiku's end. "I'm so sorry, my friend. I'm glad that Koji was able to be there for you." In spite of his earlier warnings about emotional involvement, he'd backed off, saying in a conversation the night before that Naoto had to go through whatever his life presented to him. And right now, that was Koji.

Naoto came to a stand still. "Me too." He turned and his eye fell on the papers Koji had laid on the desk a while ago. The paper he'd scrambled to clear away when they first walked in. At the time, Naoto had been too grief-stricken to notice. Now, however...

He looked closer. And pulled in a breath.

"Naoto? Are you there?"

Kiku's voice sounded as if it were coming from the end of a tunnel, as Koji's drawings, ones he hadn't seen before, came into focus. "Yes. I'm sorry."

"No problem. Listen, stay with Koji. It's quiet here. Call me in the morning, all right, to tell me how you are?"

Naoto's gaze had frozen on a perfect drawing of him and Koji, naked bodies entwined. Pulling his attention from the drawing, he concentrated on his friend. "Thank you, Kiku-sensei. I'm grateful."

"You're very welcome. If you need me, day or night, just call."

"Thank you so much." Naoto ended the call and stood, attention riveted, over what appeared to be a series of drawings on one page. He had no right...Koji hadn't shown him these, or even told him any drawings existed apart from the ones he'd modelled for.

He glanced towards the bathroom. Koji was still inside with the water running and Naoto could hear the soft scrape of a scouring pad against tile. He pictured Koji naked, bent over the tub, hard at work to make the place nice for him. So sweet.

But time was running out...

Naoto picked the drawing up. This time, he saw several other frames, a whole *manga* storyboard with dialogue and thought bubbles, an entire progression of his and Koji's lovemaking. Naoto's heart sped up even more, partly from the content of the drawings, and partly from the illicit nature of spying.

Naoto, I love you so much, Koji said in one frame as Naoto kissed the side of his neck, his arms around Koji in a possessive embrace. *I want to be yours forever.* And then Koji's thought bubble, *I can only hope you feel the same way.*

The paper shook as Naoto's hands trembled. In each frame, Koji made another heated declaration of love. And in each thought bubble, he lamented that he couldn't tell Naoto how he felt.

The water stopped.

Naoto dropped the paper as if it had burned his fingers and dashed over to the bathroom.

Koji was standing in the middle of the tiny bathroom, naked except for a pair of yellow rubber gloves. Sweat gleamed on his skin, plastering tiny spikes of his short hair to his forehead and temples.

Naoto stared at him, heart racing.

Koji loves me.

"Naoto, are you all right?" Koji's brow furrowed.

Words wouldn't come. Naoto's pulse galloped. His heart was leaping with a life of its own. His mind was blurred. All he could do was step forward, cradle Koji's face and kiss him, nip softly at his bottom lip and suckle his tongue. When he finally pulled back, Koji's face was flushed, his eyes dusky.

"Come into the shower, Naoto," he said softly. "Let me wash you."

Naoto smiled. "Are you going to wear those?" He pointed to the gloves.

Koji grinned. Damn, he had the most incredible smile Naoto had ever seen. "Of course not." He pulled them off, tossed them into the sink and turned on the shower faucets.

Chapter Eleven

Naoto followed Koji back to the apartment from the stairwell. He watched the back of Koji's head as the other man fumbled a bit with the key in the lock and couldn't decide if the pleasant tingling in his blood and brain was from the decanter of saké they'd shared at supper or just a sense of drunkenness from falling helplessly in love with Koji. The man seemed to get sweeter by the minute, the way he'd washed Naoto in the shower, then dried him off, so obviously trying to care for him the way he'd been cared for at the White Tiger. When Naoto had realised what was going on, he thought the feeling of sweetness would overwhelm him.

Koji got the door unlocked and held it open for him. "Come in," he said softly. His skin was flushed, although Koji hadn't had as much saké as he had that first time. But he also suspected Koji's gently dazed look to be from the same source as his own...now that he'd seen Koji's drawings.

Naoto grinned. "You go first. I'll follow you. I like watching your ass." Which was true. He even loved the back of Koji's neck, the way his ebony hairline was so perfect along his smooth golden skin.

A shy smile teased at Koji's lips. The look infused his large eyes. "Thank you."

Naoto followed him and pressed up close as Koji slid his shoes off. Mmm, he breathed in Koji's scent, soap and clean laundry, hair still slightly damp from their shower. He brushed a kiss on the nape of Koji's neck, just above the collar of his polo shirt and rested his hands on the man's slim hips. If this was heaven, no wonder people preferred to go there. "Did I thank you for supper, Koji-chan?" he murmured against Koji's skin.

Koji leaned back against him. "Several times. You don't need to say it again. You're very welcome."

Naoto pulled Koji to his chest and rested his chin on the slimmer man's shoulder. At this angle, his eye fell on a pile of cardboard boxes in the corner, something he hadn't seen earlier. A cold feeling spread like fire through his chest. "Are you moving away, or something?" He heard the worried tone in his voice but couldn't help it.

Koji shook his head. "No, why?"

Deep sigh of relief. "Those boxes over there."

Koji sighed too. "No. Those are some things of my stepmother's. After she died, my sister packed them up and gave them to me. I...haven't wanted to look at them yet." He turned in Naoto's arms. "There are pictures of her, though. I'd show them to you."

Koji's face was close, so close, his warm breath caressed Naoto's skin. The scent was faintly of saké and garlic, which, in this case, became a magic potion for arousal. He caught himself on the verge of saying, 'You don't have to show me them, if you don't want,' but stopped himself, recognising in that moment Koji's self-effacing way of asking for something he wanted.

Naoto nodded. "I'd like to, very much." Of course, he was wickedly curious. Everything about Koji intrigued him now and he wanted to know the man's life...as intimately as he'd known Lee's. Well, that is, until the last part.

The pang passed through him as he followed Koji to the corner. Koji was already kneeling and pulling open the flaps.

On the top was a pile of drawings. Koji lifted them out and started to set them aside, but Naoto stopped him with a hand on his wrist. "May I see those?"

Koji's cheeks reddened and he looked down, making his sexy fringe of eyelashes rest a moment on his cheeks. "I guess so. I used to make drawings for her all the time." Naoto took the pile and Koji surrendered them.

Naoto put the pile on his lap. One glance and Naoto could see the drawings were by a kid's hand...a very talented kid. The subjects were mostly mundane, pictures of a family, house, pets. Yet in spite of the subjects, Koji had already shown a grasp of perspective and shading. "How old were you when you did these?"

"I don't know. I did them over time, like between eight and fourteen."

"They're really good."

"Thank you." Koji sounded shy.

Naoto looked at every last one before handing the pile back to Koji.

"Shizuko kept everything I did," Koji said as he set the drawings aside. "Even if it wasn't something I meant to give her. If I didn't want it, she'd ask if she could have it."

"She was devoted."

Koji nodded. "Yes. She really cared about me and Gina."

Naoto's heart squeezed and he wondered if Koji was aware of how transparent he really was...and of how much Naoto appreciated being allowed these deeper glimpses into Koji's life. "How did your father meet her?"

"She was a secretary in his office. Apparently, she was attracted to him for some time and then, not long after my mom died, he started seeing her." Koji's shoulders sagged a bit. "I'm not sure that he was in love with her as much as he was desperate to find someone willing to take care of me and my sister. He couldn't deal with kids."

Apparently, Naoto thought, considering the scars on Koji's ass.

Naoto watched Koji retrieve the next item from the box, a photo album with one of those phoney red leather covers. "I made this for her on one of her birthdays. I think I was sixteen at the time." He handed it to Naoto.

Naoto took it, staring at Koji's face, wondering. Pretty unusual for a teenage boy to make such a sentimental kind of gift, especially for a parental figure. But considering what he knew about Koji—and had experienced in the middle of the night with him—Naoto had already known of the feelings between the two people.

He opened the cover. The first page was one of Koji's drawings. Incredible. A woman sitting under a cherry blossom tree, watching the petals fall around her, a wistful expression on her face, her long hair flowing. The writing said simply, *For Shizuko, Love, Koji*

"Koji-chan, this is incredible." Naoto couldn't keep the breathy sound of wonder from his tone. "Beautiful."

"You really think so?"

He fixed Koji with a look. It bothered him that Koji couldn't see his own talent. "Hell, yes. I *know* so."

Koji bowed his head. "Thank you."

Naoto turned the first page. On it was a large photograph of a woman between a sixteen-year old Koji and a girl somewhere close to Koji's age. The woman was very pretty, smiling, her arms around Koji and the girl, a birthday cake glowing with candles on the table in front of them.

"That's Shizuko," he heard Koji say. "The girl is my sister, Gina."

Naoto stared, captured first by Koji's face. Eyes sad, though he was smiling, but leaning into Shizuko, his posture conveying the affection he had for her. The next thing that struck him was the woman's hair. Long and sleek. Probably almost to her waist by the look of it falling in front of her breast and disappearing below the line of the table in front of her. "She was beautiful," he said. Indeed she was. "I see why you like long hair."

The silence that followed made him look up. Koji was staring at him. "What?"

Naoto pointed. "Long hair. I just understood. You loved Shizuko. She had long hair and she was very close to you. It makes sense."

Koji's brow furrowed. "I never thought of it that way." A sudden air of tension swirled around him.

"I'm sorry, Koji. I didn't mean to say something bad."

Koji looked down briefly. "You didn't. Don't worry. It's just that...well...I don't understand something."

"What?"

Koji drew in a deep breath. Somehow, in seconds, Naoto had managed to burrow his way in deep. Deeper than he already was Naoto understood things about Koji that *he* didn't even understand about himself. The shock of realising someone could know another person so deeply made his heart thrash. "Well, if that's true about the hair...then why wouldn't I want a woman with long hair? Not that it's so important. I...want *you*."

Naoto heaved a sigh. He looked down at the picture, his rugged face deep in concentration. Koji recognised that expression now, the set of his full lips, the way he half-closed his eyes, as if searching for the answer deep in an invisible place. A long time seemed to pass with only the occasional sound of a car passing on the street outside the building. "If you want to know my thoughts, I'll tell you."

Koji pulled in a breath. His heart beat so hard, he wondered that the sound didn't fill the small apartment. "Yes," he whispered.

Naoto looked up. His dark eyes were misted, as if the answer had come to him and made him sad before he even voiced it. "You loved Shizuko, and…it was painful for you."

Koji's chest tightened. More pain had come to him around her than he'd ever imagined he could feel. "Yes."

"Maybe if you love a man, it's somehow…safer."

Koji stared at him. Well, not at Naoto directly, because his vision was too blurred. All he could see was Naoto's hair, the glint of the lighting off the ebony sleekness. The words the man had said seemed to be like arrows, shooting into him, stirring up something wordless and visceral that made his breath come in short, hard bursts.

Large warm hands were suddenly on his shoulders, pulling him close. Naoto's broad warmth. Koji rested his forehead on Naoto's shoulder, just as he'd done the very first time they met and Naoto was caressing his back. Tears leaked from his eyes as feelings trembled through him. He was vaguely aware of the album resting on Naoto's lap, all those images contained on the pages, photos he'd meticulously arranged for Shizuko, because he'd loved her so much.

So much, it was agonising. His tears were hot, covering his cheeks and soaking into Naoto's shirt. *No. Not now.* For so many reasons, not the least of which, he was supposed to be here for Naoto, not the other way around. He felt the brush of Naoto's thumb across the tendon in his neck. Naoto's touch alone was a healing balm. An unexpected shiver of guilt passed through him, followed by an image of him and Etsu at a table, talking over dinner. An unwanted view of the near future.

"The thing is, Koji-chan," Naoto said gently, "Loving anyone, man or woman, can bring pain."

The sadness in Naoto's voice pulled Koji from his inner conflict and he remembered what Naoto had just been through, the pain that had brought him here in the first place, looking for comfort.

Sitting up, he looked into Naoto's eyes, still misted. The dark pools gazed on him with a look that made Koji feel completely naked, inside out.

His blood felt suddenly chilled. Could Naoto see so deep inside him that he knew? Knew somehow about Etsu and was trying to make him want her? Koji felt almost as he had when Miosuke had sent him on vacation—like he was losing his mind. "Are you trying to cure me?"

Naoto frowned. "Cure you?"

He nodded. "Yes, cure me so that I'll want a woman instead of you."

A hurt look clouded the other man's eyes, made Koji realise the thought had never occurred to him. "Absolutely not, Koji." His hands came out and grasped Koji's shoulders. The movement made the photo album slip partway off his lap. "Koji, please, don't think that. You're wonderful as you are. I just wanted to...understand. You're important to me. So important." Naoto bore a pleading look into his. "You're not angry at me, are you?"

Be angry with Naoto? The one person he felt was a true friend? In mere days, Naoto had been kinder and more understanding with him than anyone who knew him for years with the exception of Shizuko. In fact, Naoto deserved only the truth. He looked down. "No. I'm not angry with you. Not at all."

He heard Naoto sigh, a distinct sound of relief. "I'm glad."

"I just realised, I feel guilty to you."

Gentle fingertips under his chin tilted it up. When he did, Naoto's eyes looked relieved and still misted over. "Why?"

Koji heaved a sigh. "When I left you the other day, I went straight to my sister's house. She'd invited an old friend of hers to supper without telling me. A woman. My father pressured me to ask her out." His heart lurched. "I gave in. He wants me to marry. I don't know what else to do." He fell silent, heart racing as he waited for Naoto's response. If Naoto was going to get up and leave, now was better than later, better than after they'd had sex again and maybe fallen asleep together. Sleeping without Naoto was proving difficult enough, but having him stay the night and *then* leave…seemed even worse.

"This doesn't have to ruin anything."

Koji whipped his gaze up. "What?"

Naoto's misty expression hadn't changed. He reached forward and grasped Koji's hand. "I said, this doesn't have to ruin anything…I mean, if you were to get married." He squeezed Koji's fingers between his own and Koji could feel the coiled passion in his touch, felt that invisible something flow between them, pulling them together, as he'd felt back in the White Tiger. Naoto spoke with certainty, as if he knew Koji's feelings, the ones he'd expressed in his drawings but not out loud. He could never say them out loud.

"Many of the men who come to the White Tiger are married." Naoto went on, a hopeful sound in his voice, "It's okay. As long as they pay the bills, keep a roof over their families' heads, do the husband-father things, it doesn't matter what they do with their leisure time. That's the way it is. You could come and be with me at least once a week, maybe even stay the whole night. We'd work it out."

Koji sighed. Perhaps that was meant to make him feel better, but strangely, it only deepened his sense of despair. When had Naoto become the one person in the world he didn't want to live without? He stared down at the photo album, now on the floor, the cover closed. Shizuko would have wanted him to be happy. She used to tell him that...out of earshot of her husband—Koji's father, of course. But Shizuko wasn't here, not here to put herself between Koji's poor scarred ass and his father's strap, not here to encourage him in her conspiratorial way.

He was going to have to accept what was possible...not what he *wanted*. He nodded. "You're right." Looking up, he held Naoto's hand tighter. "We'll...work it out." When he and Naoto had become a 'we,' he didn't know. It had seemed to happen of its own accord. But that's the way it was.

"Koji-chan." Naoto's voice was nearly a whisper. He reached up and a large hand cupped the back of Koji's neck, gently drew him closer and pressed their lips together.

Koji yielded to the kiss. He loved that feeling of being gently guided, commanded...wanted. Naoto's kiss made his insides feel soft and melty. The tip of Naoto's tongue played along the seam of his lips, stole between them in warm, passionate licks against his tongue.

When Naoto pulled back, the mistiness in his eyes had turned to a look of raw desire under heavy lids. "Let's go to bed."

Without a word, Koji got up and yanked the cushions off the sofa to pull out the folding bed within. The mattress was already made up with sheets and a thin blanket, thankfully clean because Koji never used the bed. Sleeping alone all the time in his tiny place, and working the hours he did, all he did was collapse on the sofa night after night.

As soon as he'd set the legs of the bed frame to the floor, Naoto pulled him close and lifted up his shirt. Koji raised his arms and soon his shirt was tossed to the side. He watched Naoto do the same with his T-shirt, dropping it to the floor with Koji's shirt. Naoto's wide, handsome face was flushed, lids lowered now with obvious hunger. "Hurry," he breathed, shucking his own jeans as he spoke. "I want you so much."

Koji obeyed, undid his jeans and pushed them down. When they fell around his ankles, Naoto tackled him and fell over onto the bed with him, Naoto on top. "I can't wait, Koji. I'm sorry." He covered Koji's lips with his before Koji could answer.

Naoto's kisses were fevered, hot, hungry. His large muscled body gripped Koji's with a possessiveness Koji had never experienced from the other man before. Naoto had always been passionate, yet so controlled, so precise in every touch, lick and caress.

Not now. Now he was sheer raw power. Unguarded desire.

Koji gripped Naoto's back muscles, felt the hard flexing under his hands and returned Naoto's fervent kisses while he worked his jeans over his ankles, releasing his legs to wrap them around Naoto's hips. Nothing felt better than this, than being completely surrounded, enclosed in Naoto's passionate strength.

Naoto groaned into his mouth and ground their cocks together. He pulled his lips away and rose up on his elbows, staring down into Koji's face as he rocked his hips in a hungry rhythm against Koji's groin, sending sparks of heated pleasure through Koji's cock, down into his balls...through every inch of his body. "You'll see, Koji-chan," he whispered, "Nothing else matters. As long as we have each other."

Naoto's words shuddered through him with a power all their own. His hands slid to Naoto's hips, loving the power in them. "Yes," he panted, "nothing else matters."

Naoto rolled to the side then and Koji felt himself being turned onto his stomach by powerful hands. "Koji-chan," he whispered behind him. The heat of Naoto's body hovered over his back and ass, and Koji gave himself over to the feel of Naoto's lips on the nape of his neck, the tickle of Naoto's hair across his shoulder blades.

Koji closed his eyes, sank into the bed while Naoto's lips brushed over one shoulder blade then continued in tiny nips along his spine. His fingers kneaded Koji's rib cage and came to caress his ass.

Koji thrust his rear upward, needing to feel Naoto closer. With his own hand, he grabbed his cock, which was rigid.

Naoto's lips had reached one ass cheek, and they rubbed against it. Koji shuddered, a groan escaping him.

"Like that?" Naoto raised his lips enough to murmur.

Koji could only deepen his groan in answer.

Naoto chuckled and continued to fondle his buttocks, licking and kissing his skin.

"Ohhh!" the exclamation escaped Koji when he suddenly felt Naoto's thumbs slip into his crevice and spread him open.

"Koji-chan," Naoto whispered again. The sound of complete wild abandon was in Naoto's voice. Naoto's tongue brushed down his ass cheek, an erotic sweep of moist heat on the sensitive skin.

Koji closed his eyes, sinking underneath the delicious assault, then pulled in a breath as the same wet hotness licked across his hole. He groaned and fisted the sheets as Naoto licked and teased the tight opening until Koji felt his very brain would melt and his hips rocket to the ceiling.

The mind-blowing licks continued down his perineum, across the underside of his balls and then Naoto's weight was settling gently on top of him. Somehow, Naoto had lubricated his own cock and the plump head nudged at Koji's hole.

Naoto's hands closed over his shoulders. "Koji." Again, that passionate whisper full of emotions.

Koji spread his legs wider and pushed against Naoto's cock, forcing him deeper. Nothing was better in the entire world than Naoto's naked body against him, his thick cock filling him, pushing in deep.

Naoto's lips closed on Koji's shoulder, rested there while his hands slid down Koji's arms, lacing the fingers of both hands together. The weight of his lover sandwiched Koji's cock firmly against the bedding, rubbing the hard length with each thrust of Naoto's cock inside him. The flimsy joints of the bed creaked mercilessly as their bodies rocked together and Koji imagined in his blurred mind that the whole thing would probably collapse underneath them and that every neighbour in the building could hear the sounds they were making.

He didn't care. Naoto's body pressed down on him in masculine strength. All that mattered was the passion they felt for each other. Life wasn't worth anything without it. He'd never wanted to live a double life like the one Naoto had suggested, but knew he was powerless in the grip of what was happening now. He'd live that way if it meant seeing Naoto, if it was the only way to be able to kiss and touch and be in his arms.

These thoughts swirled through his brain as Naoto rode him harder. He lifted his mouth from Koji's shoulder and moaned before brushing his lips across Koji's skin. He whispered Koji's name over and over, each time pushing deep into him, causing Koji's cock to rub against the sheets until the sweet explosion came and Koji felt the warm stickiness of his climax soak into the bedding underneath him.

"Did you come?" Naoto panted into his ear.

Koji turned his head to the side, cheek pressed into the sheet. "Yes."

"Ohhh." Naoto surged inside him, several hard thrusts and Koji felt the tiny pulses against the insides of his passage as Naoto's cum filled him. With a long breath he collapsed on top of Koji. The heat and sweat of his body stuck them together and his breath fanned over Koji's skin.

After what felt like a long time, Naoto rolled off him and gathered Koji into his arms. Koji pressed his cheek to Naoto's chest and closed his eyes. He felt Naoto press a kiss onto his hair. "You'll see, Koji, I promise, it'll work out."

"I believe you," he whispered, though the sense of sadness only deepened.

"You can believe me. I know about these things."

Koji sighed. He hoped Naoto knew because he sure as hell didn't.

And he had a date with Etsu in two days.

~~~~~

I promise, Koji, it will all work out. I love you. Don't leave...

Naoto blinked. Grey daylight filtered into his eyes. The words, his pleas to Koji, spiralled through his mind, fading as he became aware of Koji's sleeping body curled up against him.

Sighing, Naoto stared up at the ceiling of Koji's apartment. That's when he realised it. The dream. It hadn't woken him as it had since Lee's death. No more dark hallways, Lee beckoning him in even though the darkness frightened him. Now he knew what that darkness been. Not so dark, but leading to a wonderful light. And yet still dark. Lao Tzu said that a man, 'preferring light, prefers darkness also is an image of the world'...

Yet, heaviness still hung in his chest.

In a little while he'd have to leave, go back to the White Tiger while Koji went to work. *No.* The thought of being out of this bed, him and Koji in separate places, waiting for the next time they could be together — waiting while Koji went out with that woman, slept with her, married her, any of it — it all sucked.

This wasn't supposed to have happened. But now it had and he had to deal with it. He'd promised Koji they'd work it out somehow. He intended to keep that promise, even if it meant only seeing Koji once or twice a week.

Who knew? Maybe it was better that way.

Savouring the quiet moment, he stared up at a network of cracks around the light fixture while listening to Koji's soft breathing. The little apartment was so dingy, the furniture battered, papers and books piled on shelves and on Koji's desk. The guy couldn't be further from the upscale urban Tokyoite so many of their generation were trying to be.

And that made him so lovable.

It also hadn't taken a rocket scientist to figure out why Koji hadn't fallen in love with anyone until now. He'd already been in love with Shizuko and had never really recovered from her death. Not to mention he probably had felt guilty for loving her.

Naoto sighed. Koji was probably one of the most complex people he knew aside from Kiku. Koji probably thought of himself as gay, but he'd been madly in love with a woman for half his life. He seemed to be drawn to people he considered beautiful and who made him feel safe. Naoto felt a wave of affection for the man. Koji apparently felt that way about *him*. To Naoto, Koji wasn't gay or straight. He was just Koji. Sweet, gentle Koji.

Koji murmured and stirred. His large eyes opened, staring right up at Naoto.

Naoto's heartbeat rose a bit. He wanted Koji to smile and kiss him and say good morning. But he didn't do any of these things.

"Naoto-chan, is that you?"

Naoto chuckled. Relief prickled through his veins. "Of course it's me." He snuggled into Koji and nuzzled the curve of his neck. Mmm, he was warm and musky. Naoto's dragon tingled. Koji had to be the most delicious human being on the planet. At least to him. "Who did you think it was?" He felt Koji's hand slip into his hair.

"I wasn't sure if I was awake or dreaming," Koji murmured. "I had trouble falling asleep last night because I was afraid you'd leave." Koji's body sagged in his arms. "You know, after what I told you."

Naoto lifted his face from Koji's neck. Waves of warmth for the man seemed to travel to every inch of his own body. "I wouldn't leave. I finally…found you. I told you, we'll work it out." He hoped he conveyed a confidence he didn't completely feel. Not because of himself, really, but because of Koji. Koji was still…fragile in a way.

Koji looked at him. Worry lines were etched around his eyes and he looked about as troubled as he had that first day at the White Tiger. He wasn't only complex, but Koji was intense as hell, as intense as any of the men of the White Tiger, himself included. "I believe you," he said softly. Though his eyes didn't show any certainty.

Leaning over, Naoto pressed a kiss to Koji's lips and then held him. The contact of their naked bodies pressed together, chest to knees, made Naoto completely hard. However, he resisted the clawing desire to start rubbing against Koji. More incredible, powerful sex would only make leaving and going back to the White Tiger more difficult. And make Koji late for work, no doubt.

He held Koji as long as he dared and then gently pulled away. "I have to get back," he murmured.

Koji nodded, but instead of rising, lay on his back, watching Naoto fish his clothing from the pile on the floor. "Do you want breakfast? I don't have anything here but downstairs there's a bakery."

Naoto shook his head. "Don't worry about it. I'll eat when I get there." He pulled on his jeans, feeling pulled, beckoned by Koji's gaze. The other man's worry emanated from him like a cloud, as it always had. Sitting down, Naoto reached out and touched Koji's cheek. "Listen, we'll call each other every day, at least once. And then, next Tuesday, I can come to get you at the hospital like yesterday, after I see Lecy and we can spend the whole time together, just like last night." He brushed his thumb along Koji's bottom lip. "Please, Koji, tell me it's all right."

Koji caught his wrist and held it, nuzzling Naoto's palm. Naoto closed his eyes at the soft warmth of the Koji's lips. A small kiss and then Koji looked up. "Of course it's all right." Now, finally, he smiled. "I already wish it was next Tuesday."

Chapter Twelve
Friday…

Time had never crawled so slowly before in Koji's life. Barely forty-eight hours had passed since Naoto had spent the night, yet it felt like a year at least. Koji lay on the sofa after his alarm clock had started screaming at six-thirty, trying to get up the motivation to rise and get ready for work.

It didn't make sense, when he and Naoto had been together, time flew like a bullet train. One moment, he was meeting Naoto in front of the hospital, then he blinked and Naoto was getting dressed the next morning to leave and go back to the White Tiger.

Now every minute separated felt like a torturously slow hour. Time was something to fill until next Tuesday, which he'd managed to do so far with work, drawing, talking to Naoto on the phone and going out after work with Hiru and some of the others. Yet, whatever he did, wherever he went, Naoto was there, in his mind. Just thinking of Naoto's face, body, hair, smile, touch made Koji mad with missing him.

Sometimes, looking up from his desk, he'd watch people around the office, talking on the phone or typing and wonder how they were getting through the day, whether they had something or someone they missed and desired as much as he missed Naoto.

Then he would turn back to his own work as time continued to crawl along, tormenting his mind, slogging along with a reminder each minute that he was going to see Etsu Friday night.

Wait! That was tonight! Shit.

He sighed and raked a hand through his hair. A sick feeling began to swirl in his gut and his breath started to get short.

Why? Why make such a fuss? He'd known Etsu most of his life. She was a nice woman, attractive and kind. He could never understand her friendship with Gina who was such a busybody. Well, that wasn't fair. Gina was a nice girl too. She meant well, was rarely catty and bitchy, just adoring of her older brother and wanted him to be happy. She just didn't know what it was that would make him happy. Because he never told her.

He sat up, still leaning back. Cancel. He could cancel. Call Etsu and tell her he wasn't feeling well. Or…he could tell her the truth. Maybe she wouldn't care. He remembered what Naoto had told him about the married men who came to the White Tiger.

It was too early to call her now anyway. If he was going to beg off being sick, he'd have to wait a little longer…

He jumped as the kung fu theme on his phone began to play. Fumbling for it on the desk behind his sofa he looked at the ID. Thank God. He clicked the button. "Naoto, hi." A thrill passed through him even before Naoto spoke.

"Hey." Naoto sounded a bit sleepy, making Koji think that he'd woken up just to call. "I wanted to catch you before you went to work." There was heaviness in his voice, something beyond the sleepiness. Koji felt it in his bones.

This sucked.

"I'm glad you called. I was missing you, Naoto." Koji held the phone tightly to his ear, as if that could bring Naoto physically closer.

"Do you have a bit of time?"

"For you, of course."

There was a long pause on the other end and for a second Koji worried that Naoto wasn't there. "Naoto?"

"What are you wearing, Koji?"

A tingle passed down Koji's arms. "Wearing?"

"Yeah. I'm trying to picture you."

"Just a pair of boxer shorts."

"Nothing else?"

"Nothing else."

"Mmm."

Naoto's murmur made the tingle continue down into Koji's cock, which stirred against the thin material of his shorts. "What about you?" he breathed.

"Nothing, Koji. I'm naked. And my cock is hard, just thinking about you."

Koji pulled in a breath. He immediately imagined Naoto, his brawny muscled body reclined on his bed, thighs spread, thick cock jutting upward. The mere image made him pull down the waistband of his boxers to free his own erection. "So is mine."

"Oh, good.. I'm imagining that I'm sucking on your cock right now. Picture me, okay? Feel my hot mouth sliding up and down, from the tip all the way down until you're cock is in my throat."

Koji began stroking himself, Naoto's voice like an erotic mantra, guiding his thoughts.

"How is that?"

Koji shut his eyes, leaned heavily into the sofa cushions. "Good," he panted, rubbing the length of his cock in quick strokes.

"I'm sucking you harder, faster. A drop of cum seeps out and I lick it up. You taste so good." Naoto's voice was silky and ragged. In the back of Koji's fevered mind, he sensed that Naoto was jerking himself off as he talked.

"When you come, Koji-chan, I'm going to swallow every drop. You're delicious, salty and sweet. I want it to hit the back of my throat, hot and thick."

That was it. The mere image of shooting into Naoto's mouth made the tension explode. Thick pools spurted onto Koji's stomach and chest. He screwed his eyes shut, stroking quickly until the last spasm passed through him.

On the other end, Naoto moaned, a sound Koji recognised as his when he was coming. Eyes still closed, Koji imagined the white milky cloud erupting from Naoto's cock, watched it coat his golden skin and washboard stomach. If only he could be there right now, he could feel Naoto's skin, kiss his lips as he came, smell the musk of sex, see Naoto's eyes look up at him with that misty look of dark hunger he often had…

"Thank you, Koji-chan." Naoto was breathing heavily, each exhalation echoing into the phone.

"I'm the one who should be thanking you." Koji's heart squeezed. If the situation were reversed, he'd be going nuts thinking about Naoto out on a date, looking to get married.

Pause. "I called you, wanting to tell you all kinds of wise things. I wanted to appear strong, so you wouldn't worry, but all I can do is tell you what's in my heart."

Koji gripped the phone tighter. Naoto sounded sad and frightened. "What is that?"

He heard Naoto exhale. "Just that I…love you. You're beautiful and sweet. And the other day, when I needed you so much, you were there. I felt…loved back."

Koji sat up, leaned forward, pressing the phone firmly to his ear again. His heart pounded and guilt spiked through him. "You were right, Naoto. You're right."

Several more breaths passed. "Good. I…don't want to lose you."

"You won't. I promise."

"Will you call me later?"

"Yes." That moment of anxiety set in, the way it always did before he and Naoto ended a call.

"Good. Have a good day, Koji-chan."

"You too." Koji paused, waited until he heard a click on the other end, then tossed the phone onto the cushion and got up to shower. How the hell was he going to get through this day? And night?

~~~~~

Koji walked back and forth in front of the restaurant. The best thing had been to meet Etsu near her work. This Indian place had been her recommendation when he'd suggested meeting her close to her office. Now, however, his stomach clenched so tightly he had no idea how he'd get any food down.

"Hi, Koji."

Koji stiffened. He pulled in a deep breath and turned around, working a smile to his lips at the same time. "Hi. How are you?"

Etsu was smiling at him in the sweet way she always had. The look made him remember all the times he'd come home from school and she'd smiled at him that way from the kitchen table where she sat with Gina. "I'm fine. And you?"

"Okay." Koji found himself wishing he could like her the way everyone else in his family wanted him to. In her stylish pants suit with a collared white blouse and her long hair in an elegant bun, she was perfect for some guy who wanted her.

A silent moment passed, filled with only the sound of traffic noise on the street. Etsu looked suddenly shy, not the image of a managing editor at a publishing house. "Have you ever been to this place before?" She indicated the restaurant behind them.

Koji blinked, as if she'd awakened him. Yet his bad dream wasn't dispelled. "No. Is it good?"

"Very. You want to go in?"

"Yes." He followed Etsu and held the door open for her. He knew he was being taciturn but couldn't help himself. All he wanted was to be cuddled up with Naoto, with a balmy spring breeze caressing them through the open window, feeding him sushi with his fingers and laughing together, kissing him...

Exotic Indian music played softly in the background of the colourfully decorated place and the scent of exotic spices floated in the air. The hostess, dressed in a traditional *sari,* led them to a booth. When she asked them for their drink order, Etsu turned to him. "Have you ever had Indian *chai?*"

He stared at her. Moments like these he saw how utterly unprepared he was for this kind of thing. "No. I...don't know what it is."

She smiled, a warm smile that didn't make him feel more of a jerk than he already felt like. "It's black tea simmered with milk, sugar and spices. Delicious. Want to try?"

He nodded, heart pounding. "Okay."

Etsu ordered the *chai* for them and when the hostess had left, looked at Koji, her smile fading. "Koji, I've been meaning to say to you how sorry I am about Shizuko-san. She was a wonderful person."

The sincerity in Etsu's voice melted away a bit of his tension and he nodded. "Thank you. She *was* wonderful. I miss her." It was the third time in only a few days someone had spoken to him about Shizuko. First his father, then Naoto, then Etsu. Until then, no one had said a word about her. Or maybe they had and he'd been so busy distracting himself with work, he hadn't heard them.

Another silence settled between him and Etsu, which she broke by asking him about his work. His answer took all of about two minutes because he gave the short version, not that he didn't want to fill up the time, but he also didn't want to be rude and bore her. In that time, the waitress brought two steaming cups and the scent of cinnamon and cloves wafted up between them. Koji lifted his cup and took a careful sip. The warm milky tea slipped down his throat in a pleasant way, but unbidden, all he could think of was that first night at the White Tiger, pouring a cup of tea for Naoto, and the brush of his fingertips as he accepted it...

"How is it?" she asked.

He nodded. "Very good. Thanks."

She smiled at him and his stomach flipped at the hopeful look in her eyes. What had Gina said to this woman about him? "I think that what you do is much more interesting," he said. Better to get the attention off himself. Besides, *manga* had been a boyhood passion, a topic they at least had in common. Etsu had always had some tucked into her schoolbag, though the ones she'd liked were geared for girls her age and of absolutely no interest to him.

She chuckled. "I don't know about that, but it's fun, especially since I like the medium so much." Before she could say anything else, the waitress came to take their order. A few more minutes passed with Etsu explaining to him about the dishes.

He was only too happy to let her order, agreeing to whatever she liked. Anything to get through the night smoothly and to get back home.

Once the waitress had gone again, Etsu smiled at him. "Anyway, you had asked me about my work." A shy look slipped through her eyes. "I'm the managing editor of the division that publishes *yaoi*."

He stiffened. *Yaoi?* Manlove *manga*? Carefully he set his cup down from mid-lift so he wouldn't spill the *chai*. "Really?" he managed to say.

She nodded. "You wouldn't believe how popular that genre is these days," she went on, "So much so that we have a division that translates the work of our Japanese artists into about fifteen other languages." She chuckled. "It's becoming a wave in its own right." She fell silent and sipped her *chai*.

Pulse rising to a gallop, he cleared his throat. Maybe…just maybe…he could tell her the truth. As if some invisible force were handing him an opportunity on a plate. Certainly a woman who read graphic manlove novels all day would be understanding, right?

While he was pondering, Etsu looked at him, obviously getting ready to speak again. "I remember you used to draw." She smiled and looked away with that shy look. "I'm sorry that Gina invaded your privacy and showed me your drawings. I always liked them."

He smiled in spite of himself, remembering that time. Gina had tried to hide her crime, but Koji noticed the tiny folds in the corners of the pages that hadn't been there before and knew immediately what she'd done. He hadn't spoken to her for a week, but then her constant pout had worn him down. Gina was his little sister after all. He'd solved the problem by hiding his most private drawings under his mattress. The ones with the samurai making love to him. "I recovered."

"Do you still draw?"

Koji's cheeks heated and his skin tingled under his collar. "Sometimes. I…work too much to have that kind of time."

Etsu nodded. "Well, I hope you're able to draw again at some point. You really have talent."

The flush in his cheeks deepened. "Thank you." Was she trying to flatter him so he'd like her more? No, he decided. He'd known Etsu most of his life. She was a sincere person.

She took another sip of her *chai*. If she was aware of his inner conflict, she didn't act so. "Do you still have your *manga* collection?"

Another thing Gina used to invade and show to Etsu. He nodded. "Packed away somewhere. Probably sitting in a dusty corner of Gina's attic. I don't have space for it."

Her smile widened. "Hold onto them," she said. "Some of the classics from our time will be worth something. I know. I have the inside track."

He found himself smiling. "Okay, I will." Some of the churning in his gut calmed down and he took another sip of the *chai*. Of course, then he wondered if Naoto had ever drunk *chai*, and if so, had he enjoyed it. There wasn't one thing Koji could do or say, not one place he could go that he didn't wish Naoto was there with him.

~~~~~

Tell her. Tell her. The voice echoed through Koji's mind during an after dinner stroll down the sidewalks of Ginza. Thankfully he had the distraction of many colourful store window displays as they chatted, mostly about *manga* and some about Tokyo in general and how it differed for her from Kyoto where she'd lived for most of her marriage.

How could he be anything but a hypocrite, acting gentlemanly, making conversation, when inside, he was wailing silently for his lover, watching each minute pass, counting down until he could go home and fantasise about Naoto, make more drawings of him and hopefully, speak to him on the phone?

"Am I making you nervous, Koji?"

Etsu's voice pulled him from his inner rant. When he looked at her, he met a sympathetic gaze. Apparently, she wasn't insensitive to his conflicted state. "I know I can talk too much sometimes."

His blood felt cold. *Shimatta.* Etsu deserved better than this. "Not at all," he said softly. "I'm just...nervous."

She smiled again. "Me too."

After a while, he hailed a taxi and accompanied Etsu home. They rode in companionable silence and he walked her to the door of her parents' house where she was staying until she could afford her own place again.

At the front door, she turned to him and smiled. "Thank you again for supper, Koji. I really enjoyed it."

"You're welcome. I liked it too. I...never had Indian food before." His heartbeat sped up at the way she was looking at him, that soft shine in her eyes and at the way she tilted her face upward. As if she wanted him to kiss her.

"I'd invite you in," she said, "But I think my parents have gone to bed. I shouldn't make noise."

Koji nearly released a deep sigh in relief. He stopped himself at the last second. Now was the perfect moment to tell her the truth. There'd probably been a million moments before this that also would have been perfect. But he'd chickened out each time. "No problem. I have to get home anyway. I work early tomorrow."

Etsu smiled. "Koji, I want you to know, Gina invited me again this Sunday. I told her I'd only come if *you* felt it was okay. I know she can be kind of…enthusiastic…and doesn't think that other people don't feel the same way."

He stared at her. Was it possible she was this considerate? If so, he didn't have the heart to tell her she couldn't come. "No, it's okay. Really."

Her smile deepened, reaching her eyes.

Kuso.

"I guess I'll see you Sunday."

She nodded, but didn't say anything. Then she tilted her face upward…leaned a bit closer.

His stomach lurched. He couldn't do this. He had to tell her. "Etsu, I have to tell you…"

"Yes?"

He sighed, heart squeezing like a worn out sponge in his chest. "I enjoyed…tonight." He leaned down and kissed her cheek. A soft kiss in which he could feel the firm smoothness of her skin. It was nice. Pretty. And she smelled like perfume.

But not what he wanted. Not Naoto. "Good night."

"Good night, Koji."

She unlocked her door and he stood, watching, until she was safely inside.

Koji stared at the door. His hands balled into fists at his sides. Disgusting the way he was behaving. How was it he could be basically honest about so many things, except this? Which was exactly why he'd avoided dating a woman. So he wouldn't have to put either of them through that…moment of truth. Etsu was nice, decent, a sweet person. She didn't deserve to be lied to. So why hadn't he?

Simple. Once he told Etsu, he'd have to tell his father. No way in hell Tashiro Watanabe would believe an excuse of *we aren't compatible*. Not when it came to Etsu, a pretty, sincere, obviously eligible woman.

He sighed. When it came to Tashiro Watanabe, Koji was still the little boy getting the strap. And sometimes it felt like he always would be.

Naoto's lover hadn't been that way. Koji remembered Naoto's story, how Lee had dropped to his knees before his mother, begging for her understanding. Since then, he'd thought many times of doing just that, of telling his father the truth and falling to his knees. He was a grown man now. If his father raised a hand to him, he could defend himself.

So would Naoto. The look on Naoto's face when Koji had told him the truth about the scars had said everything. He'd been certain Naoto would have wanted to thrash his father had he met him. That had been the moment he'd really fallen in love with Naoto. Just the way he had with Shizuko when he was eleven, the day she'd thrown herself between him and his father's strap-wielding hand. The slap of leather had landed on her, bruising her, shocking the man into stopping.

Koji watched Etsu's door a moment longer then turned. He'd already sent the taxi away already and started down the sidewalk. His family's house was a couple of blocks away, but he'd be damned before he went there. It was at least an hour's walk back to his neighbourhood, but he didn't care. What the hell else was he going to do?

Halfway there, a taxi passed by. He almost hailed it. Almost decided to go to the White Tiger. But it was Friday night. The place would be filled with guests and Naoto would be…busy. Koji couldn't bear the thought that he'd get there and Naoto couldn't be with him because he was…massaging some other guy. Or worse.

Heat prickled all over Koji's body and his heart pumped, his breathing harsh. Jealousy was one of the most uncomfortable things he'd ever felt, almost worse then the belt across his ass.

He dialled Naoto's cell phone and got his voice mail. Shit. Naoto probably *was* with someone. *Shimatta.* The pain of jealousy was unbearable. He'd had years of it around Shizuko and had never wanted to experience it again. The only way to escape it was to break up with Naoto. Yet, as the idea sank in, it made him want to cry. He couldn't do that.

Trying to keep his voice from shaking, he left a quick message and kept walking, unable to enjoy even the sweet spring night. In moments like these he knew that Hell was not a place one went to in the after life.

He was in hell right now.

How he made it to his apartment building and upstairs without going into a full panic attack, he didn't know, but once there, he stripped off his jacket, picked up his drawing pad and drew, pencil scribbling furiously on the white paper. Until the phone rang.

~~~~~

Koji picked up on the second ring. "*Moshi moshi*. Naoto-chan?" He sounded so anxious, as if he'd been waiting for Naoto's call. Well, Koji couldn't have been more anxious than he was.

Naoto leaned back against the wall and closed his eyes. The mere sound of Koji's voice flooded him, made his body erupt in tingles, like a boy with a crush. "Yes. It's me. What are you doing right now?" he asked and immediately regretted it. What if *she* was with him? What if…*shimatta*…no…Koji wouldn't jump into bed with her, would he? The thought of her…of anyone else…lying next to Koji, naked, was fucking unbearable. Shit, they'd only just begun and this was going to drive him mad.

"I'm at home. I saw her to her parents' place and left."

"Oh." Naoto tried to sound unconcerned. "How…was it?" A heavy feeling settled over his chest. He'd been spoiled having lived with Lee all that time, the way people who loved each other *should* be able to. It was *supposed* to be that way. Lovers together, sleeping curled up in each other's arms, waking up to each other, first thing. Not like this.

"Nothing happened, Naoto-chan. I just…wanted you to know."

Relief prickled down Naoto's arms. Though the heaviness in his chest remained. It was only a matter of time until Koji wouldn't be able to say that, especially if he was going to marry the woman. "It's all right," he murmured. Even though really, it wasn't all right. How could he have been so casual, so…arrogant, when he'd told Koji they could handle the situation this way? He sighed and sagged against the wall. Cool spring air wafted through the back alley behind the hotel, a spot he liked to go for breaks, to be alone. Only tonight, he didn't really want to be alone. This spring night was perfect weather for snuggling…

Naoto's dragon stirred as he pictured Koji's leanly muscled body and flawless skin. His very hands itched to cradle Koji's back as he kissed Koji hot and deep. Yet, just as quickly, his arousal faded. Phone sex just wasn't good enough right now. His entire body ached for Koji. *Kuso*. This was the crappiest time to have a hotel full of guests. The weekend crowd only cleared out in the evening. Until then, Kiku needed him. "I wish I could come see you, Koji-chan," he said, "but…weekends are…busy."

Koji's tension on the other end was nearly palpable. "Naoto-chan?"

Naoto's chest tightened. "Yes?"

"Do you…have you…you know…oh, I'm sorry. It's none of my business."

Naoto pushed away from the wall and paced in the alley. He knew what Koji was asking. This past week, he and Koji had managed to avoid this conversation. Unfortunately, Naoto hadn't been able to avoid sexual contact with a few guests. Really, like Ryu's regulars, they'd been older, wanting only a happy ending to their massage. After all, they were paying for a certain experience…

"Koji-chan, will you still…want me if I say I have? You know the difference. I explained it to you." He heard the pleading in his own voice. Not since Lee's death had he felt quite so…tormented.

"Of course I will. I understand."

Naoto halted and closed his eyes. He pulled in a deep breath to steady his pounding heart. Finally he could speak again. "I'd avoid it, if I could."

"I know."

"Koji-chan, I miss you."

"I miss you too."

He heaved a deep sigh. If he stayed outside too long, someone would have to come looking for him. "I'm sorry. I...have to go in now. Can I call you later?"

"Yes. Don't worry what time it is. I want you to call."

Naoto sighed again. "I will. Bye." He clicked off and opened the back door, wondering how the hell he was going to make it through the weekend.

Koji pressed the *end call* button on his phone and sat back against the sofa cushions.. His heart pounded and sweat heated his armpits in spite of the cool night. He sighed and set the phone down while that...feeling...that horrible monster raked at his insides. Only the sincerity and conviction in Naoto's voice soothed him. In all honesty, he himself, knew there was a vast difference between a hand job and the passionate lovemaking-sleeping together thing that he and Naoto had.

Finally, he felt calmer, calm enough to retrieve his drawing pad and make sketches of Naoto until his lover called him again.

Chapter Thirteen
Saturday…

Koji opened his eyes. He went to lift his head and pain shot through his neck. Rubbing the back of it with one hand, he became aware of the position he'd fallen asleep in, sitting up, his head tilted back against the cushions. As he rubbed the stiffness out, he grew aware that it was morning and that his drawing pad had slipped off his lap to the floor when he'd fallen asleep.

A truck chugged down the street in front of his building, the only sound in the quiet section of the neighbourhood. He sighed and rubbed his neck a bit more. When it felt looser, he started to rise and changed his mind. The heaviness he'd fallen asleep with remained, like an invisible shroud over his mind and heart.

He thought of Etsu and immediately the shroud darkened. She'd smiled at him so much, believing he was interested in her. Guilt squeezed in his chest.

Then he thought of Naoto. And craved Naoto's touch, the hard, protective warmth of Naoto's brawn against him.

Just then his phone rang. Koji started and fumbled for the phone. Naoto's name showed in the tiny window. As if Naoto had sensed he was being thought about. He pressed the button. "Naoto-chan, hi." His heartbeat sped up. "How are you?"

"I miss you. That's how I am. You sound like you just woke up. Did I wake you?"

Koji found himself smiling even though Naoto couldn't see him. "You didn't wake me. Don't worry." Even this simple conversation was good. Naoto's voice was a healing balm.

"Koji-chan, can I...may I...come see you today? Later? Just for a little while. The afternoons are often quiet. I can get away for a bit."

Koji's heart thumped. "Of course. I'd like that. When?"

"At two?"

Excitement skittered through him. "Yes, two o'clock. I'll be here." On the other end, he heard a sound like a sigh of relief.

"I can't wait to see you, Koji."

Koji smiled again. "Me too."

Naoto's happy feeling increased the closer he got to Koji's building. Getting through the day until now had been difficult. Koji saturated his mind and heart so much he had to summon all his discipline to concentrate on whatever he was doing.

Letting himself inside, he headed for the stairs and nearly collided with a man already on his way up.

"Excuse me. I'm sorry," Naoto murmured and bowed an apology.

The man nodded in return and stood aside so Naoto could bound past him. There was no time to waste. Every second that passed was another second not spent with Koji. He ran up all three flights of stairs and knocked loudly on Koji's door. "Koji-chan, I'm here." Every nerve ending in his body tingled in anticipation.

The door opened to reveal Koji's smiling face. Even in a baggy T-shirt and grey sweatpants, he was hot. "Naoto-chan."

Joy swept through Naoto. Thought melted away as he stepped forward and grabbed up Koji's slimmer form into an embrace. Koji pulled in a breath and laughed, but Naoto captured the sweet rich sound with a kiss.

Yesssss...Koji's mouth was velvety soft, delicious...Naoto slid his tongue against Koji's, tasted the moist warmth with eyes closed. With their lips pressed together, he set Koji down on his feet and pulled him closer, chest to chest. Koji's arms slipped around him and Naoto felt the press of the other man's palms into his back muscles as he slowed their kiss from fevered chafing to a languorous appreciation.

"What is this?"

Naoto's heart jumped. The voice was male. Deep. Stern. Naoto pulled away from Koji and turned.

The man he'd passed on the stairs stood in the doorway, watching them.

"Dad," he heard Koji say.

Naoto's blood ran cold and tension clenched in every muscle. So, this was the bastard who'd whipped Koji.

"What the hell is going on here, Koji? Who is this person?" Watanabe's eyes darted a suspicious glance in Naoto's direction.

"He's my..." Koji swallowed hard. "Lover." The word came out in a tight whisper.

A strange elation swept through Naoto's chest. Koji hadn't sold him out! But Koji was also terrified. His breathing was tight, stance huddled. Fear emanated from him in almost palpable waves.

Naoto stepped closer to Koji in a show of protection. Koji's glance darted to him and then back to his father whose glare had deepened, the corners of his mouth turned down. It wasn't difficult to picture this man wielding a strap in rage.

"Lover? Lover? I come to discuss important matters of your life with you and this is what I find? What about Etsu?"

"Don't worry," Naoto heard himself say. He knew he should shut up but couldn't help himself. "Koji will marry her to please you. All he ever does it try to please you."

Watanabe's eyes widened then narrowed again at Koji. "You're damn right you'll marry Etsu. You owe me this after what you did."

Naoto's face burned. "Koji has done nothing to you but be a good son."

Watanabe turned that furious look on him. "Good son, eh? Go on, Koji, tell him what you did. Tell him how you betrayed me with my own wife."

"I...I did nothing, Dad. I swear." Koji's eyes were large, glazed with fear.

Watanabe pointed at him. "I used to see the way she looked at you. You're a filthy liar. You've done nothing but dishonour me your whole life, you wretched —"

"Enough!"

Koji's gaze whipped to Naoto whose large hands shot out and fisted his father's collar. In the next second, Tashiro Watanabe was pinned, back to the wall, eyes wide, face suddenly ashen.

"Koji is a diamond," Naoto growled. "A precious jewel."

From the side, Koji could see Naoto's face was red. His thick arm and back muscles strained against his T-shirt.

"You will treat him with the respect he deserves." Naoto kept him pinned, his forearm muscles corded from the effort. "Let's see you beat him now. Scar him up some more, you sick bastard." He paused while Koji watched his father's lips work soundlessly.

"Just as I thought," Naoto went on, voice clenched. "You're nothing but a fucking bully." He pushed his face closer. "If you ever, *ever* say another cruel word to Koji or harm one hair on his head, you'll be picking your teeth up from the floor." With that, Naoto opened his fists and stepped back.

Only then did Koji realise his own jaw hung open at this unfamiliar sight. His father's shirt was rumpled, his face was flushed and his eyes were still wide, trained on Naoto as if Naoto were a tiger who would claw him to death if he moved a muscle. With an expressionless glance at Koji, Tashiro Watanabe inched his way towards the door and slipped out.

Naoto slammed the door closed in his wake and stood, back heaving, fists clenched, head bowed.

Koji stared at Naoto's back, watched the dark fall of his hair shift with his heavy breathing. He wanted to approach Naoto but found himself frozen in place as one emotion after the next churned inside him.

Slowly, Naoto turned around and looked at him. To Koji's surprise, the other man's eyes had lost their ferocity. He gazed at Koji with an almost sorrowful look. "Koji-chan, are you all right?"

Koji stared back at him. He wanted to nod, to say *yes*…anything, but couldn't.

Naoto's eyes widened. He stepped forward and dropped to his knees in front of Koji. "Koji-chan, you don't hate me, do you? I couldn't help it. You're so precious." He threw his arms around Koji, hands clutching his T-shirt in the back, and pressed his cheek into Koji's stomach. The way Lee had with his mother when he'd been terrified of losing her.

"Please, Koji, please. I'm sorry."

Finally able to move again, Koji lifted a hand to Naoto's hair and stroked it, noticing how his hand trembled. Shock warred with fear, embarrassment and other emotions in a tangle so intense he couldn't identify them. How could he be mad at Naoto for defending him? He continued to caress Naoto's hair as his feelings became clear. He was embarrassed, mortified. At his own fear and at his father's behaviour. Naoto shouldn't have had to defend him that way, hadn't had to get so angry for his sake. It was disgusting. "I didn't know he was coming," he said softly. "I swear. I'm sorry."

Naoto looked up at him, dark eyes misted yet searching. "Koji-chan, you're…embarrassed?"

He nodded. "Yes."

"Don't be, please." Naoto's cheek pressed to his stomach again and Koji felt the larger man's body sag against him. "Koji, you don't understand. I love you. I love you so much."

Koji's hand went to Naoto's hair again. Naoto was behaving exactly the way he did in Koji's drawings, saying the same beautiful things. Koji sighed. In the drawings, he could control everything that happened, make himself a brave character who deserved Naoto's love, a man who could stand up to his father and not need his boyfriend to do it for him.

In the drawings, he never had to get married and could go and live with Naoto at the White Tiger. In the world he created, there was nothing but bliss.

The reality couldn't be more painfully different.

Naoto looked up again and Koji could see tears shimmering in his eyes. His heart thumped. Naoto had been a fierce tiger only moments before and now was on his knees, crying. What kind of world did this man live in that he could experience and openly express such a range of emotion? Certainly not the same one *he* lived in, the world of silent agony and tortuous duty.

"Koji-chan, do you want me to leave?" Koji felt Naoto's fists tighten on his shirt and saw the fear of rejection in his eyes.

Koji's heart squeezed. Without thinking, he tugged Naoto's arms to make him stand. "No. I want you to sit down." He ushered the larger man over to the sofa, dropped his drawing pad to the floor and tugged Naoto onto the cushions.

Before he could sit down, he felt himself being pulled. Large arms closed around him and Naoto's lips covered his.

"Mmmnhh…" Naoto's tongue slipped past the seam of his lips, invaded his mouth hungrily.

Koji sank into the kiss, eyes closed, and slipped one hand into Naoto's hair. Naoto's fingers slid along the tendons of his neck, up and down in a caress while the other hand cradled Koji's back.

Naoto tasted him deeply, long and slow and Koji felt the other man's broad chest rise and fall against his. He was surprised when Naoto broke the kiss and held him slightly away. Naoto's eyes were still misted though now, the lids were heavy over his dark gaze. "Koji-chan, I've become a raw bleeding heart again." His voice was nearly a whisper. "I didn't think it would ever happen again, but it did." He paused and Koji watched Naoto's gaze study his. "I pray you understand, Koji-chan. Whatever you do is what I'll live with. I…can't explain it any other way. If you marry and come to me once a week, that's what I'll have. I'll live with it because I want you so much. If you tell me not to touch another man but you, I'll obey."

Koji stared into Naoto's eyes. His heart pounded so fiercely he couldn't formulate speech. What did you say to someone who was offering up their heart, body and soul to you so completely? So many times he'd wanted to say such things to Shizuko yet fear had stopped him. Every time he saw her his insides melted, his heart had gone to mush, Everything else that was described in the poems and songs happened to him. He felt them now…understood in his very blood what Naoto was saying. Only Naoto was living it while he cowered in the shadows, as always.

Something passed through Naoto's eyes…fear perhaps…or anguish. He reached up and cupped Koji's cheek. "Don't say anything yet, Koji-chan. It's all right. You've had so many demands made on you. I don't want to add to them." Naoto's thumb moved along his cheekbone. His other hand still rested on Koji's back, a warm gentle pressure that made him feel so…safe.

Desire swept through him in a sudden wave. He sank down on Naoto and covered the other man's lips with his. Naoto's lips parted on a soft groan. With growing ardour, he tasted Naoto, slid his hands over that broad muscular chest. Loved it…loved the strength, the power that emanated from him, that had defended him.

Strangely, Naoto pulled away from their kiss and squeezed Koji, just resting there, softly breathing. Time passed and Koji settled more into the simple embrace while the shock of the confrontation eased away. Perhaps they'd have a sweet visit after all. Maybe things weren't as hopeless as they now seemed.

A noise startled Koji. He lifted away, tension gripping his body.

His phone.

He looked down at Naoto who was staring up at him, his skin flushed, eyes dark. Naoto sighed. "You should get that."

Koji stared at the phone another moment. Certainly it was his father calling to berate him some more, especially for the company he kept. For a moment, he decided to ignore it, then a strange feeling in his gut made him reach over and pick it up. He looked at the ID and pulled in a breath. Gina was calling him. His gut lurched. This couldn't be good.

With a glance at Naoto, he pressed the button. "*Moshi moshi*, Gina."

"Koji-chan?"

Koji's stomach churned at the sound of distress in Gina's voice. "What is it, Gina? Are you all right?" In his peripheral vision he saw Naoto sit up.

"It's Dad. Something's wrong. He just came home and his face was so pale. He sat down and couldn't catch his breath. Jiro and I are driving him to the emergency room. Can you come?"

Koji's vision blurred. The hand holding his phone felt suddenly sweaty. "Of course. I'll leave now." He pressed the button and launched off the sofa. "I have to go. My father's on his way to the hospital." *And it's my fault.*

Naoto jumped up. "Koji-chan..." His eyes looked tortured. "I'm so sorry." He bowed his head. "It's my fault."

"No it's not." Koji pulled on his jacket even though a cold sweat had already broken out all over his body. He looked at Naoto's bowed head, at the way the man's broad shoulders drooped. The sight suddenly enraged him, made him want to pick up pieces of furniture and smash them into the walls, through the windows and scream until he had no voice left. He balled his hands into fists, dug his nails into his palms. "This is what happens because I tried to be happy."

Naoto lifted his gaze. Koji's eyes had a dark look in them he'd seen only briefly, when Koji had been showing him the album he'd made and had gotten upset over Naoto's assessment of his feelings for Shizuko. Tiny muscles worked in Koji's jaw and the slimmer man's knuckles were white from the fists he was making. Koji was wrong, of course, about the happiness thing, but now was a time to shut up about it.

Truth was, he'd pushed Koji's father up against the wall and threatened the man with physical violence. The man was no kid and now could very well be having a heart attack.

If this was anyone's fault…

"I'd offer to go with you, Koji-chan, but I think it wouldn't be a good idea." He'd consider himself lucky if Koji wanted to see him again after this.

"I guess you're right." He turned and started for the door.

Naoto followed, slipped on his sandals and went out the door with him. He remembered the hospital being only a few blocks away. With each step he told himself to go to the bus and let Koji go himself, but each step that passed, he remained at Koji's side.

Koji walked quickly, not speaking but Naoto could see the emotions churning on the other man's face. At least he didn't turn to Naoto and tell him to go away. Finally, at the hospital's entrance, Koji stopped and turned to him. "I'll call you and let you know what's happened."

Naoto resisted the overpowering urge to pull Koji into his arms. There were just so many reasons he couldn't do that now. Maybe never again. He nodded and then bowed his head. "I'm so sorry, Koji-chan."

"What are you sorry for?"

The question shocked Naoto. He straightened and looked into Koji's eyes. Koji was looking at him, that darkness in his large eyes again.

Naoto stared back at him as people passed them on either side. What was he sorry for? Defending the man he loved from a bully who'd wounded him his whole life? How could he be sorry for that? How could he be sorry that Koji's father was a hateful bastard, not an understanding, caring person like Lecy?

When he didn't answer, Koji sighed. "I'll call you. Thank you for...walking with me." After a noticeable hesitation, Koji turned and went through the glass doors.

Naoto watched Koji disappear inside. He stood on the sidewalk, his heart pounding, for what felt like hours before he finally went for the bus back to Ni Chome. He had to get back and tell Kiku what he'd done.

Ryu was in the office, dusting, when Naoto walked in. Ryu's welcoming smile faded as soon as their gazes met. He threw down his dust cloth and came right over. To Naoto's surprise, Ryu picked up his hand. "Naoto, what the hell happened? You look freaked out." He tugged Naoto to a chair by Kiku's desk and knelt down by him, still holding his hand.

Naoto heaved a deep sigh and told him everything.

Ryu squeezed his hand. "You did the right thing," he said gently. "How could you not have gotten so angry?"

He shook his head, letting his shoulders sag. "I should have controlled myself. Kiku will be angry with me."

"For what?"

Naoto caught his breath and looked up.

Kiku stood in the doorway. "What will I be angry for?"

Ryu released Naoto's hand and turned to him. "Naoto was at Koji's apartment. Koji's father walked in unexpectedly and started saying horrible things to Koji."

"I pushed him up against the wall and threatened to knock out his teeth if he hurt Koji," Naoto finished. He blew out a heavy breath and bowed his head. "Koji's father is in the hospital now. I don't know what's wrong with him."

Before Kiku could answer, Naoto dropped to his knees and bowed. "I'm sorry, Kiku-sensei. I've shamed you. I'll leave, if you wish it."

"Hell no!" Ryu was beside him, an arm across his shoulder. "Don't you dare leave. You'd never make him leave, Kiku...would you?"

Naoto tensed, avoiding the older man's gaze.

"Of course not. Don't be ridiculous."

Kiku was suddenly kneeling in front of him. When Naoto looked up, Kiku's expression showed sympathy. "I would never make you leave because you defended someone who was being abused." He grinned. "That would certainly make me a hypocrite."

Naoto smiled weakly. He'd heard quite a few stories from Ryu of Kiku's days as a *yakuza*. Kiku could be pretty tough when he wanted and it was a point of contention between him and Ryu now that Kiku had grown too passive during his practice of the White Tiger path. Naoto bowed again. Relief fanned through every inch of him and he bowed. "Thank you," he murmured.

A hand on his shoulder made him look up. Ryu was gazing at him. Sympathy radiated from his eyes.

As if it had turned a key inside him, the expression made tears sting in Naoto's eyes. Tension released and he slumped over, letting the salty droplets spill out. This had turned out to be the second worst day in his life. He'd lost Lee and now, he'd probably lost Koji.

Before they'd even really had a chance.

~~~~~

"Koji-chan."

Koji slipped his hands from his hair and looked up. Gina stood in front of him. In the back of his consciousness he felt the stiffness in his limbs from sitting in the waiting room chair for hours. "Yes?" He jumped to his feet, heart pounding.

Gina smiled. "Dad will be okay. The doctor said he had an *anxiety* attack. Not a heart attack."

Dropping back into the chair, Koji heaved the deepest sigh of relief. He knew well about anxiety attacks, considering he'd had about five hundred of them in recent years. They weren't harmful…just frightening when you didn't know what was happening to you. Tears sprang in his eyes. He reached up to wipe them away. Relief made his limbs feel like gelatin.

"The doctor also said Dad can come home now. He should just rest and he'll be fine. Will you come back with us?"

Koji stiffened. Behind Gina, he saw Jiro with their father. The older man sat in a wheelchair. The colour in his face was restored but he looked tired and sullen. The cold sweat returned in Koji's armpits and his stomach tightened again. He swallowed hard. He had no excuse to leave and go home. If he refused, Gina would want to know why. Certainly, his father wouldn't want him around, and yet Koji felt guilt pull him, like an iron rope between him and his father. He nodded. "Of course I will."

Slowly he stood and followed Gina over to his father. Tashiro Watanabe's eyes widened when his gaze met Koji's but then he looked down quickly.

Koji's blood chilled in his veins but he silently walked with his family out of the hospital to the curb where they helped their father into a taxi. Koji sat in the front seat and went back with them to his house.

As if things couldn't get worse, Etsu was standing on the front walk when the cab pulled up. She wore a smile though her eyes looked anxious. No doubt, Gina had called her friend with the news.

Koji's heart started to pound. He needed to find a private spot and call Naoto, to tell him his father was okay. Naoto believed himself at fault. Once inside the house, Koji excused himself to the bathroom and pulled his phone from his jacket pocket phone. If he spoke quietly, he could at least tell Naoto the news and then promise to call him later when he'd left.

But when he opened his phone, he found it dead. He frowned when the power refused to turn on with repeated pressing of the button. It didn't make sense. He charged the thing every night before he went to sleep. When he'd picked it up before going to the hospital, it had been working fine.

Kuso.

Koji sank down onto the closed toilet seat and forced in a deep breath. With Etsu here, there would be no chance in hell to call Naoto from the house phone. Now he'd have to wait until later. Then he remembered, he didn't have Naoto's number written down. He'd programmed it directly into his phone. His card for the White Tiger was back in his apartment and if he left now, he'd never be forgiven.

I saw the way she used to look at you. His father's words rang in Koji's mind. His father had known all this time. Known how he'd felt and how Shizuko had felt. How could he ever be with Naoto now, after this? After having tortured his father for years. Of course, he hadn't known what he was doing at the time, but it couldn't be an excuse. He'd made an attempt to be happy and look what had happened.

Koji felt darkness envelop him, like a deep cave, sucking him into its endless depths, beyond his control. The darkness stayed with him, weighed on his chest the entire evening. Etsu and Gina made supper and Koji forced himself to eat as much as he could so as not to rouse suspicion, but it was nearly impossible with his father nearby, glancing at him with a furrowed brow and then away, as if hating Koji and terrified of him at the same time.

Koji sighed and took a sip of tea, working not to let his hand tremble. He looked at Etsu, at her long hair and smooth skin. She *was* pretty and very sweet. It had been very kind of her to come over and help with supper…

He pulled in a breath. What the hell had he just been doing?

Etsu must have felt his gaze on her, for she looked up just then and smiled. Her eyes widened briefly in a way that seemed to show pleasure at him noticing her.

His gut lurched. He forced himself to return the smile and continued to struggle with his meal.

After supper, Gina and Etsu went to do the dishes, leaving Koji with his father and Jiro. He followed them into the living room and sat hunched on the sofa, staring at a *sumo* wrestling match on the television. Koji sighed. Last week at this time, he was sitting with Naoto, watching Ryu box. Two things he would never normally do. At one point, Ryu knocked his opponent down and the crowd had gone wild, everyone there seeming to sense that Ryu was the underdog coming out victorious. Koji had felt Naoto's hand around his, squeezing it, for just a moment before releasing him. And Koji had felt something he hadn't since watching the *sakura* petals fall with Shizuko — *alive*. The thought made his chest squeeze. Strange how life could become so vastly…different in the space of a few days.

The match ended and Jiro flipped off the TV. "Maybe you should get some rest, Dad," he said, picking up the empty beer bottles on the coffee table.

"Yes, I will." Tashiro Watanabe took a deep breath and pushed up slowly from his chair.

Koji sat up at attention, then rose as his father did, heart pounding. It occurred to him that the older man was exaggerating his tiredness, but then he remembered his father's expression that day as Naoto gripped his collar and kept him pinned to the wall. Guilt spiked through Koji. Perhaps it didn't matter whether his father was faking to a degree. The fear he'd experienced was real. As was the betrayal for so many years.

Clearing his throat, Koji dared to approach his father. "Good night, Dad," he murmured. "I'll see you tomorrow." He felt like an obsequious mouse…disgusting…but couldn't help it.

Tashiro Watanabe halted and looked at him. The man's brow was furrowed and his lips turned down in that seemingly permanent scowl he had. Come to think of it, Koji didn't remember the last time he'd heard his father laugh. "Good night, Koji. Walk Etsu home." Then he turned and walked slowly out.

Koji stared at his father's back. Those last words spiralled through him in an icy way. The message was clear.

Jiro cast him a sympathetic glance but went along with his father-in-law, as if the man would fall down again. As usual, there was nothing the man could do for Koji except sympathise.

Etsu was in the kitchen with Gina. The two women were laughing softly together about something, but when Koji came to the doorway, their laughter ebbed.

Koji's heartbeat started to race. "I can walk you home, if you'd like."

She smiled and nodded, too enthusiastically for Koji. "Yes, thank you."

He and Etsu both said goodnight to Gina and left. Koji walked silently at Etsu's side. He remembered the thoughts he'd entertained of her earlier and sighed. The feeling of darkness that had shrouded him earlier, now settled more deeply. "Thank you, Etsu, for helping us today."

She smiled up at him. "No problem. I understand how difficult it is when something happens with a parent." Her voice was soft, sympathetic and traitorously, Koji felt soothed by it.

"Yes, it is," he agreed.

At her door, he stood in front of her. Etsu gazed up at him with that longing he'd seen on her face since they were kids and found himself wishing she would just say the first words so that he didn't have to. She wouldn't, though. She was being proper, demure. Probably doing what she felt was necessary to impress him.

It would be so much easier if she were a bitch, hard and mean. No man would blame him for rejecting her in that case, even his father. But Etsu wasn't a bitch. Not even a little. She was sweet and kind and definitely pretty.

And she so obviously wanted him to kiss her.

Life was handing him another chance to tell her the truth.

Or...to go on with life the way Naoto had said was possible. Marry a woman and keep him on the side. At least they'd have *some* time together. That was a hell of a lot more than he'd ever thought to have at all. Two weeks ago, he'd been working himself into an early grave. Naoto had brought him back to health and that special thing had happened between them — he couldn't even think the words. Now, he had the key to fulfilling his duty and having what made him happy.

"I...should go," he said softly. Once he said the words to her, there was no going back. And he couldn't say them just yet. Tomorrow night, he'd do it. He'd kiss her tomorrow, so she'd know.

Just not tonight.

He leaned down and pressed his lips to her cheek. Like before her skin was soft and she smelled like perfume. He could get used to that...if he had to.

And it looked like he had to.

"Good night, Etsu."

She smiled but in the lamplight over the door, Koji saw the disappointment slip through her eyes.

Well, tomorrow night she wouldn't be so disappointed.

"Good night."

He waited until she was safely inside and then went home. He grabbed the card for the White Tiger and went to a nearby public phone. Thankfully he had enough time left on his phone card. His hand shook as he punched in the number and listened to it ring.

"*Moshi moshi*, White Tiger." A soft male voice answered. Not Naoto.

Koji cleared his throat. "Yes, may I please speak with Naoto?"

"He's not available at the moment. May I take a message?"

Koji shivered. If Naoto couldn't come to the phone, Koji didn't want to know what he was doing. Naoto had said he'd never touch another man if Koji didn't want him to, but Koji hadn't responded. "Can you please tell him that Koji called—"

"Watanabe-san?"

"Yes." Koji furrowed his brow.

"This is Ryu. How nice to hear from you. Naoto will be glad you called. I can have him call you back. Maybe in an hour?"

Kuso. An hour. He definitely didn't want to know what Naoto was doing. If he'd been there, Naoto would be doing *him* instead. Koji's chest tightened and he fought to breathe normally. "That's not possible, Ryu-san. My phone died and I'm on a public phone. Please tell him..." Koji hesitated. What to tell him, exactly? He didn't want to say *I love you* as a message that Ryu would hear. He took a deep breath as the words formed in his mind. "Please tell him my father is fine. Nothing is wrong with him. I will come to see Naoto on

Tuesday but I'll call him tomorrow when I get my phone fixed."

"Got it. I'll tell him as soon as possible, Watanabe-san."

Koji sighed. He would have been relieved completely had Naoto been able to speak to him directly. "Thank you very much. Um, I hope you're well."

"Yes, thank you. And you."

Koji hesitated again. An ache tightened his chest, a desire to say more, to connect with Ryu on the other end, but he couldn't. Couldn't tell him what was really going on. "Thank you, Ryu-san. Um…good night."

"Good night, Watanabe-san."

Koji hung up the phone and leaned against the wall. His breath had tightened painfully and cold sweat covered his body in spite of the cool night air. He closed his eyes a minute and worked his thoughts under control. In the future, it wouldn't be this way. They'd have a schedule. Tuesdays together. They could plan times to speak on the phone in between, maybe during the days when Koji was at work. And then, maybe, once in a while, he could go to the White Tiger on another day and be with Naoto then. It would all be arranged so that he'd never have to call and be told that Naoto couldn't come to the phone, leaving Koji jealous and wondering what his lover was really doing.

Sudden agitation made Koji push away from the wall. That nerves on the outside of his skin feeling was happening. Yet out on the street, with people passing by on foot and in cars, he couldn't very well pace and rub his scalp like a madman.

He started walking, more briskly with each step. If he was going to freak, he preferred to be in his apartment where no one could see him. No one would understand the way Shizuko had understood or the way Naoto understood him now.

As he walked, he unclipped his phone and tried to turn it on again. Dead. Stopping under a streetlamp, he pulled the sim card out. Nothing wrong with it. It was only a few months old, too. So weird. This had never happened to him before and there really was no reason. He slipped it back into his jacket and continued home.

Once upstairs, however, he couldn't shake the agitation. Before Koji had left the White Tiger, Naoto had shown him how to sit quietly and listen to his breath a few minutes each day. Koji tried to sit now and do it, but his mind fought so hard he couldn't sit still.

Launching off the sofa, he went out of his apartment, up the stairs to the roof. He paced a while on the gravel, and then walked over to the edge. Kneeling down he looked over, stared at the sidewalk below. He hadn't felt quite this hideous since that morning at the hospital last summer. He'd fallen asleep in the waiting room and had woken up to see Shizuko's doctor looking down at him with a sad expression. In that moment, he'd wanted the earth to swallow him, obliterate his mind and body so he wouldn't have to feel this pain.

That's how he felt now. What was the use of trying to be happy when it only led to this?

He leaned further over. It would be so easy. So easy to fall and end the misery. Who would care? His own father wouldn't care. He'd probably be glad.

But then...someone would care. Maybe several people. But certainly one person.

Koji is a diamond. A precious jewel.

Someone who cared enough to risk being hated or scorned for his sake. Someone who'd already been devastated from losing someone he loved, heart and soul. And cared enough to love again, in spite of the pain.

Koji froze. He pushed back, away from the wall, heart pounding. How could he have been so selfish? So cruel?

He sat, staring down at the gravel of the roof when sudden, intense exhaustion hit him, saturated every inch of his body. Without thinking, he lay back, looked up at the stars and then closed his eyes, unable to stay awake a second longer.

Chapter Fourteen
Sunday…

The second Naoto opened his eyes, he reached for his phone and dialled Koji. Koji had said his phone was broken, but maybe it was fixed now. He couldn't stand another moment of waiting. He'd been relieved when Ryu delivered a message from Koji, but sorry he'd been massaging a guest when the call came. This was going to be one of the really shitty parts about the arrangement they'd have. And if he'd heard Koji's message correctly about Tuesday, Koji must have made some kind of decision during the night.

A decision Naoto would have to live with. Even though he now wanted Koji with him day and night.

No answer except Koji's voice mail message. Naoto closed his eyes. The mere sound of Koji's deep voice flooded him. Just as he heard voices in the hallway. Sounded like they were arguing.

At the beep, Naoto pulled in a breath. "Koji-chan, I got your message last night. I'm sorry I couldn't talk to you. I…miss you…so much. I know your phone isn't working but I needed to call you anyway. I understand what you said about Tuesday. I understand. Like I told you, I'll accept whatever comes I want to be with you so much." He paused. The voices in the hallway were coming closer to his door. Ryu and Kiku. He had to finish his message in a hurry. "I'll wait to hear from you today. I'm glad your father wasn't hurt. I'm sorry about that. But…" A quick sliver of anger sliced through him. "I'm not sorry I defended you. I love you. You're in my heart all the time."

Naoto hung up and slid open his door, about to step out when the voices stopped him. They were right outside his door now.

Kiku and Ryu's conversation was heated. Well, Ryu was heated and Kiku was trying to remain calm, his attempt at control only fanning Ryu's flames.

"Kiku, no! Don't make me hide again," Ryu said. "This is crazy already. I'm sick of running from that bastard."

"Please, Ryu. You know I want to protect you."

Naoto remained still. He slid the door closed and tiptoed to his bed, but the rice paper *soji* screens did little to mute the sound and Naoto could hear every word.

"I know you want to protect me." Ryu sounded less angry now. "But I don't want to leave my home again. I feel safe here with you and Naoto."

That vote of praise made Naoto smile in spite of his distress.

"Besides, Kiku, I'm a *boxer* for God's sake. I can defend myself."

"Not against guns."

"Kiku, you seem to forget, I grew up around these assholes. Suzuki isn't going to shoot me. If he kills me, he doesn't have a chance of…well…you know."

"Shush!" Now Kiku sounded angry. Ryu had pressed the wrong button mentioning the rape again. It seemed to Naoto that Ryu was dealing with what had happened to his own body better than Kiku was. The situation was really complex and Naoto knew that Kiku, having been an underling with Suzuki, would simply have killed Suzuki at the time if he could have, if doing so wouldn't set off a whole other rat's nest of problems.

"That's it, Ryu. No more arguments. I'm going to ask Naoto right now to take you to Yokohama."

Naoto heaved a deep breath. Yokohama, the city twenty minutes from Tokyo with a huge Chinatown, where Kiku's mother lived. That's where Kiku sent Ryu each time Suzuki came to use the White Tiger's facilities. Free use of the White Tiger had been part of the agreement made allowing Kiku to leave the organisation.

"No, Kiku!"

"Naoto," Kiku said from the other side of the screen, "I'm sorry to disturb you."

Naoto slid open the door. "You're not disturbing me. Sorry I overslept. I'm almost ready to go downstairs."

Kiku's brow was furrowed. "It's all right. I need your help."

Behind him, Ryu stood, dressed in his hotel uniform, brow equally as furrowed. His nicks and bruises from his fight had nearly faded. "We shouldn't be bothering Naoto. He's got his own problem."

"It's all right. I want to help."

Kiku frowned. "Suzuki is coming tonight and—"

"Please, Naoto, try to convince him to let me stay." Ryu stepped between them.

But Kiku drew him back with a firm hand on his shoulder and Ryu yielded. "Ryu, hush. We're lucky the man brings his own pets to massage him and doesn't demand for you, or anyone else here, to rub his cock." He took a deep breath. "Suzuki wants me to call him when the weekend crowd clears out. Can you please take Ryu to my mother's?"

"Kiku—"

Kiku shut Ryu up with a hard look and Naoto could see the man who'd once been a tough *yakuza* under Ryu's father's command.

Naoto glanced between them. For the moment, he put his problem with Koji aside in order to concentrate. It was a difficult spot to be in, understanding both Ryu and Kiku's untenable positions. Kiku was Naoto's mentor, someone he wanted to obey. And Ryu, having already been shit on by his own parents and raped by a psychopathic yak, was someone Naoto didn't want to make feel abandoned again at all. He cast about in his mind for a possible compromise. Then it hit him. "Kiku-sensei, I think I might have a solution."

Kiku's eyebrows rose. "I'm listening."

Behind him, Ryu moved closer, one hand coming to rest on Kiku's arm.

"Maybe Ryu could stay with Lee's mother in Shin-Okubo. She and Ryu like each other. Lecy's a good cook and I know she'd be grateful for the company. That way, Ryu would still be in Shinjuku, practically walking distance from here. Then, if Suzuki leaves early enough, Ryu could come right home."

Kiku nodded. His broad chest heaved in a sigh. "If she is agreeable to that, I'd gratefully accept."

"Me too," Ryu said. "Thank you."

Naoto pressed the button of his phone, still in his hand. "Let me just make sure she will be home." Lecy was home and was, of course, happy to have "little Ryu" as she'd nicknamed him, come over. Naoto thanked her and ended the call. "It's all arranged. I'll bring Ryu over there around supper time."

Both men in front of him breathed relief. "Thank you, Naoto," Kiku said.

Ryu nodded. "Yes, thank you so much." The tension had drained from Ryu's classically beautiful features and Naoto's heart squeezed. He understood that Ryu felt he could deal with anything as long as he was here with Kiku and his friends.

"No problem at all, Kiku-sensei."

Then Kiku looked at him intently, brow furrowed again. "How are you?"

Naoto sighed. "Worried. I haven't spoken to Koji since we parted at the hospital. I know he tried to reach me. I called him just now but his phone is still not working. I left him a message."

Kiku paused a moment. "Do you have anything he touched?"

Naoto's stomach fluttered. He knew that Kiku could receive images that way and could tell him what was happening with Koji. But did he want to know? And did he even have something Koji had touched recently besides himself? "He touched me..." Then Naoto remembered. "And he touched this." He turned and plucked the white jade tiger off the shelf, holding it out towards Kiku. "He gave it to me as a gift. At the end of his stay here."

Ryu's eyes went wide. "Wow, that's beautiful." The envy was clear in his voice, not over the object itself, but over the obvious feeling behind the gift.

Naoto nodded. "Yes, it is."

"That will do." Kiku gently retrieved the small statue and held it. The air in the room seemed to hum with a quiet energy. Naoto remained motionless, as did Ryu.

Finally, Kiku took a breath and the spell of energy broke. He handed the small tiger back to Naoto with both hands. "He's sleeping now," Kiku said softly. "He's been battling his demons all night."

There was a look in Kiku's eyes that made Naoto think he wasn't telling all he'd seen, but the fact that Koji was all right was the only thing that mattered. He owed his head. "Thank you," he murmured. "I was worried. He feels so guilty all the time."

Kiku nodded, his expression sympathetic, as was Ryu's. "Yes, it'll be better for him when he understands he doesn't have to fight. That his demons aren't really demons."

Ryu was looking at him with a sweet smile, his eyes empathetic. He returned the smile and dared to reach out and ruffle the other man's hair before going back into his room to get dressed.

There was nothing else to do now but wait.

~~~~~

That evening, Naoto brought Ryu in a cab with him to Lecy's. It was bad enough that Suzuki was coming to the White tiger. He still hadn't heard from Koji and worried even though Kiku had offered to look again for a vision and had put his hands on Naoto's shoulders, reassuring him that Koji was still asleep.

With a deep sigh, Naoto gazed out the window as the cab pulled away from the curb in front of the White Tiger.

"Naoto, I can't thank you enough for this." Ryu's voice pulled his attention back. When he turned, Ryu's sincere gaze rested on him.

Naoto smiled. "No problem. You're been through so much already. I'm glad if this helps."

"It definitely does." Ryu sat back, his gym bag on his lap. "I'm just so tired of it, you know? Of Kiku having to jump because of that bastard." His dark eyes looked sad as the neon glow from outside signs shifted across his skin and hot pink hair. "Kiku would have ranked well over Suzuki by now had he stayed in and Suzuki knows it. That's why he busts Kiku's balls this way all the time." Ryu looked at him, eyes narrowing. "I think that's even why Suzuki…did…what he did to me. A *fuck you* to Kiku, you know, for being preferred by all the higher ups, including his own father." He sighed and looked down.

Naoto just listened quietly, sensing Ryu's need to talk. Ryu had never spoken openly like this with him and Naoto knew he'd achieved a rare place of confidence. He didn't want to do anything to violate it.

"The only reason I agree to go to Kiku's mother's place each time is because, well, I'm so grateful Kiku cares about me so much."

That last bit made Naoto sigh. He knew from Kiku that since Ryu was a kid, Kiku had acted as a self-appointed guardian angel over him and that Ryu worshipped him for it. "I understand," he said softly.

Now Ryu looked straight at him. "I know you do. Hey, enough about me and my problems. How are things with you and Koji-san now? That is, if I may ask."

"Of course you may ask." Naoto sighed and looked out the window. The cab was just entering Little Asia. Damn, the main street had changed so much in the last ten years. The place that had once been run down, a place most people didn't care to go and had now become quite the swanky destination with its array of Korean restaurants and grocers. Lee's parents had come from Beijing on the first wave of immigrants before the real estate prices had soared and had secured their little apartment and shop on one of the side streets, still quieter than the main drag. Had it still been that way, the yak whom Lee had paid to hit him might have been caught. As it was, Lee's killing remained unsolved...

"I don't know," he said to Ryu. "I...never thought it would happen like this again." He sighed. "The thing is, he's under horrible pressure to get married and well, he's got a woman."

Ryu shook his head. "Man, that's rough."

Naoto nodded. Just discussing it made his chest ache. "I told him about all the married guys who come to the White Tiger, and he wants to try and make it work even if he gets married. But truthfully, he's...I don't know...I think that will be impossible. I think he'll end up choosing one life or the other." Naoto blew out a breath, remembering the look on Koji's face when his father had gotten the kind of reprimand he'd deserved for a hell of a long time. "I don't have to tell you about violent men, Ryu-chan. His father's one of those and has Koji under his thumb like I've never seen before." Naoto felt his heart darken with those words, with the heaviness of their truth.

Ryu's dark liquid gaze was sympathetic. If anyone knew about heartache, Ryu did. "I'm sorry, Naoto. I hope so much that things work out for you two. You're both good guys and you really deserve to be happy."

Naoto smiled. "Thanks, Ryu. Funny, that's how I feel about you."

Before Ryu could answer, the cab pulled up at the address Naoto had given the driver. Naoto saw Ryu upstairs, spent a few minutes with him and Lecy until he knew that everything was okay, then left to go back to the White Tiger. Of course, Lecy saw the something was bothering him but he couldn't bring himself to talk about it with her yet.

The whole ride back, he fingered the buttons on his phone, wanting nothing more than to call Koji. But Koji had promised to call later after he'd rested. He'd probably gone back to his sister's house for supper. Unfortunately, that woman...Etsu...might also be there.

At the door to the White Tiger, Naoto paid the driver and went inside, thinking the whole time how this just sucked. Plain and simple.

~~~~~

Shizuko's face hovered in front of Koji. Then Naoto's, while oceans of long sleek ebony hair caressed his cheeks...

Koji opened his eyes. Bright light invaded them and he squinted. The images faded. A gentle gust of air, like a breeze, passed over his face.

The sky. He was looking up at the sky. But how could that be if he was in bed?

Slowly his memory trickled in. The light floating of sleep receded, leaving the heaviness of his body. His hand rested on something rough. He moved his fingers around. Gravel. Then he remembered what he'd nearly done...where he was and shame flooded him. Naoto would probably hate him if he knew. Which was why he'd never tell him.

Slowly, stiffly, Koji sat up. His body ached from sleeping on the hard gravel. He raked a hand through his hair, wondering how long he'd actually been asleep. Judging from the angle of the sun, he'd slept most of the day. Another few hours and he'd be going back to his family's house.

His gut lurched and tightened. Another few hours and he'd ask Etsu out for real.

Rising to his feet, he turned and went inside, not even glancing at the edge of the roof. As he went down the stairs, he felt the weight of his phone in his pocket and reached for it. Then stopped. No. He wouldn't call Naoto now. On Sunday, Naoto would still be busy, no doubt and it was torture to think of the exact nature of his busyness.

Back in his apartment, Koji turned the shower on in the bathroom, stripped, and looked at his reflection while he waited for the water to heat up. The dark circles were back under his eyes and his cheekbones looked too sharp again. He'd always showed weight loss very quickly and noticed it especially now, after a couple of weeks of eating more than he had in years.

He sighed. The look in his eyes was haunted again, guilty, like a whipped dog. That expression had become such a part of him for so long he'd stopped noticing it. Now, after having felt some happiness, the contrast was striking.

Did falling in love mean your life automatically got torn apart? He thought of Naoto. Naoto had been in love before and it had torn up his life. But Naoto had loved that guy Lee anyway, dealing with whatever nightmare he had to. His heart wasn't his own. Then again, Naoto was the first person Koji had met who had a real community of friends who cared about him just as he was...who actually encouraged him to be that way. Koji couldn't help but wonder what it would be like to be in a place like that, spending his days and nights with someone who saw him as 'a precious jewel' rather than as an investment. Such things weren't supposed to matter. Being a part of...doing your part...those things were supposed to matter. And he'd been doing them religiously. Yet, the result had been working himself so hard he'd risked getting seriously ill.

What he wanted also wasn't supposed to matter as long as he did the right thing.

Was working yourself into an early grave the right thing?

Steam billowed out behind him. Koji pulled himself away from the mirror and got under the hot spray where he stayed until his skin was nearly raw.

A while later, dried and dressed, he shrugged into his jacket. The phone was still in there but he didn't pull it out. There wasn't time to get a new one now. He'd have to call Naoto later tonight from a public phone. Later, when it was quiet at the White Tiger, he wouldn't be as worried about Naoto's giving some strange guy a blowjob.

Before he left, he went into the kitchen. A bottle of saké sat on the counter. He hadn't touched it in the longest time, keeping it there mostly for the rare times when Hiru had come over to hang out. He picked it up, unscrewed the cap and took a healthy swig. The burn of the clear liquid spread through his veins, made his mind soften and tingle. Tension drained a bit from his body. He started to lift the bottle to his lips for a second sip and froze, disgusted. Was this how he would deal with being married? Drink to make it bearable?

No. He practically slammed the bottle down, replaced the cap and went to leave. Passing the sofa, his fell on his drawing pad. He hadn't touched it since Friday and the latest drawing of him and Naoto, naked bodies entwined lay on the floor. A sudden impulse made Koji pick it up. He folded the cover over it and put it under his arm, as if having the drawings of Naoto could bolster him, make him feel safer.

Then, finally, he left.

As soon as he walked into Gina's house, the tension already coiled Koji's neck and shoulders worsened. Voices wafted from the dining room, Gina's excited buzz and then his father's solemn tone. His heart sped up as he set down his drawing pad and slipped off his shoes. Gina's voice grew louder as he neared the room.

For a moment, Koji held his breath. Had his father told her what happened the day before? He listened a moment. No. She was going on about clothing or something and didn't sound particularly upset. He should have known. Even though the tension between them was painfully obvious at this point, seeing as his father had barely spoken two words to him since the hospital, Tashiro Watanabe would never have told Gina something so embarrassing.

"Koji-chan, is that you?" Gina appeared in the doorway, smiling.

"Yes."

Her smile deepened and she beckoned to him. He kissed her cheek briefly and then straightened. His stomach lurched when his gaze met his father's.

The older man nodded to him and looked quickly down at his place setting.

Koji swallowed hard and walked in. The next person he saw was Etsu, smiling at him. "Hi."

He nodded. "Hello." A lump formed in his throat, vying with equally fierce tightness in his chest.

Gina held his arm all the way to his seat at the table. "How are you?" Her voice had a hushed conspiratorial kind of sound and her eyes shone. Was it possible she was this happy about his seeing Etsu?

"Great. Just great, thanks." He knelt down at his place and stole another glance at his father. The man's gaze was still cast downward. In contrast, his brother-in-law wore an especially happy expression. Koji looked around quickly to see if anyone else noticed the tension between him and his father, but no one seemed to. There was something else going on.

Gina was busy setting bowls of steaming soup at each place before kneeling at hers.

With another glance at his father, Koji picked up his spoon.

"Koji-chan."

His hand froze in mid-lift. He looked up at Gina. A huge smile stretched almost the entire width of her face. "Koji-chan, I have something to tell you."

He put the spoon down and dropped his hand to his lap. "Yes?"

"I'm pregnant. I found out today."

Whoa. Heat flushed along the back of Koji's neck. So, that's what the excitement had been. He worked a smile to his lips. "That's great, Gina. Congratulations."

Gina's eyes misted over. He'd never seen her so happy. "Thank you. I'm so glad you'll be his...or her...uncle. That means so much to me."

"Me too."

"I hope you won't mind if I make your old room into the nursery." Gina's smile faded somewhat.

Koji's heartbeat galloped. "Of course not."

Her smile returned. "Thank you, Koji-chan." She took a spoonful of soup and Koji did the same, forcing himself to eat. Koji did the best he could to eat everything put before him, so as not to appear as troubled as he felt. All the time he was aware of Etsu next to him. She'd left her long hair down tonight and every so often, he'd catch a glimpse of the light glinting off of it. And of course, each time, a pang shot through him. Wishing life were different was as agonising as being apart from Naoto. He could never come here with Naoto and have his family be as joyful about their happiness as they would be when he said he was going to marry Etsu, and then told them Etsu was carrying his baby.

He looked around at their faces again. Gina's happy chattering faded to the background as his mind swirled and his heart pounded. He'd wanted to please them so much, make them proud, able to brag to their friends about his accomplishments, his great job, his beautiful wife. He never could. He never could love the right people in the right way.

Shizuko.

The way he'd loved her had been wrong too.

Another memory flew into his mind. When he was fourteen, he'd seen her through the bathroom door, partly ajar, brushing her hair, wearing a silky nightgown. She'd been so pretty…so beautiful…and she was so good to him. His father practically ignored her. She was there to service his needs, to take care of his kids and clean his house. He'd hated his father for treating such a beautiful person that way. It wasn't his fault that Shizuko loved him. It wasn't his fault his father was an unloving prick. She must have felt as guilty as he did.

Watching the brush move down the length of her hair, he'd absolutely ached to go in there and hold her, to feel her softness, smell her skin. Feel surrounded by love.

That's all he ever wanted.

That's how Naoto made him feel.

He glanced at Etsu. She was smiling and nodding her head at something Gina was saying. He tried to picture sleeping next to her every night, except once a week when he'd be with Naoto. He tried to picture her pregnant, holding a child, a lifetime of commitment that would take him further and further away. He'd be doing nothing but working to pay the expenses, interrupted with a few moments of pleasurable escape with Naoto.

Didn't they all deserve more than that? Was this the true purpose of life? Work, fulfil your duties and then die? *No!*

Koji didn't realise he'd spoken out loud until the silence at the table penetrated his thoughts. He looked up. The eyes of the four other people were all set on him.

Gina frowned. "Koji, are you all right?"

He put down his fork. Under his father's hard, quizzical look, his heart pounded. No doubt his father wanted to reprimand him and didn't because of Naoto's warning.

Sweat erupted in his armpits. "Y…yes. I'm sorry." He forced a smile, for Gina's sake. "Just excited."

His answer was rewarded with a big smile and relief in Gina's eyes. "Of course, Koji-chan."

He looked at his sister. Terrible to ruin her special evening, so he sat back and forced himself to eat, smile and join in the conversation.

Finally, it was time to leave and Koji suggested walking Etsu home.

"Gina-chan, I'm happy for you." He kissed her cheek after rising from his seat. When he turned, his gaze met his father's. The older man looked quickly down and Koji now sensed the ripple of tension in Gina and the others. Without thinking, he knelt down and bowed to his father's profile. "Dad," he said softly when he'd straightened, "I've never meant to dishonour you or hurt you." Heart churning, he looked at his father. "But if I live a lie, then I'm already dishonouring both of us."

Tashiro Watanabe half-turned his face towards Koji. "What am I supposed to say to that?" he muttered.

Koji wiped his palms on his thighs and struggled to breathe normally. *Koji is a diamond. A precious jewel.* He sure as hell didn't feel like a precious jewel, but if Naoto felt that way, so be it. Whether he deserved Naoto or not wasn't even an issue anymore. Naoto loved him and how Naoto felt mattered the world to him. And had from the beginning.

In that moment, Koji felt something in him shift. Like a light shining down, he saw the truth of Naoto's words. What difference did it make whom he loved? He'd never had Tashiro Watanabe's love or approval…ever. Long before Shizuko was in their lives, his father had told him what a shameful boy he was. Tashiro Watanabe was angry and bitter. If Koji thought back to his earliest memory of the man, he always had been that way, probably long before Koji was born.

The weight of guilt lifted and elation swooped into the clean place inside. He bowed again. "Good night, Dad."

His father said nothing and looked back down at his empty place.

When Koji rose to his feet, he caught Gina and Jiro looking at him, a mixture of confusion and sympathy. He smiled at them and kissed Gina's cheek again before going into the front entry where Etsu was waiting for him. He slipped on his shoes, picked up his drawing pad and held the door open for her. His heart was still pounding and the cool night air wafted through his sleeves, making him aware of how much he'd been sweating.

Etsu followed him outside and fell quietly into step next to him. Koji's stomach tightened with each step. The momentum he'd had earlier was nearly lost. He had to tell her. Had to end this torment before he completely lost his nerve. Halting, he turned to her. "Etsu, I have something important to tell you."

The worry that slipped into her eyes made him pause. "Yes?"

Doubt infused him. Could he possibly be doing the right thing? "Um...when I asked you to dinner last week, it was because my father wanted me to. I had a very nice time with you," he added quickly, "but, he wants me to marry you."

Her eyes widened. "Oh, I see."

"Not for the right reason, though." Koji took a step back, wiped his palms on his jacket. His drawing pad cut into his armpit with the movement. The hurt in Etsu's eyes almost made him recant. But he couldn't. The mere thought made him want to finish that bottle of saké in his kitchen. "Don't misunderstand," he went on, "If I were to marry, I'd want to marry you. You're...one of the sweetest women I've ever met."

His words were rewarded with a smile. Then an idea hit him. He pulled his drawing pad from under his arm and opened the cover to the first drawing of him and Naoto, naked bodies entwined. "Here, this will explain what I mean." He held it in front of her, feeling his cheeks burn.

She studied it quietly for a second. Her eyes widened and she looked up. "Oh, I see." A smile came to her lips and her eyes sparkled. "This explains so much. Thank you for telling me."

In spite of himself, he smiled, then leaned over and kissed her cheek. "I'll see you to your house."

"Okay, thank you."

They started walking again and Koji nearly panted from the release of tension. The sky seemed to open up above him and he felt as if he could fly up to it. "I'm sorry I didn't tell you sooner," he went on. "It's so…" He paused in search of a word.

"No need to explain," Etsu said. Her own relief was reflected in her voice. "I actually had begun to think after dinner the other night that you really just didn't like me. I'm glad to know that's not it."

"It certainly isn't."

They went up the front walk of Etsu's parents' house and came to a standstill facing each other.

"Koji-kun?"

He froze. "Yes?"

She smiled. "Truthfully, if you wanted to…marry anyway, I would still do it. I…I've liked you for a long time. We would have our own lives, but it would help with the families. And we would still be friends, of course."

His gut lurched painfully. Could he possibly be hearing correctly? He stared at her, frozen. After all this, Etsu was still offering him a chance. He wouldn't have to lie to her. And she was pretty…

No. He couldn't do that. Not if the immediate ache in his heart for Naoto indicated what he truly wanted. Night and day. "Etsu, you're beautiful and good." He bowed. "I can't do that. I need…I…want to be with him always. It wouldn't be fair…to any of us."

She nodded and Koji could see her disappointment. "All right."

He stared down at her. Relief washed through him so hard he almost dropped the pad. "I…hope…we…can be friends."

"Of course. I'd like that."

He looked at her another moment. "I should be going."

She nodded. "Good night."

He turned.

"Koji?"

Her voice pulled him back around.

Now, Etsu wore a big smile. "Your talent is incredible. You're a true artist. If you ever want to publish a *manga*, call me at work and I'll arrange a meeting with my boss. I'm sure he'll agree with me once he sees your work. It's not usual that *yaoi* artists are men, but it certainly shouldn't make a difference with such passion and quality work as yours."

Koji stared at her. "Really?" So many years he'd wanted simply to sit all day and draw, but his father had always griped at him about not making a living from doodling. It had been only Shizuko's support that had allowed him to draw even as a hobby. Well, maybe...now...hopefully, he'd be needing that, something where he could work from...home. He nodded. "That would be great."

A quiet moment passed and he knew the next moment of reckoning was about to happen. But first, to say good night to Etsu. She'd been a true friend to him this night, in more ways than she knew. "Etsu, thank you. I can't thank you enough. For that, and for your...understanding." He stepped forward and embraced her. She squeezed him close, just for a moment. When they parted, he met her gaze, a mixture of feelings, not the least of which was that a woman who'd been taken with him in their youth.

"You're welcome. Good luck. Speak to you during the week?"

He nodded. "Yes." The cool spring air enveloped him, and for the first time, he felt the sweetness of it fill his lungs, noticed the balmy scent. And the stars dotting the night sky. Everything looked more beautiful.

Out on a busier street, he caught a cab. "Ni Chome," he told the driver. "The White Tiger hotel." He gave the specific street address and sat back.

His heart pounded as the taxi pulled out into the night traffic.

As the distance closed to the hotel, Koji's mind raced as quickly as his heart. Was he doing the right thing?

He almost told the driver to stop. Better perhaps if he called and told Naoto he was coming. But he couldn't. What if Naoto tried to talk him out of coming over? Or damn, what if he was with another guest? That would just make Koji lose his nerve completely and he needed to go through with this. He had to see it through to the end, no matter what happened.

~~~~~

Naoto needed a breath of air. Suzuki's very presence was like a choking cloud of poison. All he needed to do was see that stocky, smug-looking bastard with his neck to ankle tattoos dragging around a pathetic-looking pretty boy, to think of poor Ryu and what he'd suffered at that prick's hands.

After letting Kiku know where he'd be, Naoto went through the back door. Even in the alleyway behind the White Tiger, the cool spring air was refreshing. He dragged it into his lungs as he paced back and forth a few times before leaning his back to the wall.

Tilting his head back, Naoto closed his eyes, using the fresh air to erase the images of Suzuki in the bath with his latest pet, a twenty-three year old small cute guy he called

Yuzo. The poor *kawaii no chibi* looked at Suzuki with hatred when the yak's back was turned and Naoto hadn't missed the way the kid gazed at Kiku when Kiku came into the bath to greet Suzuki.

Ach! It sucked. He pulled in a deep breath and switched his thoughts to Koji. He would call soon...

His eyes popped open at the click of the back door.

Kiku poked his head out. He grinned when his eyes met Naoto's. "Naoto, there's someone here to see you."

Naoto pushed away from the wall. He didn't have any regulars who asked for him. "I'll come in."

"No, hold on. He wants to go out there." Kiku disappeared.

And then, Koji appeared in the doorway. Koji's large eyes stared at him, uncertain, as if afraid he were bothering Naoto. Under one arm, he held a drawing pad. "Hi."

Naoto felt his entire insides leaping. "Koji-chan." Without thinking, he grasped Koji's hand and tugged him outside. Behind them, the door clicked shut. "Koji-chan, you're here. I can't believe it." He pulled Koji into his arms and kissed him, leaned back against the wall and tugged Koji against him, rubbing their bodies together as if he could climb inside the guy. The sound of the drawing pad sliding to the ground whispered up through the air.

Koji's lips yielded to his, head tilting back and Naoto tasted Koji's tongue in languorous, hungry strokes. Like coming home to a warm fire after being out in the snow, Koji's warm hard body moulded against his. Koji's shirt rubbed his nipples into immediate hardness and he felt Koji's hands fist his vest.

Finally, he pulled from their kiss, breathless, to stare into Koji's face. So hard to believe he was actually here. "Koji-chan," he whispered.

"Naoto, I can't do it."

Naoto's blood went cold. "Can't do what?" Oh shit!

Koji's bottom lip trembled. "I can't get married and only see you once a week. I just can't."

Naoto's hands slipped away and he felt as if his legs would buckle. "Are you telling me it's over? That you can't see me anymore?" He began to feel as if giant hands squeezed his neck, choking off his breath.

Koji's brow furrowed. He was still breathing heavily from their kiss. "No. I'm telling you that…I want to be yours forever. I want to be with you every day. And every night. I…told Etsu the truth." His eyes were wide, staring into Naoto's. "I love you. I want to be yours forever." His hands roamed over Naoto's chest, pushed his vest open and rubbed over his nipples. "I love you so much."

Before Naoto could answer, Koji kissed him, a hot moist kiss. The wild Koji who'd made love to him while dreaming.

Naoto moaned. His body hardened and he sagged against the wall while Koji trailed kisses over his jaw, down his neck, to his chest. Naoto pulled in a breath. A hot tongue licked across one nipple, teased and feathered it to hardness. He slipped his fingers into Koji's hair, unable to move. Koji kissed his way across Naoto's chest and tongued his other nipple, sucked it to a small peak.

Damn…

Fingers scrabbled at the button of Naoto's shorts, got them open and then an eager hand slid down his cock and cupped his balls.

That immobilised him completely.

"Naoto-chan," Koji murmured against his skin, then continued his trail of kisses down Naoto's stomach.

Koji was dropping to his knees…That hot tongue slid up the length of Naoto's dragon then captured it in moist delicious suction.

Naoto shut his eyes. He couldn't move. His fingers worked in Koji's hair, followed the bobbing movements of Koji's head as Koji swallowed his cock to the root then slid back up. Then down again.

Damn…good thing they were in the back alley. No guests came back here. They were alone.

Koji groaned, a soft sound that vibrated through Naoto's cock. His balls tightened. His belly tightened. The sight of Koji on his knees, head bobbing out here in the cool air. His Koji, who wanted to be with him forever.

It was too much. Naoto exploded. Koji's hands gripped Naoto's hips and Koji held on, swallowed Naoto's dragon cloud greedily. Naoto sagged back, empty and his cock slipped out of Koji's mouth. He tugged Koji up and smoothed Koji's hair back, seeing drops of his cum gleam on the other man's lips and chin. "I want you inside me, Koji-chan," he panted. He pushed his shorts further down then reached out and undid Koji's pants, tugged them down, along with his briefs. Then he turned, offering himself.

"Naoto-chan, are you sure?"

Naoto nearly burst out laughing. Koji didn't realise he'd already done this. For a second, Naoto almost confessed it to him, then stopped. Koji would be embarrassed and start apologising when all Naoto wanted was the heat between them. Confession was for another time. "Of course. Please." He wet his hand with spit, reached around and slicked it on Koji's erection. Koji pulled in a breath and groaned. Naoto turned and braced his hands on the wall. "Please, Koji-chan."

Without another word, Koji came up behind him. Naoto guided the head in and hitched a breath. He pushed back against Koji. Even the first push was blissful. Koji inside him, filling his tight channel, spreading him open.

Koji groaned and Naoto felt the other man's hands on his hips again. "Naoto-chan..." He slid in and out, faster, harder. The movement rubbed Naoto's prostate and he nearly jumped out of his shoes. Sparks of pleasure danced through his whole lower body and spread like a blissful fire through his chest.

Koji's fingers dug into his hips. Naoto felt him stiffen and then the hot gush inside him. Koji collapsed against his back. His ragged breaths sifted through the fall of Naoto's hair.

Naoto closed his eyes. He took hold of Koji's hands and pulled the other man's arms around him. The musky scent of sex warmed the cool air.

"Naoto-chan, when we parted at the hospital, I think I made you afraid that we wouldn't be together. I'm so sorry."

"Don't worry." Naoto didn't want Koji even to finish that sentence. "I understand. It doesn't matter anymore. You're *here*."

Koji squeezed him tighter. "I want to be yours forever," he said again. But then his brow furrowed. "Is that...what you want too?"

Naoto turned in Koji's arms so that Koji's dragon slipped out, leaving a strange absence in his body. No matter. Koji was here. There would be many more chances to have that feeling again. He turned Koji so that the other man's back pressed to the wall and gazed into Koji's huge, magical eyes. *I want to be yours forever.* Those words…he'd seen or heard those words before. Then it hit him. Koji's drawings. The declarations of love he'd written on them over and over. He was saying them out loud!

Now, in the aftermath of bliss, the words sifted more deeply through Naoto's consciousness. Another wave of pure, sheer joy swept through him. He stepped closer to Koji, filling the space with the warmth of their bodies so close together.

Cupping Koji's cheeks, he kissed him then pressed his forehead to Koji's. Tingling heat travelled down every vein, lit every nerve ending of his body on fire with joy. "Of course that's what I want, Koji-chan," he said softly.

Koji's beautiful smile replaced his worried look. "Me too."

Me too. The words travelled like a sweet liquid fire through Naoto's veins. "There's one other thing I want," he whispered.

Koji's hand laced into Naoto's hair. "What? Anything."

Naoto smiled. "I want forever to begin right this second."

About the Author

Award-winning, multi-published author of erotic romance, Sedonia Guillone spends her days writing deliciously naughty romances — when she's not cuddling with the man she loves or watching kung fu and samurai films and eating chocolate.

Sedonia welcomes comments from readers. You can find her website and email address on her author bio page at www.sedoniaguillone.com.

Tell Us What You Think

We appreciate hearing reader opinions about our books. You can email us at sedonia.guillone@gmail.com .

Other Ai Press books by Sedonia Guillone

Aki's Love Song

Taming Kate

Fallon's Jewel

Cowboy and the Crow

The Delightfully Wicked Punishment of Takashi Yamashita

Master of Ecstasy

Lion's Lover

Lady of Two Lairds

Soy Sauce Face

The Completeness of Celia Flynn

Blind Love

Whether you prefer e-books or paperbacks, be sure to visit Ai Press on the web at www.ai-pres.net for an erotic reading experience that will leave you breathless.

www.ai-press.net

www.ingramcontent.com/pod-product-compliance
Lightning Source LLC
Chambersburg PA
CBHW061132200626
46817CB00016B/916